The Neurology of Angels

A NOVEL

Krista Tibbs

To Melanie,
Congratulations!
Krista T.

Published in the United States by Friction Publishing, Massachusetts

2008 Friction Publishing Trade Paperback Edition

ISBN: 978-0-9818803-0-3

Library of Congress Control Number: 2008905977

www.neurologyofangels.com

Printed in the United States of America

10 9 8 7 6 5 4 3 2 1

Sick children are angels on loan.
—Elizabeth Rose

PHASE I

1

Cambridge, Massachusetts

#423—THIS IS THE ONE.

Galen wrote the words into his notebook and yawned. Beside him, a hum emanated from a gently rocking platform of vials. He tugged on a pair of latex gloves and wrapped masking tape around each wrist to secure the fraying cuffs of his lab coat, then he settled onto a stool and drew a rack of slides across the counter. He slipped the first slide off the rack and positioned it under the microscope, looking at it for only a moment before replacing it with the next. He stifled another yawn.

His eyes scanned the second slide, left to right, and stopped. Galen squeezed his dark brows together and leaned closer to the eyepiece. He increased the power on the lens then grabbed another slide and another. His breath came faster as he registered the discovery: the blue-stained tissue of the control specimens was marred with black clusters of dead cells, but the slides treated with formula 423 were spotless. With trembling hands, he adjusted the focus. Not a fleck of black on 423, just a blue sky of healthy tissue.

The ocean rushed in his ears, and a memory of apple shampoo and caramel hair swept across his heart.

Galen's hand shot out for his notebook, knocking it to the floor. His long arm swung down to retrieve it. His pulse raced as he examined each page from the past week, searching for—hoping for?—a mistake. There were none. He switched off the platform, confusing the liquid against the walls of the vials. The tissue he had prepared before work that morning would be enough to repeat the final steps. He looked through the microscope again, like a kid peeking at his birthday presents.

As Galen reset the experiment, he recalled a dream from the night before. He had been by *her* bedside again, after her beautiful mind became trapped inside the paralysis and her weakened body was already buried beneath the covers. Again he had gathered her close and strong and vowed to make her well. But in his dream, she lived.

Galen's watch alarm startled him. He hurried to clean up; Linda would make him suffer if he were late for Lamaze class again.

After so many trials, so many failures, maybe 423 would finally be the cure. But then what? The words "this is the one" were written before every experiment in his notebook, part of him certain each time that it was true. But as the pile of notebooks grew, and the dozens of failed formulas turned into hundreds, the realist in Galen stopped thinking beyond the lab. So although he knew he'd have to do human studies to get FDA approval, he didn't know how. Mice, he could order from a catalog; he doubted the same was true for people. He had no idea how a drug was scaled up from the lab bench to commercial manufacturing. He had no idea how it got distributed around the country. How long would it take? How much would it cost?

The unknowns of success hit Galen in a wave of fatigue. He was overwhelmed with dread for the level of communication it would require to find partnerships for funding, convince the medical community of 423's merit, collaborate on research designs, and coordinate with the FDA. Maybe tomorrow's results would be another disappointment, and his life would remain predictable for a while longer.

He put the negative thoughts out of his mind. This experiment would confirm his findings. And when it did, Eddy would handle the rest.

Arlington, Virginia

ELIZABETH FORCED HERSELF to remain seated in the red leather chair opposite Dr. Frio's desk. She had kept the appointment with the genetic counselor for nothing more than a reason to get out of bed.

"I thought Mr. Rose would be with you today," Dr. Frio said as she flipped through a file.

"He—he couldn't make it."

"That's fine. You'll have the paperwork to take home. I'll start by saying that neither you nor Mr. Rose is a carrier of any of the usual diseases for which we screen: certain cancers, cystic fibrosis, and so on. Here is the list, for your records." She slid a piece of paper across the desk. Elizabeth looked down at it but didn't pick it up.

"At your request, we also ran some of the less established screens and found nothing of note there, either." She held onto the second piece of paper. "However . . . ."

Elizabeth looked up. She couldn't speak but pleaded with her eyes that the doctor not say more. She was sure that if she heard what was to follow *however*, the fragile seams holding her together would disintegrate.

But Dr. Frio continued. "Per your consent, we ran some additional tests that are in development." She laid before Elizabeth three photos labeled *EIF*, each displaying what looked like stereo equalizer bars. "These are pictures of a section of a normal gene sequence compared to yours. You can see there are some differences. Based on these tests, we think that you and Mr. Rose both have variations in an enzyme called the eukaryotic initiation factor, or EIF, which is necessary for proper development of brain cells."

3

Elizabeth stared blankly at the photos. Her mind wasn't processing the words, only the thought that if she didn't speak, the world might continue to turn.

"Clearly, your brain cells and your husband's have developed normally." Dr. Frio hesitated.

Oh no, please don't say it.

"But both of your abnormal genes will likely be passed on to your children, should you choose to have them. EIF is implicated in a number of fatal childhood diseases, leukodystrophies in particular."

"I'm pregnant."

Dr. Frio sat back in her seat. Elizabeth thought she had succeeded in stopping the bad news, but after a moment, the doctor pressed on. "Unfortunately, we are not far enough in our research to be able to conduct neonatal testing or to quantify the risk for you, but I would estimate it to be relatively high. So while your pregnancy certainly complicates the situation, it doesn't change the nature of the decision. Of course, you don't need to terminate the pregnancy today. It's certainly something you should discuss with Mr. Rose."

"He's dead."

This announcement effectively ended the conversation. After a long period of Elizabeth staring at the graph and Dr. Frio staring at her, Elizabeth—still in one piece—walked out the door.

2

GALEN AND EDDY crunched over half-frozen mud puddles on their weekly jog past Harvard University. As always, they slowed when they neared their former dormitory. The windows were lit with activities from indoor Frisbee on the first floor to debates on the sixth, where a wide screen television streamed election results.

"Who do you think will win the district?" Eddy said. "My money's on Jenkins. I don't necessarily agree with all his politics, but he's the most likely to actually do something about health care in this state." He paused to catch his breath. "I mean, the system's a mess. Government should be taking better care of people." After a moment of silence, Eddy said, "Don't you think?"

"You know I don't watch the news."

Eddy looked sideways at Galen. "Ever the conversationalist." He sprinted ahead.

Galen responded to the challenge, glad for the chance to burn off his anxiety. He did have something to discuss with Eddy, but not yet. Twenty minutes later, both panting and covered in sweat, they stomped in a tie on the ground step of Eddy's apartment building.

Inside, Eddy kicked off his sneakers. "Anybody home?"

"I'm in the nursery with Linda," his wife called.

Eddy clattered inside a utility closet. To Galen's amusement, he emerged with a six-pack of beer. "Joy would kill me in a jealous rage if she knew I had this."

They cracked open the cans and moved into the living room, where Eddy reached into a box next to the couch. "Look what we found when we were clearing out room for the nursery." He held up a heap of charred black plastic. "Remember that tailgate party at the Yale game? In the snowstorm?"

Galen groaned. "You kept the tarp?"

"It was so darn funny, we needed a souvenir. You trying to rig it up to keep Linda dry, and the more you tried, the madder she got, because the wind kept flapping it on her head." Laughing uncontrollably, Eddy could hardly get the words out. "I can still see your face when it blew off and landed in the bonfire!"

Galen balled up the tarp and launched it into the next room. But he couldn't help laughing as well. Despite the inauspicious beginning, he and Linda had married just a few months later.

Eddy clicked on the television, and Galen wandered behind the couch to look at the portrait of the two couples on their shared wedding day, posing before the Atlantic Ocean. Joy and Eddy could have been models for the portrait frame; she was tall with long, red hair blowing back toward the water, and his blond locks and carefree grin belonged at the beach. They were a glamorous contrast to the incongruous couple with self-conscious smiles: Galen, lanky and pale from too much daylight spent on research, and Linda with an oddly dark tan and platinum up-do.

Galen could feel Eddy's eyes on him as he scanned a new screen of photos from college. He knelt to look at one snapshot in particular. A twenty-year-old Galen was seated on a boardwalk bench. *She* stood behind him with her cheek pressed to his, her lean arms and caramel hair draped over his shoulders. Eddy's hands formed rabbit ears behind them, and they were all laughing toward the camera. The picture was inscribed to her brother: *Hey Eddy, Thanks for being my #2 fan. Love ya.* It was signed with a well-practiced illegible flourish. Galen smiled, remembering her insistence that an aspiring actress needed a distinctive

6

autograph. He studied her face for some hint of the brain strokes that would take her from them a year later.

He stood up. "How are your folks?"

Eddy let out a breath. "Good. My mom still worries about you, but she finally accepts that you haven't been spending all that time in the lab trying to create the Fiancée of Frankenstein." Galen's jaw dropped. "Oh, come on. Sis would have been the first to laugh at that."

Galen shook his head but smiled again. He leaned against the arm of the couch. "Of anyone, I'd think your parents would support my compulsion. To spare other people what we went through."

"No one asked you to give your life to it."

Galen shrugged. He gulped his beer then held the can up. "To new life. And whatever loophole got us into the club."

"Speak for yourself. I'm going to kick butt in the fatherhood department." Eddy bumped cans with Galen. "To riding my coattails."

Galen smirked and took the empties to the closet. He returned to the living room with more beer and handed one to Eddy, then he inhaled and announced his news. "The experiment worked."

"Quiet a sec."

The television journalist was saying, "Exit polls have Jenkins in the lead."

"I knew it!" Eddy clunked his can on the coffee table. Galen dropped onto the couch. "Sorry for my lack of enthusiasm, buddy, but you swore you were on the verge of a cure about four hundred compounds ago."

"Four hundred and twenty-two."

"Yeah, so no offense, but I'll believe it when I see it."

Another district winner said, "Thank you, Massachusetts. Together, we will stop corporate greed and give the government back to the people."

Eddy flung a coaster at the television. "Corporate greed is employing half the people in this state! Including me!" He turned to Galen. "And give government back to 'the people'? Who does he think runs the corporations? Martians and puppy dogs?"

"Speaking of running companies . . . 423 needs a business plan. You have the skills."

Eddy hesitated a split second before he said jauntily, "Like I said, when I see it." He turned back to the television.

Galen was confused by his friend's reluctance. Eddy had been enthusiastic in the past, even recommending Galen for a job and sharing work projects so he could have flexible hours to continue his research. But somehow he must have known Eddy would have reservations, otherwise why would he have been nervous to bring it up? Galen chased the near-comprehension around his mind, his heart beating fast. He wanted to catch the insight and pin it to a piece of glass to study its innards, catalogue the evidence of feelings, and model their cause and effect so he could replicate the human understanding that was so difficult for him to find and hold. But like so many dreams, it began to dissolve then disappeared, and he was again isolated inside the mist.

Their pregnant wives' voices bubbled down the hall. Eddy widened his eyes in mock terror. "They're coming back. Hide the beer!"

Galen swallowed the last of his drink, and with it, his disappointment.

THE EVENING AFTER the meeting with the genetic counselor, an unseasonably warm breeze blew over the back lawn, and frogs peeped in the distance as though winter weren't coming. Sitting on her porch swing alone, Elizabeth felt more lost than ever. When preparing a legal defense, she had always found an angle, no matter how hopeless the situation. She tried to remember how she had maneuvered her brain to work that way, to consider her options.

Dr. Frio had suggested terminating the pregnancy. Elizabeth's soul cringed at the thought, but maybe it was just that easy. Without the fear of raising a baby—a sick baby—alone, maybe she could focus on overcoming her loss. She was only twenty-eight. She still had time to try again with someone else, to have a healthy child and a husband and the life she had planned. She leaned her heavy head against the swing and closed her eyes.

She was standing motionless by the side of the road, taking in the accident scene: the truck on its side, the tree in the road, the lights of the ambulance. She imagined the policeman before her was an actor in a movie, his every word of explanation scripted. She stared past him. The paramedics were approaching. They weren't talking or working, just walking, with a man on the stretcher between them. Elizabeth could only see his feet, draped with a sheet and rolling toward her ever so slowly up the hill. The rest of the man's body came into view. His face was covered.

Elizabeth's hand instinctively shielded her stomach. "I'm sorry. I'm sorry. I'm sorry," she whispered to her husband so recently in the grave and her baby so helpless inside her.

3

EDDY AND JOY were waiting for Galen in the lobby of the auditorium. "You came," Galen said.

"It's your life's work, buddy. We wouldn't miss it."

"Where's Linda?" Joy asked. "It's starting to fill up in there, so we should get seats now if we want to be near the exit."

"At home."

"Oh, dear, is she okay?"

Galen nodded. Eddy and Joy exchanged a glance, and there was an uncomfortable silence as they all acknowledged the slight. Joy reached up to fix Galen's tie. His spine was starting to curve, his body betraying a desire to be hunched over the microscope, or mounting slides, or performing any other of the calming monotonies of everyday research.

Abruptly, Joy said, "You left her alone?"

"Well, I—she told me . . . ." Galen choked on the ever-ready guilt.

Joy said, "Eddy, give me the keys. I'll stay with her."

"Hon, she's a grown woman."

"She's a pregnant woman in her third trimester."

"So are you."

"There's safety in numbers."

"That doesn't even make sense. Look, I'll drive you." He grimaced at Galen. "I'm sorry, buddy."

"I shouldn't have . . . ." Galen looked toward the building, then at Joy, and back at Eddy.

"Don't be silly." Joy took the keys from Eddy's hand. "Galen needs a friendly face in the audience. Linda and I will be fine together." Eddy shrugged and watched his wife waddle out the door.

"Do you think I should . . . ?" Galen wasn't sure how to finish.

"She's just being a mother hen. We were going to get a parking ticket anyway. Let's go in."

Inside the auditorium, Galen stood behind the stage curtain and tried to read his shaking index cards. He could still hardly believe that, among the hundreds of proposals submitted to the pilot clearinghouse, his had been one of the seven chosen. This presentation to local investors was the opportunity he needed, the first step from mice to monkeys—and then to humans.

Of course, 423 would need a real business plan before investors would offer him real money. But at that point, surely Eddy would join the venture. Galen just had to deliver the presentation.

The lights dimmed and the projection screen flashed on. When the audience quieted, Galen was introduced, and he maneuvered himself to the podium. He tried to swallow. "As we know, the role of hemoglobin in the blood is to transport oxygen from the lungs to the rest of the body." Fumbling slightly, he advanced to a slide of the brain covered in blood vessels. "Nerve cells use more oxygen than most muscles, so—" He cleared his throat. "So, I hypothesized that there is a different globin specific to the brain. My experiments have shown that this 'neuroglobin' does exist."

Galen's fingers trembled against the touch pad of the remote control like an SOS, skipping ahead several slides. There was polite coughing in the auditorium while the screen flashed blue, white, black, and red, as Galen quickly reversed the slide show.

"Today's presentation will focus on the role of neuroglobin in stroke, specifically ischemia-induced stroke." He consciously tried to deepen his voice back to normal. "We know that prolonged constriction of blood vessels, ischemia, slows the flow of oxygen, and lack of oxygen can cause cells to die."

As Galen spoke, his posture grew straighter. "The literature shows that the cerebral cortex is affected by ischemic stroke three to four times more often than other areas of the brain. I used a custom-derived stain to mark the neuroglobin in six different sections of the mouse brain." He felt a shiver of anticipation when he projected six enlarged microscope slides onto the screen. "The section with the densest blue is the cerebral cortex." Excited murmurs rippled through the audience.

"I have demonstrated that where the brain is more sensitive to stroke, there is more neuroglobin. It's not clear whether neuroglobin is born in greater density in those areas or expressed there in response to trauma, but in either case, it is clear that neuroglobin has a role in protecting cells from death by oxygen deprivation and therefore protects the brain from stroke."

Several people left their seats to approach the stage, and others conversed animatedly in small groups in the aisles. Galen allowed himself to relive the rush he had felt at each small discovery leading to this one, an addiction that had compelled him to continue the research long after his heartache had abated.

When most of the audience had returned to their seats, he continued. "Too often we academics focus so long on figuring out the how and why that we rarely get to the what-can-we-do-about-it." Heads nodded with encouragement. "The second half of my presentation is about a potential treatment. In a follow-on experiment, I induced ischemia then infused the mice with neuroglobin extracted from cerebrospinal fluid. Here's a sample from the controls, with no neuroglobin, and you can clearly see lesions where the oxygen-deprived cells have died."

His next slide elicited gasps. "And here are the treated cells, fully intact."

A crescendoing hush absorbed his words while he described his attempts to develop a synthetic neuroglobin that would not be rejected by antibodies—the six years of research, the careful logic that led to the next experiment and the next. There was silence when he showed his final slide, the exquisite blue tissue treated with 423.

Galen fielded questions about his scientific method, his literature review, and his reasons for refuting other hypotheses. After nearly an hour beyond the allotted time, the facilitator announced that only one more question would be allowed. A bearded man wearing suspenders to hold up his sagging green workpants stood in the middle of the audience. He said with a drawl, "Looks like this neuroglobin doesn't work too well. Stroke is pretty common." There were some uneasy chuckles in the crowd.

Galen smiled and relaxed his shoulders. This was the doubt he had been hoping to hear. "The brain is a complex and delicately balanced system that is constantly striving for equilibrium. For all we know, our blood vessels are normally on the verge of constriction, and every tension headache could be the precursor to a stroke, but we're fine because neuroglobin is doing its job."

Galen descended from the stage into a sea of suits. He was handed business cards right and left, accompanied by requests to talk about developing 423.

When it was over, Eddy was waiting for him outside. "Why are you still here?" Galen's blunt question was inadequate for the appreciation he felt.

"I'm taking credit for all your work. I have a dozen job offers already." They grinned at each other.

"Run my company." Eddy's grin froze, and Galen immediately regretted bringing it up again.

But Eddy ignored the comment. "I didn't realize you had it in you, buddy. If you'd turned on that charisma as my wing man, we could have sowed some serious wild oats."

On the drive home, the two men recounted their college escapades in tribute to the caramel-haired girl they had both adored: her sweet-talking them to every dance club in Boston, where she selected co-eds for Eddy to pick up; winter vacations with their family in the Berkshires, singing karaoke with the locals; and summers at the shore, where she had claimed with pride that every bikini there was eyeing her guys.

Linda and Joy greeted them with a huge congratulations cake. Galen gave his wife a long and hearty conciliatory smooch, to his friends' applause, and he felt the happiest he had ever thought he could be. Until later that night, when his daughter was born.

Holding Alexandra—Lexi—Galen's priorities became clear. The bundle in his arms was joy incarnate and underscored the importance of his work. Lexi had ten fingers and toes and a healthy genetic profile, but he knew that at that moment, somewhere, someone else's child wasn't as lucky.

ELIZABETH ROCKED BACK and forth in a ray of sunlight. Her baby Sera gazed up at her, listening to the chimes tinkling in the soft May breeze. The delicate round eyes turned to ovals then crescents as Sera drifted to sleep. Elizabeth tilted her head back against the chair to rest her cramped neck and shoulders. She noticed the peeling border of angels circling the nursery and made a mental note to fix it. The note was so far down on her To Do list, she would be lucky to get to it before Sera turned ten. If she turned ten.

Elizabeth banished the thought from her mind and surveyed the room, across the vacuum tracks on the pink shag carpet, over the neatly folded clothing on the changing table, to the stack of half-read legal documents on the lamp table. She spoke to the picture of a man wearing a *#1 Dad To Be* t-shirt and a wide grin. "We can't do it all." She smiled at the precious bundle in her arms. "But we're going to be okay."

She rocked forward to transfer the baby to the crib then picked up her papers and went downstairs to work. Her firm's latest commission was a consultation to the government on a class action lawsuit against the U.S. Food and Drug Administration. FDA had not approved a treatment for spinal cord injury because it could cause brain tumors, and patients were suing to overturn the decision, to gain access to treatment if they chose to take the risk.

At the office that afternoon, one of the eager new talents had proclaimed his disgust over their firm's participation in a defense that would withhold drugs from patients who needed it. A more experienced colleague had launched an equally passionate counterargument that if the judicial branch were allowed to overturn the FDA's decisions governing safety, it would mean the system of checks and balances had failed, and the U.S. as they knew it would end.

Elizabeth and her husband had bickered like that when they first met. Their avidly opposing viewpoints and growing relationship made them a good team in the courtroom, and they had been on their way to greatness. Now she struggled on each case to remain unbiased, trying not to wonder how she would feel if the patient were Sera.

4

EDDY SAT IN his cube with his head in one hand and a pen in the other, editing yet another training manual. It was hard to concentrate. Would his life always be training other people but never doing the work himself?

His mind had been in turmoil since Galen had offered him a partnership for the third time. Galen had made a half-dozen business plan presentations without success, but Eddy knew that the science behind 423 was solid, so securing funding was only a matter of time. His friend had pitched hard to his ego, making Eddy feel that his business degree, two internships with start-up companies, and charisma would ultimately convince an investor to back the project.

There was a stirring in Eddy's stomach when he thought about quitting his job and teaming up with Galen. Starting his own business would be a thrill, something he had always wanted to do. But the voice of his conscience, sounding annoyingly like his father, nagged him. *What if it doesn't work out? You have responsibilities. Who's going to feed and clothe Abigail while you chase a dream?*

The squirm inside was something else, too. Not jealousy—that was almost laughable. Galen's success would be a reflection on Eddy, in any case. Since freshman year, Eddy had been the one to hype Galen's confidence, expose his humor, make him an honorary fraternity member, coach his running technique, and draw him out to meet people—including Eddy's sister, the girl who had started it all. So, why didn't he want to work for Galen? Inexplicably, Eddy remembered the stray dog he'd adopted when he was twelve and the incomparable emotion he'd felt sneaking leftovers to the woodshed and seeing that tail wag in gratitude.

A tone from his computer reminded him of the training session starting in five minutes. He was relieved to have something else to occupy his mind for an hour.

After the presentation, several people congratulated Eddy on their way out:

"First mandatory training I didn't sleep through."

"You should be a politician with theatrics like that."

Eddy returned to his desk feeling proud, as he usually did after a session. The thought of leaving this job to do something that he wasn't sure he'd be good at, that depended on other people for success, and that had no security terrified him.

But if he and Galen could make a go of the business, the financial rewards would be unlimited. To have a home with no mortgage, send Abigail to college without debt, buy a new car, sail summers on the Vineyard, retire early, travel the world, and not least of all, feel fulfilled by his job—who didn't want those things, the

American Dream?

But Eddy didn't want to rack up debt on a venture that still had so much risk. Of the two college buddies, Eddy had always considered himself the more adventurous one, pulling pranks with the Harvard underground, taking skydiving lessons to Joy's chagrin, and striking up conversation with any stranger on the street, to Galen's admiration. But was a financial adventure in his repertoire?

He complained about his job, but it wasn't so bad. He had regular hours, good pay, and stability. The truth was, even though it was the loss of Eddy's sister that triggered the research,

Galen's commitment to 423 went beyond channeling heartbreak. Eddy wasn't sure he shared that ambition.

He plugged headphones into his computer and cranked the volume, hoping the electric guitars would drown out his thoughts.

The timing just wasn't right. Maybe in a few years, when he had some money in the bank, he'd be able to venture into something new and take bigger risks. It was fine for Galen, who had lived on the edge of poverty growing up. But Eddy's father had always provided, so it would be much harder for Eddy to learn to live with less.

Plus Galen and Linda didn't exactly have a model relationship. Linda often griped to Joy that she'd married for strong and silent, not oblivious and distant. It had to be stressful living with the specter of bankruptcy and paying the rent with a credit card. Eddy didn't want to be exposed to such insecurity.

So, he would tell Galen he was declining the offer for the sake of his daughter and his marriage.

5

THE CLICK OF Galen's dress shoes on the marble floor echoed off the twenty-foot ceilings of the investment firm lobby. He approached the receptionist and tried to act as if he had signed the logbook a thousand times, but his signature was as wobbly as his legs.

Between working full time and spending off hours trying to finish supporting experiments, Galen had slept little more than four hours a night in the past six weeks. His only sacred time with Lexi now was when she cried in the middle of the night. Despite his fatigue, he smiled to himself, thinking of her tiny hand on his cheek and her head nestled against his neck. Moments like those made him feel like he had won the Nobel Prize, which was a needed boost after he presented to investor after investor, his initial confidence crumbling more with each handshake: *Call me when you have a patent. Interesting idea, needs a patent. I'd like to consider it, but in this economic climate, I can't risk anything without a patent.*

Galen had been reluctant to apply for a patent and start the twenty-year countdown to the day he would have to relinquish ownership of his work. But he had finally done it, because something had to give. Since he had finished his thesis and no longer had student access to the university, he had been renting lab space from an independent company. But his grants had run out, and his loan application was turned down, which meant when the month ended, his research ended. All the years of work would languish in a drawer unless he had money, and a patent seemed to be the only route to get it.

Galen stepped on the elevator and pushed the button for the 34th floor. He winced, having forgotten the blistered finger he had scorched on the toaster this morning in his distraction.

The elevator seemed determined to stop on every floor. Trying to diffuse his impatience, Galen pulled an envelope from his briefcase. It was a piece of letterhead from the biggest investment firm in Boston, and on it was scrawled a date and time and a note: *Only come if I'm your last chance.* Today was it. He would be meeting with the last interested investor, which was a long shot, at best—at worst, a cruel joke. But joke or not, Galen had to find a way to communicate this time. Otherwise, 423 would die in his mind, where no one else could hear it screaming.

When the elevator finally reached his floor, Galen stepped out to face the only door in the hall. It was marked *Amos Theriault, President.* Galen placed one hand on the metal doorknob and one palm flat against the cool pane of the window, imagining success through osmosis. He turned the knob and pushed.

An apprentice to Grizzly Adams stood to greet him. Amidst the spacious office and shiny, contemporary furniture was the plaid-clad and suspendered Amos Theriault. He shook hands with Galen over the orderly desktop and said with a Smoky Mountain drawl, "Alright, stake your claim."

Galen assumed he meant the presentation. His eyes darted around the office, but he didn't see a projector screen, so he removed his computer from its case and balanced it awkwardly on his knees.

"For crying out loud, use the desk, son."

Amos cleared a corner for Galen to place the laptop. Galen turned it so both of them could see the screen, twisting his legs to squeeze closer to the desk. He opened his PowerPoint slide presentation of 423 and launched into a condensed version of his dissertation. Amos asked few questions about the science.

Galen next clicked to the screen containing a table of the basic stages of clinical development. "These are my time and cost assumptions at a birds-eye view. I figure drug can be made in the lab for the first couple of small trials, but obviously we'll need to scale up to a contract manufacturer for the bigger pivotal trials."

Clinical Studies	Time	Cost (in millions)
Phase I Safety	6 months	$2 M
Phase II Safety and Efficacy	1 year	$6 M
Phase III Efficacy #1	2.5 years	$37 M
Phase III Efficacy #2	2.5 years	$37 M
TOTAL COST FOR DEVELOPMENT*	6.5 years	$82 M

*Cost includes treatment, data, FDA filings, and manufacturing

Galen went on. "Fifty thousand people suffer from ischemic attacks or stroke each year. My target population is the three percent of those who are under twenty and have a recurrent condition. That means in the next two years, there will be approximately three thousand patients in the U.S. who will need the drug. I cite only U.S. numbers, because assuming dosing every six months, we'd have to charge $7,500 per patient per dose just to recoup the cost of development. Of course we'd have to charge something on top of that in order to start developing the next drug and to provide a profit for shareholders. Which brings me to my profile of the company—"

"Son, this is crazy optimistic." The man's bushy, gray eyebrows were struggling to leave his forehead.

Galen was stunned. He reexamined his chart. He thought his problem was being too pessimistic, assuming higher costs and longer timelines than investors wanted. He did think it was outrageous to ask patients or insurers to pay $15,000 per year, but that was how the numbers worked out. He answered slowly, "I'm not sure what you mean."

Amos turned the screen toward Galen, to the effect of shaking a fist in his face. "First off, the average cost of a single Phase Three study in humans is ninety million, and you think you're going to finish the whole damn process for less than that. Second, the average time for clinical development is seven to ten years, but apparently you're better than average, even though you've picked the rarest patients you could think of. Third, you're assuming that every person who has the disease is going to buy your product, when a third of all Americans are underinsured, let alone that insurance won't cover this right out of the gate."

Galen's foundation was shaken. He wasn't sure whether to continue his presentation or drop to his knees and beg.

Amos leaned forward over the desk. "You don't know what you're doing, son. You need a management team."

Galen struggled to keep the heat from rising under his brand new blue shirt collar. The liberal use of the word "son" and the reminder that his best friend had abandoned him were more than he could swallow. He might doubt himself, but he never doubted 423. Galen slid forward in his chair. "Sir, 423 works. But I can't get a management team without money. And if I can't get money without a management team, then we're both wasting our time."

Amos waved his hand in the air. "Don't offer money; offer risk and reward. Starting a company isn't about job security."

"Why would smart people go into debt for little more than a pipe dream?"

"You're doing it."

"And I question my judgment."

"Don't you believe your product is worth the risk?"

"Don't you?"

Amos' face softened, and he studied Galen through half-closed eyelids. Galen was tempted to break the silence but could think of nothing more to say.

Suddenly, Amos surged from his chair and banged his fist on the desk. "I can't sell wants! The horse comes first!" His fuzzy gray hair stood out straight.

Galen could only blink.

"You're approaching these meetings like open auditions at a talent agency, like you can just bring your great idea and expect someone else to develop you into a success. But we're investors, not implementers! Good ideas are a dime a dozen, son."

Galen's anger, humiliation, and exhaustion took over. He stood up. "With all due respect, I came here for a check, not a lecture." Then he walked out.

6

AFTER GALEN LEFT Amos Theriault's office, he rode the subway in a daze, lost in the flow of rush hour, carried off at Harvard Square and into Peet's Coffee. He sat with his lower limbs folded under a table, his hands wrapped around a cup, and his mind spinning in circles, trying to figure out what had possessed him to throw away his dream. The minutes ticked by as other patrons came and went. Linda called to find out where he was. Galen told her where, but not why.

The enormity of Eddy's rejection flooded Galen with nausea. Like brothers, they had their roles; Galen's place was science, and Eddy's was people and business. All along, Galen had been thinking of it as Eddy's company. His friend had as much reason to want it to work, so he would come around. But he hadn't, and now the opportunity was gone. Like all roller coasters, Galen's science had taken him for a seven-year ride but went nowhere. He reached for a trashcan.

The door flew open in a gust of December air. Grateful for the refreshment, Galen closed his eyes. When he opened them, his vision was filled with a scruffy beard and copious plaid.

"Son, you have solid ideas and a decent delivery once you get going. Your business plan needs work; the financials are weak. But you know that now."

Galen's mouth fell open. Amos Theriault didn't sit.

"A CEO who knows what he doesn't know is worth his weight in gold."

Galen stopped breathing. CEO?

"An investor worth his weight can see through the polish on a presentation to the spit and elbow grease behind it. I have good eyes, and I think you have some good spit."

Did he say "spit"? Who was this guy?

"Son, I never do this, but I'll give you a quarter million of my own and an appointment with my colleagues in six months."

Galen blinked his bleary eyes again.

For the first time, Amos laughed, as if Galen's stupefaction were a delightful response. He dropped a business card face down on the table. A name and number were written on the back. "Myesha Knight has led finance and clinical and regulatory operations for four start-ups that IPO'd for millions. I recommended you."

Galen managed to hold his projectile excitement inside long enough to thank the man and pick up the card.

"I think you have what it takes, son. And that's the last time I'm going to say it."

PATRICIA CHEN HAD a plan: go to medical school, complete an internship at a prestigious hospital, spend a few years as a clinical research investigator, then build a career at the U.S. Food and Drug Administration approving new treatments for neurological diseases. She stopped outside the modern orange brick office building in the government complex and smiled with satisfaction at the engraved sign: *FDA Center for Drug Evaluation and Research*. The plan was right on track.

She entered the wide glass doorway and showed her new ID badge to the security guard then marched toward the elevators to ascend to the next phase of her life. She was sure this building housed her destiny.

At her desk, she opened the folder of her first assignment as assistant medical reviewer for a new product for fibromyalgia. The company had just finished the last stage of clinical trials.

Patricia considered it her job to ensure effective drugs were available for people who needed them. This new drug could free millions of people from debilitating pain. She would be part of history. Her life was turning out exactly as she had designed it.

PHASE II

7

THE KITCHEN TABLE was covered with paper, and Galen was typing on his laptop, in the same position he had been for several days. He hadn't blinked in hours. He paused and wrinkled his eyebrows, shuffled several pages, then looked up at the calendar on the refrigerator. A fat blue circle marked the day the next progress report was due to investors—three days away.

Two years ago, the development of 423 had suffered a number of setbacks that cost fifty percent more than planned and six months of development time. After Galen had finally found an appropriate monkey model for the disease, an outbreak of E. coli at the lab killed most of the research animals, then the acquisition of replacement monkeys had been held up in bureaucratic red tape around the breeding facility. The adversities quickly made Galen and Myesha a good business team, and her military efficiency neutralized his tendency toward dread and avoidance. Finally, a Phase I study was nearly complete and showed 423 was safe to use in humans.

The current progress report was a critical piece in convincing investors to fund the multi-million dollar Phase II study that would demonstrate the drug's effect and build the safety profile. Galen and Myesha still didn't agree on the target population, so they were presenting two possible scenarios. With the economy in a slump, very few early development projects were being funded anywhere in the industry, so their justifications for both had to be rock solid.

From behind Galen's chair, Linda slid her arm around his neck and kissed him on the ear. He tried to ignore her. She put her hands through his hair, and he tilted his head sideways, twitched like a cow swatting a fly. She jerked her hands away and clanked the dishwasher empty. He asked, without looking up, "What's wrong?"

When she didn't answer, he kept typing. She eventually returned to the living room, siphoning all of the breathable air from the kitchen. Galen sighed impatiently and saved his work.

He found her sitting on the couch reading a novel. He stood in the doorway for several minutes. She didn't lift her eyes or turn a page. "If I don't do this report right, all these years were wasted."

"I want to have another baby."

A white flash of irritation crossed his mind. Immediately, guilt stabbed his stomach, and his back started to curve. "Three days."

"We shouldn't have to talk about it." She turned a page.

Galen rubbed his temples. "Why are you telling me this right now?"

Linda finally looked up. "After we had Lexi, when you were applying for your patent and working full time, you were too tired. So I put on a smile and waited. When you were trying to get your initial funding, you were too worried. So I put on a smile and waited. Now that you have the funding, you still don't have time, because there's the next milestone right on top of us. So when, Galen, when do I get priority?"

Galen's vision faltered, and the living room furniture bounced and slid toward him. Linda's head went in and out of focus, and his feet turned numb. He loved his wife, he loved Lexi, and he loved 423, yet he was in danger of failing them all.

But if he had failed one child, why would Linda want them to have another? Galen had a vague impression of being manipulated. He forced his eyes to focus on her face, which was sharp with accusation. "I'm trying," he said, "and you're pretending to be happy. I don't understand how to work with that."

"I'm trying, too, Galen. But what I can't understand is why your work means more to you than your family."

"It's more than work."

"Okay, fine, so you're helping someone else's family someday, sometime in the future. At the expense of your own."

Galen had a sense of déjà vu from his childhood. He didn't want to think about it, so he left Linda mid-conversation and returned to the kitchen table. It wasn't long before his attention was again fully concentrated on his task.

IT TOOK SEVERAL meetings and follow-up calculations, but 423 funding was finally approved. To release their many months of tension, Galen and Myesha took advantage of the crisp October day to run the trail around the city reservoir and renew their argument about trial design and target product label.

Myesha said, "Acute treatment. In hospital. Immediately after stroke. Objective to minimize damage from—" She gasped for air. "Oxygen deprivation."

Galen jogged easily. "I invented this drug for *recurrent* stroke. I don't want people to have to have an attack before getting treatment. So I say preventative dosing, regularly every three months."

Myesha stopped and leaned over with her hands on her knees. After she caught her breath, she said, "First of all, I hate you; you didn't even break a sweat. How the hell do you keep in shape with the number of hours you spend at your desk?"

Galen handed her a bottle of water from his pack. She took a swig. "Second, it takes a lot longer and a lot more people to measure prevention. Plus it's just plain hard to prove a black hole. Remember Y2K, the big computer glitch that was going to bring the world to a screeching halt at the end of the millennium? There were a lot of programmers working on that, and nothing much happened. Were they just awesome programmers, or was Y2K just not that big of a deal? How do you prove it?"

She took another drink. "Third, if you're enrolling people who have had multiple strokes in the past, they could be coming into the trial with some brain damage we can't even see." Galen listened intently. "They could have wildly different responses to 423. Do you really want funky variable data to be the first thing that we try to market? By the way, 423 needs a real name."

They started to jog again. "Finally, we're talking about putting stuff in the cerebrospinal fluid. Foot-long needles to the back every three months for the rest of their lives could scare people off. Especially because the subset you want to target are kids. So we need to start with something that's a single injection that could be unequivocally successful, like acute treatment after a stroke. That'll get the word out that 423 works. Meanwhile, we go back and do a trial to prove chronic dosing is preventative, so by the time it's approved, four CSF injections a year will be an acceptable evil."

Galen crunched over the fallen leaves and breathed in the pungent change of season. He didn't want to lose sight of his goal, to treat kids with the rare recurrent condition. But he didn't want to be too stubborn to hear reason. Myesha's arguments made a lot of sense. And since there was no consistent, long-lasting treatment for any kind of ischemic stroke, did it matter where they started? "You're right. We just need to get our product out there so at least some people can benefit. Then we go back and do the hard stuff later."

After several seconds, Galen noticed Myesha had stopped running. He turned around to see her standing in the middle of the trail with her hands on her hips. "The 'easy stuff' you're referring to is finding six hundred patients who'll sign up to be in a study for a year or more, not knowing if they'll get the real thing or placebo, then making sure eighty doctors in eleven countries perform physical exams and neurological exams and brain scans and every other study procedure in the exact same way and document it. Then we convince the FDA that it was done right. Then we do the same thing all over again to make sure it's reproducible. And *then* we can apply for marketing approval to 'get our product out there'." She started running again and passed by him. "Hard stuff *later*. You're funny."

After their run, Galen showered at the "office", which Myesha joked was a loose sense of the word, at best. In reality, the space Galen had rented for their company was a warehouse in Cambridge that a developer had started to convert to condominiums but abandoned mid-project. Their compartment had a fifteen-foot ceiling, exposed pipes, two concrete pillars and a concrete floor, an iridescent purple throw rug and matching couch, and a permanent scent of turpentine. There were three chairs, two stools, and eight long tables spaced along the walls, which served as desks, storyboard, and document assembly line. Galen pulled out a set of dress clothes from one of the filing cabinets, where he kept supplies for contingencies.

Outside the subway station, he stopped at a flower vendor. There were no roses left, so he purchased a pink carnation. When Galen arrived home, Linda looked up from the kitchen table without expression. He extended the flower.

"A carnation, really?" she said.

"The investors gave us seven million."

She gasped. Her eyes followed him to the refrigerator, where he pulled out a bottle of wine, to the cupboard where he brought down two glasses, and back to the table where he poured her a toast. She jumped up, threw her arms around him, and kissed him like she hadn't done for longer than he could remember. "Oh, Galen, now we can have a house and get Lexi into a good pre-school and—"

"Wait, slow down. We didn't win the lottery." She pulled back. "It's like the Tour de France; we just got the yellow jersey for another day. There's still the mountain climb."

"You know I don't watch sports."

He placed his hands on her face and kissed her forehead. "I mean, it's just like Phase One; we get half now and the rest if we

33

show the right progress. Meanwhile we have to manage the budget to the penny."

"Then what are we excited about?"

He perplexed his eyebrows. Wasn't it obvious?

She drew in a long breath. "You do get a bigger salary out of it now, don't you?"

"A little, but still just enough to live on. Until we have something substantial to sell."

"And when will that be?"

He thought about it. "Well, I suppose we could sell out to another company now, but I don't want to do that. We could go public to raise funds. In either scenario, we'd have good take-home money in maybe a year or two. But my ideal would be to raise enough private investment to hold out until we can market 423 ourselves and build a real company. That'd probably be three or four years, maybe more, but then our future, and Lexi's future—and a new baby's future—would be set."

Linda's face was stone as she grabbed the wine and took a drink then plunked the glass down, sloshing its contents onto the sideboard. Galen overcompensated by sipping carefully and gently setting his glass on the table. Linda wouldn't look at him; she just stared at the little puddle of wine, occasionally shaking her head.

She didn't speak to Galen for the rest of the night. After dinner, she took a book to bed, and as soon as he came in, she closed it and shut off the light. The following evening when he got home, the apartment was empty, and there was a jar of peanut butter beside a loaf of bread on the counter. A voice mail from Eddy told him Linda was spending the night there. The next evening, Galen came home to a warm kitchen smelling of chicken potpie, his favorite. Linda handed him a plate and a kiss. "Congratulations. And now we look forward to the next phase." Galen was confused but relieved.

8

PATRICIA CHEN'S PROUDEST moment at the FDA so far was being a signature on the approval for the fibromyalgia drug that was giving hope to thousands, if not millions. She was now the lead medical reviewer for a new drug for stroke, Lexistro, that she was sure was going to be just as much of a miracle.

She finished reading the submission for the Phase II study and decided to take a rare long lunch break. When she returned, she noticed a strange electric hush in the halls that increased in intensity as she neared her team's suite. When she passed her boss' office, he waved her in. His face was somber. He slid a letter across the desk, and she read it with increasing shock and dismay.

Patricia spent the rest of the week in strategy meetings with other toxicity reviewers. Patricia pored over all of the data she had evaluated since she joined FDA, looking for some clue to this outcome. Her search yielded no relief. Sadly, she signed all the forms and went straight home to bed, where she stayed until the cold, gray morning when the newspaper headlines read, "Death Prompts Withdrawal of Promising Fibromyalgia Drug".

ONE OF THE firm's senior partners tossed a brief onto Elizabeth's desk. "I need you to try this case."

She read the title. "Fibromyalgia? But I haven't been in a courtroom since . . . ." As usual, she couldn't finish her sentence.

"I know," he said sharply. "And the two of you were a damned good team. But this firm couldn't afford to lose you both." His voice softened. "You need to get back in the saddle, Liz."

He was right. But without her husband, she would be on the high wire without a net, a place she had never been before. She flipped through the brief of the firm's most prominent case. Well, why start small? "Okay, I'll do it."

At home that night, Elizabeth sat in the rocking chair next to Sera's bed and watched the hands of the clock tick to midnight. She prayed thanks for another year of her daughter's health. She's still fine, she said silently to the ever-present picture of Sera's father, so there's no reason I can't spend time on my career. Maybe I'll take her for the genetic testing this year and prove it to them all. Maybe the fibromyalgia case will settle out of court. Maybe I'll start dating again.

"It's my happy birthday, Daddy!" Sera said in the dark. Sera talked to her father's picture as if she knew him. It had disconcerted Elizabeth at first, but then she figured like mother, like daughter. She was thankful they both had something to make him feel closer, as Elizabeth was beginning to forget more and more.

It seemed strange that she could forget anything about someone who had been so substantial. He had made her feel safe and warm and intelligent and beautiful and delicate and strong, all at once. She spewed ideas to him, and he listened to her with admiration, if not always agreement. With him, she could have had her career and family and continued to write poetry and enjoy other pastimes that, as a single mother, she had to forgo. Sera was worth a thousand frivolous hobbies, but Elizabeth often wondered if she would ever feel close to a man again. Or if she would forevermore be isolated, guarded, and have to rely on herself alone. The loneliness was daunting; sometimes she just needed his arms around her.

Sera was sitting up in bed, telling some crazy story. Her silvery brown hair flew about her, glowing in the moonlight. She had her father's boisterous personality in addition to his Irish eyes. Her development was progressing on track with no symptoms of a genetic defect. If anything, she was hyper verbal.

When Sera finished her story and looked expectantly for her mother's response, Elizabeth scooped her into a hug. "You are Daddy's angel gift to me!"

Sera said, "I know."

EDDY TURNED THE volume up so he could listen to the eleven o'clock news while he finished putting together Abigail's big girl bed. It was a surprise for her third birthday, along with the new bedroom that he and Joy had been decorating in secret since they moved into their new house.

The newscaster was saying, "Dozens of fibromyalgia patients testified to Congress today, urging the Food and Drug Administration to return their drug to the market. They claim to understand the risks and want the option to decide for themselves."

Eddy stopped his hammering when he saw state representative Kevin Jenkins, whose career he had been following for years, and who was likely to run for the senate in the next election. "Mr. Jenkins, after hearing the testimonies today, what do you think about the fact that the grieving family has launched a lawsuit against the makers of the drug? They claim that the risk of death was known to the company but not released to the public or the FDA."

Jenkins spoke directly into the camera, his tone earnest and grim. "This situation illustrates that there are at least two viewpoints in every story. I believe there are still lawyers in our legal system with the will to get this verdict right—for both parties."

Eddy studied the statesman's face during the rest of the interview. Surely, the man was on one side or the other; no one could truly be neutral, and both sides couldn't be right.

THE OFFICE WAS filled with moonlight, but Galen leaned under a small drafting lamp to examine several large sheets of paper that were taped together and laid lengthwise on the table. The pages were full of notations: arrows, symbols of periodic elements, circles, green pluses, red minuses, and question marks.

Myesha joined him at the table. "Learn anything new?"

"Yes!" Galen said with exasperation. Ever since he heard the news about the fibromyalgia drug, he had been obsessed with the potential downstream effects of 423, now called Lexistro. "Let me ask you something." He pointed to a line on the middle sheet of paper. "If you introduce neuroglobin, its degradation releases the heme portion, which is necessary for regulation of stress proteins and EIF2-alpha, but the hemooxygenase—"

"Whoa, can you discount your words a little? You're talking out of my price range."

Galen looked up in surprise and laughed. "Sorry." He balanced on a stool across the table from Myesha and sprawled over his drawings. "Neuroglobin, even what we make ourselves, eventually gets broken down and cleared out of the brain. I don't know exactly how long that takes."

She pulled over a stool opposite from him. He said, "One of the breakdown products is going to be heme, same as with hemoglobin." Myesha leaned in to peer at the drawings while Galen spoke. "Either the heme stays intact and gets used to regulate different processes, or it gets broken down further. If it stays intact, the cerebrospinal fluid surrounding the brain has material that sticks to the used heme and takes it to the liver to be discarded."

Myesha's hand traced his words on the page. "Yeah, I'm following."

"Alright, the rest of the heme breaks down into bilirubin, carbon monoxide, and iron, all of which can be toxic. Bilirubin can kill brain cells, particularly astrocytes. That's okay, because we know all of our monkeys had *more* astrocytes after getting Lexistro, although I don't know why. But carbon monoxide can bind up other hemoglobin and keep it from distributing oxygen."

Myesha sat up. "So just by using our brains, we're making stuff that's killing off our brain cells? Geez, no wonder we've been dying since the day we were born."

"Hah. I never thought about it like that. Maybe we'll stumble onto the cure for aging!"

"I could stand to get back a few years."

"Tell me about it." Galen stood and leaned under the lamp again. "Just like every other system in the brain, it's moderation that matters. Bilirubin can have positive anti-oxidant effects, and some level of carbon monoxide relaxes blood vessels."

Myesha raised an eyebrow. "You're saying at the right levels, carbon monoxide might actually help to *prevent* ischemic stroke."

"Exactly!"

"So it's a lot like men, not good or bad, just shades of imperfect."

"I don't know whom you're calling imperfect." Galen straightened up with an exaggerated huff, hitting his head on the lamp, to Myesha's great amusement. "Okay, wisecracker, here's my question. How do we manage the level of CSF so that enough heme gets discarded in the liver, and there is not too much left to break down, but there will be just the right amount of anti-oxidants?"

She said, "We could hire Goldilocks. I hear she's been out of work since the three bears defamed her."

Smiling, Galen waved Myesha away and walked over to the refrigerator. He realized for the first time that he had actually made friends with Myesha, beyond just a colleague. It felt like an accomplishment.

Myesha shook off the bottle of water he offered to her. "Sorry, I'm a little punchy. Seriously, my answer is that I don't think we can. Regulate the CSF, I mean. I'm sure there's an even more complicated process in the brain for that, and we have to trust it to work."

She pulled her briefcase across the table and rummaged through it. "We just have to keep doing what we're doing, making sure that we don't give the drug to anyone who might show signs that their system isn't working. So don't give it to anyone with a history of jaundice, because they obviously have bilirubin issues. Don't give it to anyone who's had carbon monoxide poisoning. And warn people against dehydration. Then you just monitor everyone else, and if they show signs of the bad stuff, you stop giving them the drug and hope they go back to normal." She pulled out a set of keys.

Galen leaned against the windowsill, his back to Myesha. Her answer was logical, but he was dissatisfied. "It's all so imprecise."

"Welcome to clinical research. It's why we do small safety studies and pay the participants handsomely."

"But we didn't pay our Phase One participants."

"That's because they were *patients*. When companies do safety studies on healthy people, it's okay to pay them. But if we need to enroll people who already have the disease, committees on human research generally consider payment coercive."

Galen whirled toward her, stirring enough air to cause the big sheets of paper to slide off the drafting table. "It *is* coercive; that's the point! Otherwise we're just exploiting sick people for being desperate enough to sign up for an experiment."

Myesha held up her hands in surrender. "I don't make the rules. But just remember this conversation when enrollment of the trial is going slow, and cut me some slack." She hopped off her stool. "See you later."

Galen lay awake for half the night thinking about the drug development process. It had more moving parts and checks and balances and complicated downstream effects than any biological system he had ever studied.

9

PATRICIA'S ONLY THOUGHT in the few months after the drug withdrawal was that she had approved it, but it wasn't safe. *Someone died because of me.* Her guilt was exacerbated by news articles condemning the FDA for being careless pawns of the pharmaceutical industry.

Even after she had testified at the hearings, Patricia had combed through the data time and again, looking for clues. She didn't want to find out that she had missed something, but what she did find out was equally disturbing: there was no data to overlook. The company's application for marketing approval was complete and adhered to regulations. Years of clinical research had shown no hint of the catastrophic outcome.

Veteran reviewers explained that it was a numbers game. When a serious outcome was rare, such as three in ten thousand, if only two thousand patients were enrolled in all of the clinical trials, that rarity wasn't likely to manifest during development. Moreover, once the drug was on the market, there was little control over whether patients took it as prescribed and the consequences if they didn't.

Finally, she had to admit that it was just bad luck. But she vowed to change the odds for the future.

ELIZABETH INTERRUPTED HER boss during lunch to tell her the good news. "FDA reviewed the evidence and agrees there was no malicious omission!"

Her boss kept eating. "That's great. Now maybe the family will finally agree to a settlement."

Elizabeth pulled up a chair on the other side of the table. "But why would we agree to a settlement now? We could win outright in court."

Her boss put down her fork. "Elizabeth, of all the associates in this firm, you know the most about the law. But to be a great *lawyer*, you need to understand the moving pieces *outside* the law. It's all about perception. So it doesn't matter what the company did or didn't know or who said so; the longer this drags out in the press, the more the company's stock goes down. Because at the end of the day, the gossip is always going to be that the big, bad pharmaceutical industry harassed a grieving family to make a buck. So just settle it."

PATRICIA STOOD IN front of the bulletin board and gaped at the day's posted news article. It suggested the FDA was in cahoots with the company in the fibromyalgia debacle and was sweeping evidence under the rug. A colleague stepped up behind her. "You're missing the point of this board."

She didn't acknowledge him.

"The point is to ridicule a particularly disgusting piece of journalism each day. It's supposed to take the bite out of it, not give you another tool to flog yourself with."

Patricia thought if she ignored him, he would go away. But he continued. "Look, no one is ever going to pat you on the back for approving a drug, no matter how many people it saves. But they'll sure get you if you approve one that isn't perfect. Heck, now they're even suing when you *don't* approve it. So your options are either to take this stuff to heart and make decisions that cover your own butt, or to struggle every day to do what's right and make light of the crap that comes with it. The point of this board is to encourage the latter."

In general, Patricia thought this particular colleague was an arrogant jerk, but he had a point today. She had reviewed all of the fibromyalgia follow-up data in support of a return to market and was cautiously optimistic that the drug was still worth the risk, but she hadn't acted yet. Because she still feared that she might be wrong.

Once she admitted to herself what was holding her back, Patricia signed a renewed approval for limited distribution. Although fear served a primal purpose, she wouldn't allow herself to be governed by it.

ELIZABETH EXTENDED THE contract and a pen toward the pharmaceutical company representative. The family had agreed to a settlement, and the drug would be available to patients again, so it was a good outcome. "Thank you, my dear," the elderly gentleman said, taking the pen. He leaned over the conference table and perused the pages. "It's just too bad this has already done its damage."

"How so?" she asked politely as she crossed her legs and leaned against a chair, expecting another lecture about stock prices and the media.

"Well, the drug has been pulled, of course."

"I thought the FDA re-approved it."

"They did, but it's too risky for us to put it back on the market." He put his pen to the signature line.

Elizabeth grabbed the page away, causing the ink to streak off the edge to the conference table. "What do you mean?"

His white eyebrows rose high, and he studied her for a moment before answering. "We're only re-approved for a very limited population. You've seen the size of this settlement; it won't take many deals like this to overcome our revenue. Sometimes, we have to cut our losses."

43

Elizabeth dropped her professionalism and asked in blunt astonishment, "But what about all the other patients?"

He gestured her to a seat with an expression of compassion. She collapsed into a chair. "We also have the most effective cholesterol medicine in the country. If our company goes under, what about all those people?"

Elizabeth regained her composure. "That's a bit melodramatic."

He smiled. "Yes, we are are solvent with that product. However, the point is valid; this business is about choices. Not only ours, but those of every person who affects the economics, including the family who chose to sue."

Elizabeth wondered how much her husband had sheltered her when they worked on cases together. He must have allowed her to remain starry-eyed and adamant to protect her idealism. Because, she realized now, the situations they defended couldn't have been as straightforward as she had always believed.

"What would make you sell it again?" she asked.

"My dear, nothing short of a guarantee against further lawsuits can resurrect this product."

Elizabeth vowed to herself to make it happen.

10

THE PARTNERS ANSWERED Elizabeth in resounding unison. "No."

She stood at the front of the conference room in her best power suit, the most inspired she had ever been. "I've been researching this for weeks. It can work." Five pairs of eyes were on her, and she made contact with each one as she spoke. "The principle of double jeopardy is that the defendant can't be tried more than once for the same offense. My argument is that the offense in this case is simply that the pharmaceutical company didn't know all of the side effects. They did nothing wrong; they followed the regulations, and they disclosed everything there was to disclose, including the theoretical risk of serious complications. But in no study did any of the animals or humans actually develop those complications. So until the point of that first death, when the drug was immediately recalled *voluntarily by the company*, both the FDA and the patients who took the drug knew everything the company knew."

She noticed that the youngest partner, wearing a suit designed to blend in, was watching the others as Elizabeth talked. She spoke to him directly. "As long as the company continues to disclose new information, why should they be sued again? There's an element of the unknown in any new product, and consumers have the right and *responsibility* to understand that. FDA requirements are a hard balance between ensuring a treatment is safe and ensuring it's available, so when a drug is first approved for market, it means only that the *odds* are that the benefits outweigh the risks. There is no guarantee."

"You're arguing that this man paid for the privilege of being a guinea pig without consent."

Instead of answering the younger man, Elizabeth turned to the founding partner, whose attention lately was more on her grandchildren than the firm. "I'm arguing that he paid for the opportunity to be spared from pain. A terrible tragedy occurred, but that doesn't mean a crime was committed. Why should the company shoulder all of the risks of the unknown?"

"Because they're getting all of the reward."

"Are they? The patients who are no longer in pain got a pretty good benefit, I'd say. But it is true that the company sees the monetary reward. Which is exactly why they have agreed to donate half of their profits from this drug to the national fibromyalgia support organization." She saw one of the senior partners shaking his head, so she approached his chair and set a term sheet on the table between him and the other senior partner. "The product price and definitions have been negotiated as part of the settlement. It's essentially an enormous insurance premium against the unknown that caps the company's liability at half. The support organization has no limits on what they can do with the funds, aside from agreeing to handle any future patient claims like this one. It's a win-win."

"The courts will never agree to this. It's preempting the right of future victims to obtain compensation."

She crossed her arms and stepped back. "That's funny, I thought our legal system was about justice, not payout." The air chilled. Had she gone too far?

Her boss stood up on the other side of the room. "Elizabeth, we admire your creativity, but I told you, it's ultimately about perception. This solution may be rational, but it's complicated. So in sound bytes, it's just smoke and mirrors and more ammunition to say that deep pockets got the best defense again, so the little people got screwed."

Elizabeth was ready with a counterargument. "As you pointed out, perception affects stocks, which is the company's concern, not ours. The company is willing to see this through to court if the family doesn't agree to the new settlement. The company could get away with paying much less and just cut their losses, but instead they're taking the risk to get this drug back on the market, because it's the right thing to do. That has to have spin."

Her boss said, "Right depends on where you stand."

Elizabeth gestured toward the term sheet and walked slowly around the table as she talked. All five heads swiveled to watch. "The company will pay all of the family's legal bills, medical bills, ancillary expenses, and funeral costs, plus three years' worth of the deceased's full salary for the family to get back on its feet. The rest of the settlement goes to the support organization. So if this case is an isolated tragedy, the fibromyalgia community still benefits."

Ignoring Elizabeth, her boss placed both hands on the table and leaned toward the partners. "No jury will accept that. They won't be faced with the whole community; they'll face one family who lost a loved one. And they'll want payback."

"If the judge and the family agree to the settlement, we'll never have to see a jury." Elizabeth stopped at the front of the conference room. "Either way, here's my case: If the objective of the lawsuit was to make the company pay, it worked. If the point was to help the family recover financially, that worked, too." She scanned the room slowly, her gaze meeting all five, and all five again. "But if the objective was for the family or their lawyers to get rich off the loss, that's unacceptable. No amount of money will make real pain go away."

She didn't have to say, *believe me, I know*. Half of the people in the room had been involved in the insurance settlement from her husband's accident, and Elizabeth could see on their faces that they heard her. As distasteful as she found it, she knew they also heard what she would sound like in front of a jury and a television camera. They agreed to let her try.

JOY WAS PULLING macaroni and cheese from the oven when Eddy arrived home from work. "You're just in time," she said. "Abby, honey, why don't you get everybody a plate?" Abigail reached as high as she could to grab the tumbleware plates off the counter.

Eddy kissed his wife on the cheek and sniffed the casserole dish. "Mmmm."

She elbowed him. "Don't be stealing my aroma."

He filled three water glasses and helped Abigail carry them to the table. "I had a meeting with my boss today about reorganization."

Joy spooned macaroni and cheese onto Abigail's plate. Abigail sniffed loudly. "Mmmm."

Eddy grinned at Joy, who rolled her eyes. "Good, isn't it, kiddo?" Abigail nodded vigorously and shoved a spoonful into her mouth.

"Reorganization? Meaning what?"

"Oh, he just wanted to offer me a promotion."

"Honey! That's great!" Joy hugged him. "Why didn't you call me? What's the new job?"

"If I accepted it, I'd be coordinating training for all of New England." Eddy made a face at Abigail, to avoid looking at Joy.

"I'm so proud of you! What an opportunity. Will you get a raise?"

"I would. It would mean more hours and travel." Eddy focused hard on loading his spoon. "Abigail's going to be starting school soon. She'll need help with her homework."

"She won't have homework for a few years yet!"

"But she'll have school plays or something." Abigail was mirroring him whenever he took a bite. He raised his spoon slowly, she raised her spoon slowly. He lowered his quickly, she lowered hers quickly. He chomped a big bite off it, and she did the same, and they both grinned as they chewed.

Joy said slowly, "Are you thinking of not taking the promotion?"

"Well . . . no. I just wonder if it might have been better timed when Abigail was a little older. If you don't want me to do this, it's no problem. I can always ask for it later." He finally turned his head to Joy.

She was studying him. "Abigail is always going to need her dad around; there are some things money can't buy." She paused, still eyeing him. "So you would turn it down? If I asked you to?"

He knew she was offering him an out. He would have asked if she was disappointed in him for not wanting the promotion, but he didn't want to know the answer. "If it's best for you and Abigail, then I won't take it." Their eyes were locked. She nodded slightly.

He released the breath that he hadn't been aware he was holding. Abigail was watching them intently, so Eddy made a big show of gobbling the rest of his macaroni and cheese. Her little face broke its concentration, and she giggled her ready giggle.

AFTER A WEEK of negotiations with the prosecuting lawyer and the judge, Elizabeth came home from the courthouse triumphant. Sera pointed to the television screen. "Mommy's on teebee!"

"As we have been reporting all afternoon, the judge in the fibromyalgia lawsuit has agreed to a ground-breaking and controversial settlement. The lead counsel for the defense, Elizabeth Rose, told Channel Five News that the verdict was a victory for health care torte reform and urged viewers to be knowledgeable consumers and read the details of the settlement, which are available at dcnews.org. The family's lawyer declined to comment."

That night after Sera went to sleep, Elizabeth sat at her desk in the dark, pondering her firm's share of the settlement. She tried to think of it as making money off predators who made money off sick people, but she only felt guilty for taking money away from the drug company, and therefore away from progress.

She also worried that, although it was a step in the right direction, it was not sustainable. Support groups were not designed to handle patient claims, and she doubted how well they could process that volume of money. If this were going to become a norm for the future, the best solution would be a central repository for all punitive damages, structured expressly for that purpose.

Elizabeth turned on the computer and navigated to her bank website, where she opened a new savings account and labeled it *SEED*. She would transfer into it the punitive portion of her client fees. She didn't know what she would do next, but she liked the image of her inkling taking root.

When she finally went to bed, Elizabeth talked softly to the picture on the nightstand. "I did it, hon. You weren't with me, and it's been scary as hell, but I did it. And I want to keep doing it. Is that okay?" She watched the picture for a moment then let out a breath and closed her eyes. "Thank you," she whispered.

PATRICIA'S COLLEAGUES TRIED to get her to talk about the fibromyalgia verdict, but she had nothing to say. She didn't care about the money, and she would have been just as relieved to have the product off the market as on. In any case, she had work to do.

She had listened to one too many pieces of advice in the midst of her turmoil, now everyone was full of it, lobbying bits of wisdom into her office as they passed. Some were insightful, others intrusive, and most, frankly annoying. One stuck in her head like a bad jingle: *Your perspective depends on your experience to date; were you burned for access early or for providing it too late?*

Patricia tried to think of the tragedy as her defining moment and focus only on what she would do with the knowledge. She was more conservative with all of her projects. She never finished a review early, and she championed requirements for additional data prior to market approval. She had asserted herself onto a task force for regulation changes and was compiling transcripts of every court ruling and Congressional hearing on guidelines related to the Federal Food, Drug, and Cosmetic Act and the FDA Modernization Act, so she would be one hundred percent informed.

When Patricia took a rare break to go out to dinner with friends, one of them asked what had kept her so busy for the past several months. She told them, "My job is to first do no harm, and it's harder than it sounds."

PHASE III

11

GALEN WANDERED IN marvel through his state-of-the-art laboratory, not touching anything for fear it might shimmer away like a
hologram. After all those years of stealing time at the university,
here was a lab, his for the running.

Even Galen had been shocked when the first large pivotal
trial for Lexistro enrolled twice as quickly as planned, and the
interim results showed that Lexistro was phenomenally effective
in reversing ischemic stroke. His company had reached the holy
grail of clinical research, to stop the study early and be approved
for market almost immediately. The clinical development process
for Lexistro had taken barely five years, barely half of the typical
timeline. Galen and Myesha appreciated the exceeding rarity of
their success.

When they sent the market application for Lexistro was sent
to the FDA, Galen felt like an artist selling his one-of-a-kind
painting. But in the few short years since then, the bittersweet
had turned to fatherly pride as Lexistro became the mainstay
treatment in the first hours after stroke, as critical as epineph-
rine for bee stings or aspirin for heart attacks.

The company now had a name, Biolex. The warehouse was still headquarters, but the company currently leased the whole building instead of just one compartment. The purple couch was gone, and the bare floors and folding tables were replaced with plush toast carpeting and real office furniture. Galen owned the old compartment and had it made over into a post-modern condominium for himself.

Galen breathed in the sanitary air of the new lab. It didn't yet feel lived-in; no formaldehyde or xylene had been spilled on the countertops to give the air flavor. He peered over the shoulders of two technicians who were running some of his latest experiments. "How's it going?" They both jumped back from their microscopes. Galen sighed inwardly. CEO was a title that never did fit him, and he gladly would have given it up to go back to the microscope himself. He gave kudos to the technicians and reluctantly left the lab to return to his office.

Galen had planned to continue developing new indications for Lexistro as the next steps for Biolex. While he was ecstatic that Lexistro was a first-line treatment *after* stroke, he had always intended it to be a *preventative* treatment, so Myesha and her new clinical staff were running the trials necessary to get the product approved for chronic use. Galen had once again been appalled at the process, that for every different kind of disease or population, they had to spend more time to run more trials, even though his product was on the market already. Rationally, he knew that a drug could act differently in different diseases, or in children versus adults, so they had to conduct studies to know for sure. But emotionally, it was maddening to think of the people who couldn't get the treatment in the meantime.

Galen would have put all of the remaining research funding toward using Lexistro for other, more obscure, conditions, but Amos had said, "It's a damn good thing you have me, son. What are you thinking, lashing all your horses to one hitch?" So the company had hired a scientist to work on new ideas, and the new senior management team was considering partnerships and other ways to diversify their pipeline of products in development, to insure the company in case of failure.

Amos constantly reminded Galen that only one in ten thousand compounds made it from lab bench to market, and Myesha had told him more than once that he couldn't be so naïve about things like pricing. "Economics is an art," she had said. "Pricing may seem straightforward on the surface—set the price high and sell less or set the price low and sell more—but there are a lot of things to consider when you're deciding how much is enough. How much would you pay to save a year of your life? Or five years? Or ten? We could charge anything for this drug. We could charge a billion dollars, and the one billionaire who was going to die from stroke would pay it, and we'd be sitting high on the hog."

Galen had protested earnestly. He wanted the drug to reach as many people as possible.

"Of course you do," she had said. "And despite popular opinion, so do most of our investors. The trick is to find the lowest price that will earn enough profit: one, to be worth the risk of further investment; two, to provide funds to develop your next product; and three, to get you some real furniture so you can trash this nasty couch!" Galen had almost kept the purple couch for sentimental value. He smiled to himself at the thought.

Galen had offered to step down as CEO a number of times to make room for someone with more intuitive business sense, but Amos insisted that it was Galen's "pie-eyed pink spectacles" that made Biolex the darling of the media as well as Wall Street. Galen's company philosophy prompted calls from senators, fellow entrepreneurs, and students with a dream.

Galen contemplated the banner hanging in the hall on the way to his office, the same banner that he had insisted be hung in every laboratory and suite of offices at the company.

> ### FORMULA FOR SUCCESS
> People > Profit
> Accessible = Available + Affordable
> ($ Profit / $ Goal) X (% Accessible) = % Success

Biolex investors believed Galen's formula would be the secret to the company's longevity. Galen was privately glad he let Amos keep bullying him out of quitting, because for the most part, he still enjoyed having power behind his convictions.

He leaned against his real mahogany desk while he checked his voicemail and gazed through the picture window overlooking the Charles River. Galen still felt out of place in the luxury, but Amos insisted that their surroundings were critical to their continued success. "Perception is reality to Wall Street, son."

Amos never let Galen forget that despite the media attention, their company was still young and still dependent upon revenue from only one product. "The market's just a rodeo. It only takes one bull to make you, but the faster you ride, the harder you fall. And you won't win the gold buckle without a few broken bones."

Galen glanced toward the bottom drawer of his filing cabinet. He had more than a few broken parts. His mind unwittingly returned to the day he had held Lexi tightly while Linda packed the car. His ex-wife hadn't looked at him as he fastened their daughter into the seat, fumbling with the buckle, unable to see through his tears. Despair was streaming quietly down Lexi's cheeks, too; she understood as a pre-schooler does, the emotions but not the logic. If there was any logic. Galen tried to smile as he waved to them driving out of the yard, but the bewilderment on Lexi's face broke his heart and still haunted his dreams.

12

LEXI PLUNKED OUT a scale on the cream-colored baby grand piano. She tried to keep her mind off the surrounding bay window that was inviting her to leap into the color and warm wind that smelled like back-to-school. She was sure that placing the piano here was just another of her mother's subtle forms of torture. The filmy beige curtains blew around her, and she swatted them away with one hand, striking a wrong note with the other. She fought the urge to slam down the keyboard cover.

Her mother, Linda, got up from the couch to tie back the curtains and tuck Lexi's hair behind her ears. Lexi cringed. She vowed to practice hard until supper and not miss any more notes. She was still practicing when her father, Roger, came home from work. He went upstairs to change his clothes while Lexi repeatedly banged out the notes to "Mary Had a Little Lamb". After five minutes, he called from the top of the landing. "Alexandra, give us a rest, please!"

Lexi abandoned the piano and dodged up to her room to brush her hair so it wouldn't be its usual curly mess at dinner. She heard Roger and Linda in the kitchen, setting the table. She wanted more than anything to help them. She imagined it as a family event just like Sera, her next-door neighbor and best friend since kindergarten, did with her mom. Lexi and Linda would laugh and hug each other, and they would sit and talk about their day, and Lexi would get lots of praise and hardly any criticism. But Lexi stayed upstairs until she was called, having sensed at an early age that she was not welcome during couples time.

ELIZABETH HUNG UP the telephone and resumed her seat across from Sera at their little round dinner table. "Three kids in your class were absent from school today, so you're staying home with me tomorrow until the bug makes it rounds."

"Woo hoo!" Sera's delicate arms shot into the air. "Can I stay up tonight and watch music videos?"

Elizabeth assumed a stern expression. "You know the rules: regular bedtime, plenty of sleep, drink your water. It isn't a holiday."

"I know, but it doesn't hurt to ask, right?" She flashed her mother an impish grin.

The next afternoon, Sera knocked on the door to Elizabeth's home office. "Mom, I'm bored." She sighed dramatically and fiddled with the fringe on her sleeve.

"Did you do yesterday's homework?"

"Yes."

"Exercise?"

"Yes."

"What's your reading assignment?"

"*Anne of Green Gables*, but I'm done already." Sera sighed again.

"Okay," Elizabeth said, with a knowing smile. "Just let me finish this, and we can do a crossword." Sera darted down the hall to find the newspaper.

Elizabeth sealed the stack of envelopes on her desk and put them in the basket to take to the post office the next day. For the past year, she had been sending periodic mailings about Vanishing White Matter disease to companies and scientists researching the brain. She wanted to keep her daughter's illness at the forefront of their awareness. The mailings included clippings about VWM, a copy of her and her husband's EIF gene sequence, and a copy of Sera's, which confirmed the congenital defect. Her letters rarely received a response, and when they did, it was never more than a courtesy form letter. But she persevered, hoping she was planting a seed. Today's stack included Galen Douglas, an executive profiled in *Money Magazine*. Elizabeth had seen Linda reading the article before the girls' latest school play and had paid closer attention than usual, because it wasn't Linda's typical genre of reading material.

Elizabeth finished up a few more tasks, and twenty minutes later, she and Sera sat on the floor, the newspaper spread between them on the coffee table. "I got six across!" The clue read, *To bother incessantly*. Sera had written her answer in large wobbly letters: *LAUREN*.

"Who's that?" Elizabeth asked.

"Lauren Gates. She always asks me why I stay home from school so much."

"And what do you tell her?"

"I just say my mother makes me." Sera rolled her eyes. "But she tells everybody I only do it for attention." Sera dropped her head and doodled on the newspaper. "Lexi knows about my disease. She still likes me."

"Would you feel better if more people knew?"

Sera pondered her mother's suggestion while she braided several strands of fringe. "Lauren and her friends would probably say stuff anyway." Sera looked up. "I get mad when they whisper about other kids."

"Sweetie, that's because you care about people."

"I do!" She threw her hands in the air. "But I don't know how to make them stop."

"Why do you think they do it?"

"I don't know." Sera tore off a corner of the newspaper and folded it into a tiny clump.

Elizabeth wrote in an answer: *POWER*.

Sera sat up. "Yeah, it's like if they tell secrets, they can run the school, because people are supposed to feel scared or embarrassed or something."

Elizabeth leaned in close to look Sera in the eye. "I'll tell you a secret. People can't make you feel anything unless you let them."

Sera scrunched her nose. "That's too hard. We should just take away all the secrets, so they don't have anything to whisper about."

Fair enough, Elizabeth thought. They worked a little longer on the crossword, until the doorbell rang. It was Lexi.

"Hi Mrs. Rose. I brought Sera's homework."

"Come on in. Just wash—"

"I know, wash my hands, and the Lysol is under the sink." Elizabeth smiled and stepped aside for Lexi to duck under her arm into the house. Lexi sprayed the textbook with disinfectant and scrubbed her hands in the kitchen sink.

Sera came out of the living room. "Aw, homework?"

"There isn't much. Just math," Lexi assured her.

Sera groaned. "Can Lexi stay, Mom?" Elizabeth hesitated. "Come on, Mom. You know I'll get it all wrong if I do it by myself."

Elizabeth looked back and forth across the room at the two pleading girls. She scrutinized Lexi's face. She wasn't a nurse, so she didn't know when someone else's child looked ill. But there was no hint of a flush or other signs of fever, and her eyes were alert. Elizabeth turned to Sera, who was doing her best sad puppy imitation. What would be the point of saving her daughter's life if she didn't let her live it? "Okay." The girls squealed and ran up to Sera's room before Elizabeth could change her mind. She knew her struggle would only get harder as they grew up.

The next morning, Elizabeth was startled awake by the telephone. It was Linda. "I'm sorry to call so early. I just thought you should know that Lexi has the chicken pox. I hope Sera's okay."

Elizabeth was already putting on her slippers and housecoat when she thanked Linda and dropped the phone. As she rushed to Sera's room, her doctor's words reeled through her mind:

Symptoms of VWM are worse after infection. Avoid infection.
Elizabeth stopped to compose herself before turning the knob on
Sera's door.

"Mom, I'm itchy."

13

FROM THE FRONT porch, Eddy watched Abigail busy herself stirring and pouring and positioning the wares on the lemonade stand they had built out of two TV trays and a multitude of cardboard boxes. She stepped back from the stand and surveyed the setup. She straightened the sign reading *$5 Lemonade* then flipped another sign to *Open*.

Eddy immediate bought a cup. "Yum, that's the best lemonade I ever tasted."

"You don't have to overdo it, Dad."

Joy met them on the lawn. "Speaking of overdoing it, isn't five dollars excessive, even for the best lemonade Dad ever tasted?"

"No, I figured it out. I have to sell—hold on." Abigail touched her thumb to each of the fingers on her opposite hand. "Five times one is five, five times two is ten, five times three is fifteen, five times four is twenty, five times five is twenty-five—five cups of lemonade to make enough for my share of the bike. Then after lunch we can go to Wal-Mart to get it, and I can ride some before supper."

Eddy suppressed a smile and glanced at Joy, who was doing the same. She said, "Summer vacation is still a few weeks away. You don't have to make all twenty-five dollars this morning."

"Yeah, but why wait?"

"It's up to you. I'll have to pass on the lemonade, though. I can't afford five dollars." Joy turned back toward the house.

"Dad did."

"That's why I only have a quarter in my pocket; he spent all my money!"

Abigail eyed her father sternly. "You didn't spend your share of the bike, did you?" Eddy assured her that he had not.

Two hours later, when Abigail came inside for lunch, she threw her signs and plastic cups onto the counter and sat down heavily at the kitchen table. She bit miserably into her sandwich.

"So are we going to Wal-Mart today or what?" Eddy asked.

"Don't tease," she said, spraying egg salad onto the table.

Joy said, "Swallow before you talk, please. Do you want some lemonade to wash that down?"

"Mom!"

"Oh, sorry." Joy handed her a glass of water and winked.

"You guys aren't funny." They ate without talking for a few more minutes, then Abigail said, "Well, at least I made five dollars off Dad."

"I hate to break it to you, but you owe me four for the cost of goods, remember?"

"I thought you might forget about that." She pulled the crumpled dollar bills from her pocket and handed them to him.

"You're going to let her give up already?" Joy said.

Before Eddy could answer, Abigail said, "Are you going to make me stand out there all Saturday? It's stupid. Nobody wants any lemonade."

"I did, but it cost too much."

Abigail pondered her mother's statement over the rest of her sandwich. She counted on her fingers, and her eyes rolled up in concentration. With the last bite of sandwich still in her mouth, she pushed back from the table, grabbed a marker and her other materials from the counter, and ran outside.

"You're excused!" Eddy called after her.

"Don't choke on that!" Joy said.

After Eddy finished his lunch, he went out to check on progress. The sign in front of the stand now read *25¢ Lemonade*.

At supper several hours later, Abigail could hardly contain her excitement. "I made five dollars today!"

Eddy smiled at Joy. It was amazing how much one afternoon could change an eight-year-old's perspective.

"What does it cost to make cookies? Maybe tomorrow I can sell cookies *and* lemonade! Then I would definitely have my new bike before summer!"

That evening, Abigail pedaled her old bike to the store and spent three dollars on a package of pre-made cookie dough. The next afternoon, she and Joy baked it for the requisite fifteen minutes, and in an hour, Abigail had sold the full dozen to her parents, the minister, the retired couple next door, and two kids from across the street. She returned to the store with all the money she had just earned to buy another package. While the next batch was cooking, more neighbor kids gathered on the lawn.

A couple of the community busybiddies marched over to speak to the Parker parents. As Eddy was bringing out the plate of cookies, one of them said to him, "We think it's cruel of you to allow your daughter to flaunt her party in front of the kids she didn't invite."

"It's not a party, it's a lemonade stand. I know it's hard to tell, what with the sign and all." He kept walking.

They bustled after him. "It's still rude. Not all of the kids have fifty cents for a cup of lemonade."

"It's only twenty-five cents for a cup. Fifty cents gets you a cookie, too." He set the cookies onto the stand and winked at Abigail.

"In any case, it's just not right to leave those kids out because their parents don't have much to spare." Hands on hips, they peered at him.

He faced them to say, "Ladies, if those kids are so thirsty, maybe you should buy them a cup." He was normally the golden boy of the neighborhood, but it was hard to be polite when he was protecting his daughter.

"We shouldn't have to. You should be teaching your child about fairness."

"At the moment, I'm teaching my child about the value of a dollar."

"She can still learn that if she charges ten cents instead of fifty."

"She can charge whatever she wants to. It's her lemonade stand."

"Don't you think that's raising her to be a bit greedy?"

Abigail's eyes moved from her father to the women and back to her father, and her lower lip began to quiver.

"Excuse me, but I don't need you to tell me how to raise my daughter. So, if you'd please go back to your own yards, we have work to do."

They turned to Abigail. "Dear, don't you want to include all of your friends?"

Eddy stepped between Abigail and the two women. "Get. Off. My. Lawn. Please." They walked away in a huff. Eddy turned back to Abigail, who was scribbling on her sign. The other kids were staring. "Abby, kiddo, stop that. You want to make enough for your bike still, right?"

"I d-d-don't want to be g-g-greedy." She crossed out *50¢* and wrote *10¢*.

"I'm not going to let you do that."

She wiped the back of her marker-stained hand across her eyes. "Then I'm not going to do the lemonade stand anymore."

Eddy knew this stubbornness was only a preview of the teenage years to come.

The next batch of cookies was sold out within ten minutes after the new sign was hung. Abigail left Eddy at the stand while she pedaled as fast as her little legs would take her toward the store to buy two more batches of cookies with all the money she had earned that day and the two dollars left from the previous day. Kids swarmed the yard while the batches were baking. By the time Joy set the steaming tray on the stand, the lemonade was gone. When the cookies ran out, the kids standing in line started to chant. "We want chocolate chip! We want chocolate chip!"

"I'll go get more." Abigail dumped her change onto the table and counted frantically. Tears spilled onto the pile of pennies. "Daddy, I don't have enough."

Eddy immediately rounded up the kids and ushered them out of the yard. Their mantra trailed off, and he returned to sit next to Abigail on the grass behind the stand. "It's okay, kiddo. We'll think of something else to do next Saturday."

"I don't want a new bike anymore."

14

ELIZABETH BERATED HERSELF for letting the chicken pox virus into the house. She had called the doctor, who told her to keep Sera from scratching her way to further infection. She also told Elizabeth that Sera must have caught the virus at school earlier in the week rather than from Lexi's visit, because chicken pox doesn't manifest overnight. Instead of being reassured, Elizabeth felt more vulnerable. It was another class of dangers that she couldn't predict and therefore couldn't prevent.

Sera spent her convalescence covered in calamine lotion with oven mitts affixed to her hands, commiserating over the speaker-phone with Lexi. Linda called to check on Sera, which Elizabeth appreciated. She went out of her way to avoid spending time with Linda outside the girls' school events, and she wouldn't have been surprised to learn Linda did likewise. Their relationship had stalled at just neighbors three years before, one day shortly after Sera's symptoms had appeared.

On that dreaded day, Sera's kindergarten teacher had called home concerned that Sera's coloring worksheets, which were previously neat to the point of compulsive, now displayed little more than scribbles. The teacher was concerned that it was an emotional reaction to some problem at home, but Elizabeth knew it was far worse. The neurologist and genetic counselor had confirmed, as well as they could at the time, that Sera had leukoencephalopathy with vanishing white matter.

After the diagnosis, Linda kindly invited Sera over for a play date and made tea and offered a sympathetic ear. Elizabeth voiced in hushed tones her struggle with whether and when and how to tell Sera about her disease.

Linda responded, equally discreetly, that Elizabeth should keep it to herself as long as possible. "Something I've never told Lexi is that Roger isn't her biological father."

"She's adopted?"

"More or less. The point is, she's happy. She has a real family now. Sometimes you have to make hard choices to protect your kids."

"Was her father . . . not good to you?" Elizabeth asked.

Linda shifted in her chair and averted her eyes before she answered. "The thing about my ex is that he was so goddamned honest and smart and hardworking that I never felt like I could do or be anything good enough. But he had the heart of a little boy, so I felt awful for feeling awful about it. I probably shouldn't have married him, anyway—we'd only known each other a few months—but he was so intense, like I was everything to him. It's hard to turn that down. But it gets to be a burden."

Elizabeth remembered how her heart had warmed to the man's image. It was then she had realized that she and Linda could never be friends. They valued different things.

"I've thought a lot about why he even married me," Linda had gone on. Elizabeth let her talk, recognizing that it was the first time she had told the story aloud. "I think he was collecting family. Not in a creepy way, but just . . . sad. That he needed it so much. His previous fiancée died just a year before we met, and he wasn't really over her. He wouldn't admit that, but he spent the entire eight years of our marriage making a business out of her memory."

Elizabeth thought of the picture in her room. It was now eight years for her, too, and she wasn't sure she was over it.

Linda had told her that her husband's business was the reason she moved Lexi away. "It only took a few months for him to stop visiting. He still wrote, but who knows how long that would have lasted, and I couldn't stand to hear Lexi ask about him. So when Roger proposed, it just seemed like fate for us to disappear. I did love Gal—him, and I know he loved Lexi. But she deserved better. And she was young enough to forget."

Elizabeth was sure that in the same circumstances, she would have made different choices, but she didn't judge Linda. When a person does what she thinks is right, there is only one choice she can make; everything in her life has led to the beliefs she holds in that moment.

Still, Linda seemed defensive. "I was right, you know. I saw someone taking pictures a while back, and I'm sure it was a private investigator. So Lexi's father knows where she is, but he didn't come for her. What I'm saying is, if the truth is going to hurt, why tell it?"

Elizabeth had told Sera everything that afternoon. She was still amazed by how tranquilly Sera had accepted it. Elizabeth believed it was her husband's ultimate gift, to go on ahead so their daughter would know someone would be with her on the other side. She often imagined him harassing Saint Peter with his gift of gab, while he waited through each passing year, ready to meet Sera with a hug as big as a lifetime.

Since that conversation with Linda, Elizabeth and Sera talked about everything. And Elizabeth felt a sad curiosity every time she saw Lexi with her "real" family.

The chicken pox must have been a feeble strain, because it cleared up in only a week. The morning the girls were to go back to school, Elizabeth poked her head in the bedroom door to tell Sera to get a move on, and she saw a pile of discarded clothes on the floor. Sera said, "I'm coming," as she yanked on a sweatshirt and a pair of elastic pants. Elizabeth was ready to chalk up the pile and attitude to preteen fickleness until Sera shoved her feet into a pair of clogs, making a sorry-looking outfit. Elizabeth observed that all of the discarded clothes had buttons and zippers.

She watched Sera as they walked down the hall. Sera seemed cautious, and she placed her feet deliberately. At breakfast, she was uncharacteristically quiet. Elizabeth asked her gently, "Do you need to stay home a little longer?"

Tears squeezed out of Sera's eyes. "The world is crooked, Mom. It feels like it's all under water, and my fingers don't work right."

Elizabeth's heart pounded for the next three days—when Sera stumbled on her way to the bathroom, when she couldn't think of a word for the crossword puzzle, and when she slept. Elizabeth called the doctor, even though she knew no one could help. Not only was there no cure for VWM, but there was no treatment. The best the experts could suggest were universal measures, to avoid germs and stay hydrated. So when Sera was awake, Elizabeth forced her to drink water, not knowing what else to do.

By the fourth day, Sera's coordination had improved. On Friday morning, she bounded down the stairs in a shirt bedazzled with snaps and jeans with zippers along both legs. Elizabeth wrapped her in a bear hug. Then they drove to school as if it were just another day.

15

GALEN WAS SURE astrocytes would be Lexistro's downfall. For years, he had known that particular type of brain cell was more prevalent in monkeys given Lexistro, but he hadn't yet figured out why. He hadn't worried about it until this week. At first, he was convinced astrocytes were multiplying into tumors, but Myesha reminded him that no tumors had been reported—yet. Now he thought it was worse than a tumor; the astrocyte expansion was the precursor to a supernova.

If Lexistro exploded and destroyed astrocytes—which release oligodendrocytes, which create myelin, which insulates nerves— the effect could be as bad, if not worse, than a stroke. Without myelin, a person would lose control of signals from the brain to the body.

Galen felt sick to his stomach. He pulled from his desk the mass mailing he had received a few days before. The cover letter was signed *Sincerely, Elizabeth Rose*. Attached was a copy of a newspaper clipping, "Boy's Fatal Brain Disease Results in Important Finding":

One family's courageous act may help countless others with loved ones suffering from a debilitating illness. A generous donation of brain cells was made following one boy's eight-year battle with a rare inherited illness known as vanishing white matter disease (VWM).

Symptoms of VWM are typically slow development or difficulty walking and talking, often worse after an infection or minor head injury, followed by interludes of normalcy. Children with VWM often suffer seizures and lapse into coma before reaching their teens.

Through this donation, scientists have learned that in VWM patients, the type of brain cell called astrocytes are sickly or missing. There is currently no treatment for VWM.

The last paragraph still made Galen's heart skip a beat. If Lexistro eventually killed astrocytes, and anyone gave Lexistro to kids, it might cause VWM. Galen couldn't live with himself if that happened.

VWM is like shaking a snow globe, he thought. There is a flurry of symptoms, which eventually settle until something, such as infection or head injury, shakes them up again. It was clearly a disruption of homeostasis. But how? He had to figure it out.

The thought of snow globes, like most things, made Galen think of Lexi. He could no longer concentrate, so he clicked off his computer and rolled his chair over to unlock the bottom drawer of the filing cabinet. He withdrew a stack of black and white photographs and spread them on his desk. In all of them was a little girl with light wavy hair, photographed just out of reach— through the bars of the playground at school, through the picture window at her home, and through the windshield of a surveillance van.

The year after the investors promised seven million dollars for 423 was the worst of Galen's life. There was an upset victory in the presidential race that caused the stock market to crash in the uncertainty, and the investors reneged on the second half of the deal. So Galen drastically scaled back the Phase II study, leaving just enough to keep it going, praying there would be some hint in the meager results that would support further development when the economy turned around.

Shortly thereafter, Linda asked for a divorce and moved Lexi to Pennsylvania with her parents. Galen had fought it, but during the hearings, Linda's lawyer had asked, "Would a man with his daughter's best interest at heart quit his job and put his family into six figure debt?" The question had triggered Galen's deepest doubts, and at the crucial moment, he couldn't speak. The statement and his silence had hung in the air like a death sentence.

Galen sent Lexi a postcard every day and traveled from Massachusetts to Pennsylvania every other week, first by air, then by train, then by bus, until too soon he had depleted his meager personal bank account and what was left of his credit. He and Linda agreed that the sale of the house would cover child support for the foreseeable future. Galen hid that he was subsisting on a bulk stash of cheese and crackers.

After several weeks of not seeing Lexi, he received a picture of an airplane that she had colored with every crayon in the box. Desperate, he withdrew research funds, intending to sacrifice 423 to kidnap Lexi and bring her home. He rushed around the office, threw together a bag of clothes, scribbled a note to Myesha, and grabbed his keys and coat. But when he turned back for his ID, he suddenly saw his situation the way the judge saw it. He lived between two concrete pillars, surrounded by folding tables, his clothes in a filing cabinet. Even if he weren't arrested, where would Lexi sleep—on the purple couch?

So he had to be content with calling her. Then suddenly, Linda's number was disconnected. He sent a letter to her home, but the envelope was returned, *addressee unknown*. He had called Eddy, begging for news. Eddy suggested a private detective, and Galen couldn't admit that he could barely afford to eat.

So he used the only resource available to him, his telephone. Galen called every pre-school in the state for registration information. He told the truth at first, but the schools were not allowed to give out information. He tried lying, telling them he needed to obtain Lexi's records for an emergency. They couldn't help with that either. He called his local doctor to find out if her records had been forwarded anywhere, but they hadn't. He called his lawyer, whose only free advice was to hire a private detective. He consulted the Internet, but even search firms that cost twenty dollars were $19.23 more than he could find in the folds of the couch. Linda's parents wouldn't take his calls. The last number he had for her brother was disconnected.

When all of his options were exhausted, he spent countless hours on long runs along the Charles River, hoping to be numbed by the cold. It was only when the Phase II study results turned out definitive beyond their wildest imaginings that he had felt some glimmer of hope that life might go on.

The first time Galen had money to spend, he had hired a private investigator to find Lexi. By then, she was already five years old. It didn't take long for the investigator to bring back the pictures of her in her suburban neighborhood, and the one of Lexi being pushed on a swing in the yard with her new father broke Galen's heart again. He had asked himself over and over, if he barged back into Lexi's life, would it be good for her, or would he be doing it only for himself? As always when it came to personal matters, Galen didn't know the right answer. He had a nagging feeling that he would disappoint his daughter just as he had disappointed Linda and his own mother. Could her new father do better?

Galen had stared at the pictures for hours and days and weeks, until he finally decided that she looked happy, with no trace of the three-year-old's tears he had carried in his memory. As unfair as it was to him, he couldn't burden her with his grief and ruin the life he wanted for her. So he had asked the investigator to transfer the records to his lawyer and had his accountant set up a trust fund to come due just before Lexi turned sixteen, in time for her college applications. He wondered whether some undeniable gene would lead Lexi to science, but more than that, Galen hoped she would have a well-rounded life, better than his own. He also asked his lawyer to lock away all records of where she lived, in case his resolve faltered, as it often would.

He put the pictures away and turned his mind back to the newspaper article. He stared at the doodling on his desk pad. Something about it nagged him, but he still couldn't focus. So he stuffed his sketches into the envelope with Elizabeth Rose's letter and went for a run to clear his mind.

EDDY TOSSED THE day's newspaper into the magazine rack. "How's the homework?" he asked Abigail, who was kneeling at the coffee table.

"Okay. I'm almost done with math, though. Then I have to do grammar. Yuck."

"I hear you, kiddo." He patted her on the head. "Tell your mom I'm going out for a run, okay?"

She nodded, already immersed in her next problem. He grabbed his keys and left the house. As he stretched on the front lawn, he surveyed their three-story house with the graying cedar shingles and two-acre lot. It was their dream home, with a wood shop and garage for Eddy and the most modern of kitchens for Joy. It was out of their comfortable price range, but they had bought it last summer when Abigail started having friends overnight. Joy could be the hostess she was so good at being, and Abigail could be popular under her father's watchful eye. Eddy hadn't anticipated that parenting would require so much coordination, but he was proud of how well he took to it.

Eddy jogged down the street toward the beach, thinking about the latest and greatest stock market news about Biolex. Galen was probably a multi-millionaire by now, lucky dog. Eddy had long ago stopped wondering whether he should have accepted the partnership. Eddy was making good money for his job level, and he had a terrific family. Still, he hadn't talked to Galen in two years.

Eddy told himself it wasn't jealousy, just a by-product of the divorce, since Joy and Linda had been close. At the time it had happened, Eddy could do nothing but watch his friend wander through the process, signing whatever his lawyer put in front of him. Galen moved into a corner of his rented office space rather than the spare room Eddy offered. Joy's analysis was that the company was as much Galen's family as she and Eddy were.

One evening shortly after Lexi disappeared, Eddy dropped by to convince his friend that a run would do him good. Galen laced up his sneakers but didn't move from the chair. He slumped over his lap, as if sitting up required too much energy. Throughout the divorce, Galen had developed a permanent stoop, but at that point Eddy could see that even his t-shirt sagged over his shoulders, and his normally pale skin was pasty. Eddy only then realized how powerfully present Galen had always been, even when he didn't say much. His absence was discomforting.

Eddy knew there wasn't any battle he wouldn't fight to be close to his daughter, and of all the differences between him and Galen, that was the biggest. They hadn't spoken since.

Eddy reached the shore and started to climb up the rock wall. So maybe he wasn't particularly fulfilled or challenged at his job, and maybe he would have to work until he was sixty to pay for the house, send Abigail to school, and maintain their lifestyle. But he worked at a company second only to the government in job security.

He couldn't help thinking he was turning into his father. Well, he could do worse. He stood on the wall and watched the ocean waves. That's the one thing they were missing, a boat. Maybe he would work until he was sixty-two so they could get a little one to take out on the weekends. He could already imagine their space at the dock and the Saturday night soirees that would make them famous.

16

WHEN ELIZABETH PICKED up the girls from school, Sera was her usual chatterbox self as she and Lexi climbed into the back seat. "Lauren is a bully, and that's a fact." She jerked the door closed. "Hey, Mom, we want to do my idea on Monday."

Elizabeth looked into the rearview mirror. "I don't know if we can do it that soon, sweetie. Your teacher probably has plans for Monday's class."

"But we talked to a bunch of kids at recess, and we're all ready!"

Rarely able to resist Sera's enthusiasm, Elizabeth contacted the girls' teacher, who was amenable to Sera's idea and contacted the school psychologist, who helped Elizabeth persuade the other parents. They managed to pull the plans together for the following Thursday.

"Everybody, please be quiet," the teacher said to the restless classroom, swollen with visiting parents. "We're going to start today with something a little different. Please say hello to our guest."

"Good morning," came the chorus of response.

"Good morning, everyone." The school psychologist leaned against the blackboard. "Can any of you tell me what gossip is?"

A boy sitting in the front row waved his hand. "It's when someone says something bad about you that isn't true, but everybody believes it anyway."

"Well said." The boy beamed at the psychologist. "Sometimes gossip has a little truth in it, and sometimes it's about good things. That's what makes people want to listen." The third-graders were wide-eyed, poised for the discussion. "What we want to do today is help everyone in the class learn something about everyone else so you won't be tempted to listen to gossip. Miss Sera Rose is going to start us off."

Lauren Gates whispered loudly from the back of the room, "Figures." She received a kind but stern elementary teacher glare.

Sera maneuvered to the front of the classroom, and Elizabeth held her breath. Sera had such a big personality that even her mother often forgot how fragile she looked. Her lime green jean jacket made her face seem more pale than usual.

Fearless as always, Sera spoke with a loud and steady voice. "Most of you know that I stay home from school a lot. But you don't *really* know why." She looked pointedly at Lauren and friends. They stared back. Sera turned her attention to other parts of the classroom. "It's because I have a brain disease. I'll probably die from it when we're in junior high." There was a collective gasp. "It gets worse after I get an infection or something, so I stay home to keep from getting sick, that's all. Lots of people can't do stuff like everybody else."

A boy with curly blonde hair reluctantly stood from his desk in the back corner of the room. Like a new member of Alcoholics Anonymous, he said, "I'm a Jehovah's Witness." He went on in one breath. "That means I can't pledge allegiance to the flag because it's not God but I'm still an American your turn." He sat down and pointed to a girl in a pink hoodie who was standing with her mother next to the windowsill.

The girl said in a small voice, "My brother has Down's Syndrome. He's really sweet, and we love him a lot." She looked up at her mother. "It makes me sad when people talk about him behind my back." There was uncomfortable energy in the room as kids squirmed or turned to look at someone else to deflect the blame. The girl spoke up loudly and looked over to the center of the classroom. "He's not a freak. And neither is she."

The girl she pointed at said, "My family has a funeral home. It's not creepy; we help people with arrangements so they don't have to do it when they're sad."

"That's right, thank you," the psychologist said. "You see, everyone, what you hear from other people isn't always the whole truth. Does anybody else have something they want the class to understand?"

The class clown raised his hand. "I farted in gym class once. It's only because there was beans at lunch that day."

Trying to suppress a smile, the psychologist said, "Thank you for sharing that. Does anyone have some *good* gossip?"

"I'm related to the drummer in the Electric Watermelon Band," said the girl next to Lauren Gates.

"Oh, like fiftieth cousin once removed," Lauren scoffed.

The girl spat back, "It's still related!"

"Okay, now. Anyone else?" A rush of confessions followed.

"My grandpa won the megabucks, so now we're kind of rich."

"I used to be on commercials before I moved here."

"I'm adopted."

"I don't have anorexia. Everybody in my family is skinny."

"Everybody in my family is fat. But my uncle is really funny, and he's famous."

"My uncle was in jail. He's not bad, just stupid."

"I have dyslexia, which means I see weird, so I don't read fast. I'm not stupid."

"I saw heaven once." The room fell quiet. An ethereal girl sitting in the front row said quietly, "I was skating and fell through the ice. In the hospital my heart stopped, and there was a light like real warm sun."

The psychologist gave everyone a moment to absorb the news then smiled at the girl before he said, "I hope now your classmates are a little less of a mystery."

The teacher stood. "Thank you, Doctor. Everybody say good-bye to your parents then open your English books to page twenty-five."

Several kids pushed excitedly toward the rich kids with the famous relatives while Sera walked over to where Elizabeth and Lexi were standing. The girl who had the near-death experience weaved around the other kids bidding farewell to their parents and approached Sera. "I know what your name means."

"Really? What?"

"Angel."

Sera nodded. "That makes sense."

LATER THAT WEEK, Lexi had dinner with the Roses, and Sera insisted they watch the news together, to hear the coverage from Elizabeth's latest case. It was supposed to summarize the last three months of hard negotiations to ensure patient rights at the same time as fighting the rising cost of health care and maintaining incentives for research. But in ten seconds, there was only time for good or evil, so Elizabeth knew the story would just imply that she and her firm were puppets for the pharmaceutical industry.

They waited as snippet after snippet tantalized them to keep watching through the commercial to the next segment. During one commercial, Lexi said, "The news is kind of like gossip, isn't it?"

Elizabeth saw through the third-grader's eyes that there was no depth to the reports anymore, only the juiciest bits of the day, and minimal continuity with broadcasts the night before or after, let alone months apart. Although she told herself she had been working within the system to make her point heard, she realized the sound bytes and word-of-mouth that had been bringing her firm business and growing her seed fund were little more than rumor. She immediately switched off the television.

"Hey, your part didn't come on yet," Sera said.

Lexi looked at Elizabeth with an expression of guilt too heavy for an eight-year-old. "I'm sorry to make you mad."

Elizabeth reached over and squeezed her hand. "Oh sweetie, I'm not mad. Let's just talk about something else tonight."

Sera and Lexi soon found another interesting topic. Listening to them chat, Elizabeth missed her husband still. She missed having someone to talk to about her ideas and her fears, and especially now, the seed fund that her partners dismissed as her "little experiment". She had considered testing her pipe dream though an application process for people who needed medical treatment they couldn't afford. She would require that recipients read a brief about one of the cases whose settlement fed the seed fund and require that they also suggest a way to provide some kind of service to the public as payback. But she didn't know where to start.

Elizabeth had been saving all of her regular income to afford a treatment for Sera, if there ever was one. She knew their life wasn't a movie, so she wouldn't find a cure herself. But she certainly could prompt everyone else to hurry up, which she would do in her research and development speech at the policy session in Washington, DC next month.

17

FOR WEEKS, THE VWM article pervaded Galen's thoughts. It had read that the EIF2-beta enzyme is critical in making astrocytes, and VWM patients have faulty EIF. Galen had a vague sense that the astrocyte connection was important in a way he hadn't yet considered. He had drawn sheets upon sheets of neuronal maps, trying to trace the process. The huge pages were permanently spread across his kitchen table.

Galen got up in the middle of the night, as he often did, and trailed his finger over the drawings. He talked aloud to sort his thoughts.

"Trauma triggers stress proteins. Stress proteins clear away other kinds of faulty proteins to help the brain adapt to stress. Adapting to stress requires astrocytes to regulate the flow of cerebrospinal fluid that bathes the brain."

He closed his eyes and tried to picture his own brain at work. So maybe when there's trauma like an infection, VWM patients have a bigger than normal shift in fluid volume that sends the whole system out of whack for a while, like a car fishtailing on the ice. Could be.

He opened his eyes to talk over the left side of his drawing. "Astrocytes trigger neuroglobin to flow through the CSF and regulate the oxygen level. Neuroglobin breaks down into heme and carbon monoxide. Carbon monoxide can reduce stress and turn off stress proteins."

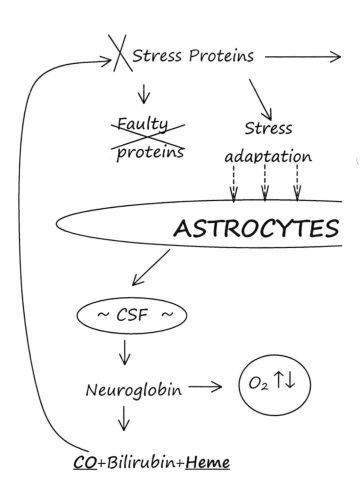

He slid the paper across the table and ran his hand along the right side of the picture. "The electrical balance of sodium and potassium depends on astrocytes. Stress proteins trigger EIF2-alpha, which is heme-regulated. Heme also regulates EIF2-beta. In VWM, EIF2-beta doesn't make astrocytes correctly."

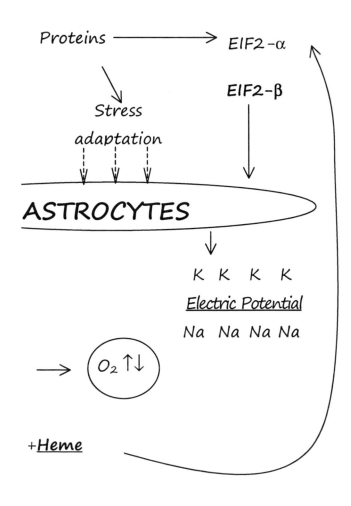

It was all just a jumble of disjointed information. Galen couldn't put his finger on where the concepts converged. Even so, he felt invigorated.

Linda used to tell him not everyone enjoyed a challenge as much as he did. He wondered now if that was her first hint to him that she planned to leave. Or had she just decided it one day? Galen knew only too well that sometimes people did that. He went back to bed, trying to put the thought out of his mind. But he dreamed the rest of the night about the last time he had ever seen his mother.

Just he and Lexi had taken the two-hour drive. He coaxed his car onto a gravel lane marked with a metal sign rusted by ocean air, its peeling paint barely readable as *Hidden Pines*. He drove slowly along the treeless rows of trailers. One site was occupied by a bus decorated in psychedelic style, its transience a stark contrast to the site next to it, barely recognizable as a mobile home behind the built-on porch, extended living room, and empty flower boxes hanging from each window. He steered around a string of forgotten Christmas lights still clinging to the discarded tree at the edge of the lane and pulled up to a single trailer with a ragged gray-and-white-striped awning over the door.

He hauled Lexi out of her car seat and crunched over the icy snow, picking up a candy wrapper on the bottom of his boot. He shook it off as they waited on the front step. His mother came to the door showing even fewer teeth than the last time he'd seen her, belying her mere forty-nine years. She reached for Lexi, who buried her head in Galen's shoulder. Galen kissed his mother on a sour cheek as he passed her grandchild to her.

A pitcher of Tang was waiting on the small round table inside the trailer. Galen poured a glass and sat on the paisley couch, faded despite the plastic covering. Lexi shimmied off her grandmother's knee when she saw a stuffed horse in the corner. She rode until the wilting Christmas bow fell from its ear, and Galen felt the ever-ready guilt. But he had come as soon as he got the time. "When did you get the TV?" he asked. He never had one growing up, just another thing that kept him from fitting in.

"Where's Linda?" his mother asked, her accent sparing the "r".

"She had things to do." The statement was met with silence. "So, ma," Galen said, changing to the other touchy subject. "I got funding for my project." He drew out *goawt* and *proaw-ject*, letting his own accent return. Always when he visited, he became acutely aware of his controlled diction, which sounded pretentious here.

He was reminded of the caramel-haired aspiring actress, never far from his thoughts, who had spent long weekends practicing enunciation in his dorm room. She wanted to learn the "proper" inflection for a down east accent. He wanted the opposite, to sound like he was from the Berkshires, believing it would cure his self-consciousness among the Harvard elite. That was before he realized his phobia was rooted far deeper than diction. Alone, he endured every social situation through a fog of bewilderment and dread, but her eyes cut the fog like a laser beam, guiding him through what to do and say. He had nicknamed their engagement bands his secret decoder rings.

"So now you look after your family like a real man?" his mother said.

Galen forced himself to sit up straight. "I want something more than living paycheck to paycheck. I don't want Linda to ever be in the position you were."

"Bite your tongue. You're not going anywhere."

"I'm not planning to. But you, of all people, know good intentions can go astray."

"I don't want to talk about astray." She raised herself off the couch and grabbed the pitcher from the table.

Galen followed her to the refrigerator, Goliath in a dollhouse. "It's only because I appreciate how hard you worked to send me to school without . . . help."

"And now you're just like he was, obsessed with making a difference, whatever that means."

"What's wrong with that?"

"Just don't let it eat you up."

He pulled a roll of money from his pocket and tried to hand it to her. He hadn't been in a position to offer for years, but time hadn't changed her reaction: she waved it away with a scowl. He wouldn't leave it on the counter, knowing from experience that it would stay there, absorbing salty dampness through visit after visit, until someone broke in and stole it. He put the roll back in his pocket and scanned the familiar kitchen. "I'll fix that faucet for you."

She shrugged. "Neighbor's faucet is leaking, too. Don't stop at me just because we're family."

The cloak of responsibility, moldy with disapproval, was suffocating and bending him under its weight. Lexi tugged at Galen's pant leg. His salvation. He rushed to dress her in coat and mittens and escaped outside to the playground.

He realized as he pushed Lexi on the rusty swing set that it was no escape, because each creak reminded him of the hours he had spent listening to his parents fight as he swung higher and higher, wishing to fly away.

It was always the same argument, every time his father returned after a month or two months or a year: Why couldn't he take a teaching job in town? Because people were already lined up to teach the privileged. Why did he have to think of everyone else first? Because he wanted to do some real good. Why was good only real in the underprivileged backwoods of somewhere else? Because he wanted to make a difference.

Galen tried to make his father proud enough to stay. He studied hard, excelled at sports, and became the handyman for all of the elderly folks in the trailer park. But it wasn't enough. When Galen was fifteen, his father left for the Smoky Mountains and never returned.

Galen pushed Lexi again and she squealed. His mother's expressionless face watched them from the window. Galen had spent his childhood trying to make her smile. The more she disapproved, the harder he tried. Linda finally told him that it wasn't personal, that his mother had long ago decided it was easier to be unhappy than to hope.

Lexi giggled as she went higher. Galen had once thought those giggles could soften some of his mother's bitterness, but now he was afraid of how much it could poison Lexi in the process. Galen had to protect his daughter from the vague sense of failure that had plagued him since boyhood. That was when he decided it would be the last time they'd ever visit.

After the divorce, once Galen had accepted that he would never see his daughter again, he tried to reconnect with his mother. He sent a letter to her and a check to the nursing home where she lived then. Both were returned, unopened.

18

SERA WAS STILL sleeping when Elizabeth kissed her goodbye before she left for Washington, DC. Her mother-in-law was in the kitchen with a travel mug of coffee.

"I really appreciate your watching Sera today."

"Of course, she's my granddaughter. Now you go talk some sense into those politicians."

Elizabeth rode the train into the city and stepped outside Union Station into a circus of media and security stretching all the way to the Georgetown University Law Center. She walked the several blocks to the McDonough Hall building, where she passed through a metal detector at the makeshift security station. At the registration table just inside the entrance, Elizabeth exchanged her invitation for an ID badge, a three-ring binder labeled *Fourth Annual National Town Hall Meeting*, and a ticket for the reception that evening. She went straight to the moot court auditorium where the health care panel discussion was being held and found a seat near the front.

The first page of the binder was an agenda for the symposium, including three parallel policy sessions: foreign, economic, and other domestic. Each session was comprised of several subtopic panel discussions. The information sheet described the process for the day: first the six panel members, all of them senators from a random selection of states, would sumarize their perspectives on pros and cons of the current system and ideas for reform, if necessary. The session would then be opened to fifty pre-screened members of the audience, who were each allowed three minutes at the microphone.

Elizabeth checked her badge, number twenty-seven. She would certainly get her three minutes, maybe before the lunch break. She flipped through the months of research notes that she had used for the screening application. Elizabeth had had no idea what criteria the selection committee would use, so she had just written her honest opinions on the topic of drug development. There must have been some merit in her application, because an invitation had arrived in the mail in February, six weeks before the meeting.

The session commenced, and Elizabeth was immediately impressed by the candor of several panel members, particularly Senator Kevin Jenkins from Massachusetts, who was as astute in praising what worked in the U.S. health care system as he was about criticizing it.

The presentations and questions from most of the first twenty-five audience participants were also thought-provoking and covered a wide range of health care issues: Medicare, private vs. public insurance, national systems, medical errors, long-term care, response to epidemics, vaccines, quality of care, indigent care, medical savings accounts, the cost of prescription drugs, and importing drugs from other countries.

With issues so vast and intertwined, it seemed ludicrous to Elizabeth that Congress still operated mainly without the aid of computer models, as if each member were a processor unto himself and could see every moving part and plan thousands of scenarios to understand the effect of every issue on every other issue in the short term and the long term, well enough to make the most equitable decisions, all without being swayed by his own special interests. It was no wonder that Congress always seemed at an impasse, and that when decisions were made, they had enormous unintended consequences. But this symposium wasn't about resolutions; it was about stirring up a stagnant debate. And the twenty-sixth person was at the microphone.

Adrenaline rushed through Elizabeth's veins. She smoothed her pencil skirt and tried to breathe normally. She considered her three minutes to be the biggest closing argument she had ever made. When it was her turn, she provided figures about the rising cost of research and the fact that the return on investment of tax dollars in the National Institutes of Health was orders of magnitude lower than the ROI of private investment in the pharmaceutical and biotechnology industry. She referenced a Government Accountability Office report about the decreasing number of new drugs being approved by FDA and provided analyses of the ever-widening gap between the new treatments available and what Medicare covered. She stopped short of quoting her least favorite senators to point out their partisan bent and lack of understanding about the issues. In conclusion, she told them pointedly that insufficient accountability to Medicare dollars and NIH grants, together with elected officials' reluctance to make difficult political decisions, had created a system that cost too much and produced too little.

When Elizabeth was finished, one weary senator said, "Mrs. Rose, you've made an admirable case for industry, but your suggestion to abolish Medicare and give the money back to the taxpayers is a bit one-sided. If you were a mother of a child who had a disease and no access to medicine, I doubt you'd think the same way." He looked down at his day's agenda in dismissal.

Elizabeth counted to three before she responded. "With all due respect, sir, I am. And I do." Her words echoed in the auditorium. The panel looked up, and she felt the eyes of the audience upon her as well. She was exposed for only a second before she mustered her legal persona, the one that could separate her feelings from her logic, show only enough emotion to make her point, and not enough to discredit her professionalism. She stood in the aisle in front of the microphone, her voice unwavering. "My daughter has a fatal illness. Seven years ago, there was a major scientific discovery, but there has been no progress since. As a mother and a taxpayer, I want to know why."

There was an uncomfortable pause, and a junior representative on the panel took the opportunity for a sound byte. "I agree that NIH is sadly under-resourced, and I, for one, am committed to doubling NIH funding over the next four years in order to find cures for diseases like your daughter's."

"Sir, perhaps I was unclear." Elizabeth spoke calmly, though her blood was boiling. "I'm not here to provide a poster child for NIH funding. That budget has doubled again and again, a half billion dollars over the last decade. I am here to ask what has been cured. If not my daughter, then who?"

A third panel member spoke. "Ma'am, we have to represent a broad constituency. Setting priorities is a complicated matter."

"I didn't claim it was easy. I even question why it's Congress' job at all. But since it is, my question is simple: What are the priorities and what progress has been made? I'm not asking this question on behalf of just myself. If my tax dollars have cured someone else, I can accept that. What I cannot accept is that instead of making the hard decisions so at least *someone* who donated the tax money sees the benefits, funds are sprinkled so thin that progress takes decades. My daughter has a prognosis of ten years. She turns nine next week."

There was silence in the auditorium. The countdown clock displayed fifteen seconds. Since no one was making a move to answer her, Elizabeth pitched a final plea. "If you can't voice your priorities because of politics, then I beg you to let citizens and companies keep our money, so we can use it to drive the work that we find truly important *now*."

The audience erupted into applause.

AT THE END of the afternoon, Elizabeth decided to skip the evening reception and handed in her badge. The woman managing the registration table said, "Mrs. Rose, Senator Jenkins left a message that he would like to speak with you before you leave, if you have time."

Elizabeth looked from left to right for another Mrs. Rose. "Uh, sure." She fidgeted with the zipper on her briefcase while she waited for him to answer his page. She had written plenty of letters, but she had never spoken to a senator in person before, and she had just depleted her bravado.

After only a couple of minutes, the registration lady pointed and Elizabeth followed her gesture to see someone shaking the hand of a tall, pale man with an earnest expression. Elizabeth thought he looked familiar and felt an inexplicable tug at her heart. The tall man turned away and Senator Kevin Jenkins strode toward her.

During the session, Elizabeth had thought he must be fresh from university, but as he came closer, she could see flecks of gray in his black hair. He wore a gray silk shirt and black suit to mirror his features, and she admired that his cornflower blue tie was the perfect match to his eyes. She was sure the ensemble was carefully chosen as a subliminal message of sincerity.

After they had introduced themselves, he said, "I was hoping to hear more of your thoughts after your provocative statements during the panel session."

She blushed. "I'm sorry about the tone. I was just trying to make a point."

He touched her arm. "Don't apologize. You were right on target. Access and *availability* of health care, including new treatments, is something of a cause for me. My hobby is collecting thoughtful people to debate the issues, and you seem like just my type."

Elizabeth smiled self-consciously and followed him to the reception room. They claimed a small corner table away from the clusters of people around the other participating senators.

He said, "Usually when I bring up the 'a' word, 'accountability', the response I get is, 'Basic research can't be measured.' I'm most curious to hear your opinion on that."

Elizabeth's composure returned as she answered. "Industry does it; companies are accountable to their shareholders. Taxpayers are shareholders in the government, so we deserve no less."

He swept two glasses of wine off the tray of a passing waiter and handed one to Elizabeth. "How would you respond if I said you've made the opposite point, that companies just do what is profitable? Government grants exist to fund the research that wouldn't make money in the private sector. It's that truly basic type of research that takes time to quantify; you can't accelerate the discovery process."

Elizabeth leaned into the table. "Can't you? What about the Human Genome Project? That's pretty basic research, yet when the government was challenged by a private sector effort, the HGP finished two years earlier than planned and surpassed its goals."

"Maybe they got more resources."

"I don't know. But I'm sure they got more urgency. The private project intended to patent thousands of genes. There's nothing like an intellectual property competition to clarify objectives and set the pace of achievement." Elizabeth sat back. "You know, as much as no one likes to admit it anymore, money has been the catalyst for life-altering discoveries throughout this country's history. But in the end, it's all just about setting milestones and measuring progress. Government should be able to do that."

Senator Jenkins nodded and sipped from his glass. "All federal agencies actually are required by law to set goals and demonstrate results for their programs."

"Sounds good, but so do a lot of laws. Does it actually function that way?"

The Senator smiled. "Well . . . it's much better now than it used to be. In 1998, NIH measured performance by the amount of dollars sent out the door—the more the better." Elizabeth's eyes opened wide. "You seem surprised. Isn't that all that matters, how much money we give out? Senator so-and-so spent twenty million dollars on a program to improve literacy, but his opponent only wanted to spend one million. Makes for pretty scathing press."

Elizabeth knew he was being facetious. She was sincere in her response. "But how many people learned to read? If ten new readers cost twenty million in one program but ten thousand new readers cost only one million in the other program, that would be a different story." She set her glass on the table. "Senator, I'm really pleased to have had a chance to talk with you, but I want to spend some time with my daughter this evening, so . . . ."

He pushed back from the table. "Please, call me Kevin. And I have to get back myself. My daughter lives with her mother in Manassas, and she's waiting for me to pick her up to go for barbecue at Hogs on the Hill, which I've been told is 'all that'."

Elizabeth laughed at the familiar tween phrase. "I live just outside Manassas, and let me tell you, Hogs on the Hill is, indeed, all that."

"Can I give you a lift home, or did you drive in?"

"I took the train, but I couldn't trouble you—"

"It's no trouble for me. Maybe for you, since I intend to continue our conversation."

"Well, I am a glutton for punishment." They smiled easily at each other and headed out to the car.

When they had settled into the back seat and given the driver directions, Jenkins resumed the discussion. "So let me ask you this."

"Uh oh."

"You can't say I didn't warn you."

"Carry on, then."

"Okay, to sum up your opinions, you think that government is more or less pouring money into a faulty system and that privatizing it will solve the world's problems."

"I didn't say it was *all that*." Elizabeth mirrored his grin. "But I do think if the private sector took over, the health care system would be more efficient. And yes, more successful too, in making sure there are new treatments, and that people can get them."

97

He shrugged. "I don't know that the private sector has the conscience for it. They've been free to do so for at least the last six decades, and access hasn't exactly improved."

"I disagree." Elizabeth adjusted her seatbelt and leaned back into the corner of the door so she could face him while she talked. "About the private sector being free from government, I mean. There has always been the expectation that individuals can go to the government for help. As long as that's the case, that's where the energy will be spent, because it's easy money. But if we just had faith in American ingenuity—" She made sure she had his attention before continuing. "If you left health care alone—if you truly left it alone—cottage industries would find a way to make a sustainable business of providing access, then every under- or uninsured person would go from being 'the needy' to being needed, as a potential source of revenue. I'm not talking about insurance; I'm thinking a whole different system where a person's regular income isn't the only thing that determines their value."

"So, you're saying I'm right; as long as there's a possibility that government will regulate away profits, no business is going to make the effort to provide health care to the poor."

She crossed her arms and sat back in her seat. "I think I've just been spun."

A horn blared and a car passed so close to Elizabeth's window that she could feel the vibration as it went by. She held her breath and watched the driver intently until he had successfully navigated the traffic and broke into an evenly moving section of the highway.

Senator Jenkins spoke again, drawing her mind away from the road. "What if I said it isn't the government's job to fund research to develop new drugs?"

"Why not?"

"Well, we can't cure everything, so Congress would have to choose one illness over another. The government shouldn't make that kind of decision."

She expected another facetious grin and was stunned to get none. Elizabeth turned completely sideways in her seat. "But you *do* make those decisions. When you pass laws that create a cost structure that stifles research and development, you're choosing to support illnesses that have treatments over those that don't. For every million people in this country who are underinsured, there are another million living with a disease that has no cure. Yet the budget for programs to help the underinsured is fifty times the budget for programs that promote research. Fifty times! Whenever you vote to fund a program, you're making that choice. I personally find it shocking that you don't even recognize what you're doing."

The Senator's tone was calm and even. "We fund social programs that get health care to the people who wouldn't otherwise be able to afford it. That's what government is supposed to do— help the needy."

"Is that your interpretation of the Constitution? To be a Robin Hood Congress that redistributes wealth to the people *you* decide need it more? Even if it's hard-earned wealth?" Elizabeth strained against her seatbelt trying to see the Senator's face in the dimming light. She narrowed her eyes and sat back slowly. "You were baiting me, weren't you?"

Senator Jenkins' brow drew up and released his grin. They were both laughing as the car pulled into Elizabeth's driveway. "Thanks for the ride. And the conversation."

"It was my pleasure. I hope we can talk again."

Elizabeth replayed the afternoon in her mind as she ascended the front steps two at a time. Her mother-in-law greeted her at the door with a finger to her lips. "Sera fell asleep on the couch. I didn't want to wake her."

Elizabeth's maternal radar went off, and her smile vanished. "It's only seven o'clock, why is she so tired? Was she walking well? How's her speech?" She rushed toward the living room.

"Don't worry. We just danced around so much, she tuckered out." The elder Mrs. Rose followed Elizabeth into the next room. "I could use a nap myself. So could my ears. Honey, there is nothing wrong with her speech!"

Elizabeth saw for herself that Sera's color looked normal, and she appeared to be breathing regularly. Elizabeth relaxed. "Thanks so much for watching her."

"Chatterbox aside, she's a special girl." They hugged and her mother-in-law left. As Elizabeth carried Sera upstairs, she berated herself. She had been arguing that her daughter didn't have much time and meanwhile was losing a whole day with her. She tucked Sera into bed and kissed her on the forehead.

Elizabeth took the picture from Sera's nightstand and brought it back to her own room. She lay on the bed without undressing, holding the *#1 Dad To Be* photo to her heart. The people who don't have a Sera have little motivation and leverage for a cause. And the people who do have a Sera don't want to sacrifice the little time left. It's no wonder that nothing changes. She punched her pillow then rolled over and buried her head.

The realization made her appreciate the difficulty of Senator Jenkins' cause. But Elizabeth couldn't bring herself to be a martyr; the Senator would have to carry the flag without her. She vowed not to lose another precious moment with Sera to any-thing—not career, not causes, not worrying, not even to teenager-mother bickering if they had the good fortune to survive that long.

"HEY DAD, TURN that up," Eddy called toward the living room as he and Abigail cleared the table after dinner. The television blared loudly. "Today's Town Hall Meeting in Washington, DC attracted over two thousand participants representing forty-six states."

Eddy's mother walked into the kitchen. "Grammy, do you want to see my Junior Achievement project?" Abigail said. "It's on economic incentives and compound interest rates! If you give me ten dollars today, then I could have eleven dollars next year. Isn't that cool?"

"Economics in elementary school? Heavens, what have you been doing to this child?" Eddy's mother said.

"Not my fault," Eddy laughed. "Abigail roped me into volunteering. We do projects with the kids about managing finances and work ethic, and stuff like that. It starts in kindergarten. What is it they say, Abigail?"

"Habits are formed in youth!"

"Whatever happened to reading, writing, and arithmetic?"

"Don't worry, Mom, they get that, too. It's a good project."

"Well then, let's go see."

Abigail dropped her handful of forks loudly into the dishwasher and dashed up the stairs.

Once the clanging stopped, Eddy could hear the final sound byte on the news segment. "I, for one, am committed to doubling the NIH budget over the next four years."

Eddy's father switched the channel in irritation. "That was the sound of our taxes going up."

Eddy made an effort not to slam the door as he closed the dishwasher. "At least the guy is committed to something," he said. Joy gave him a supportive smile as she put away the leftovers into the fridge. Eddy's inability to find his calling was their current late-night discussion topic.

"Notice he's only committed until his next election in four years." Eddy's father got up from the couch and looked out the picture window. "So, what's the deal with this boat in your driveway? I had to park on the street. Don't boats belong in the water?"

"Wow, you're funny, Dad. And you'll probably get a kick out of this: the docking costs more than the boat did. So until my next bonus, we just have to haul her with us."

"You ought to be saving those bonuses of yours for retirement. You don't know how long you're going to be able to work. Did you hear the Fed lowered interest rates a full point last week?"

"Why?"

"Who the hell knows why economists do anything? Health stocks are up, inflation is down, fishing is good, but China's still communist. Go figure. My point is you have to take responsibility and plan ahead."

At the inevitable "r" word, Eddy's blood pressure started to rise, until Joy put a cool hand on his forearm. He closed his eyes and exhaled. Sometimes he wanted to spend every cent he had, just to spite his father's unsolicited advice.

GALEN HADN'T LEFT his apartment since he'd returned from the symposium in Washington. He had run into a former labmate and learned new information about the effect of oxygen levels on brain health, so he was up for the fourth midnight in row, scribbling on his flow diagrams, trying to figure out how it worked.

Galen opened the window to clear his mind. The metallic air of a lightning storm pressed through the screen. The tang reminded him of cross-country races through damp autumn woods—pumping his muscles until they burned, adrenaline coursing, breath coming ragged, hitting the wall, and pushing, pushing, pushing until he broke through to the exhilarating exhaustion of the finish line.

Science was his rush now. "Too much oxygen can be toxic, especially to oligodendrocytes," he told the hardy, wet pigeon on the windowsill. "You need oligodendrocytes to make myelin. But too little oxygen can kill astrocytes. You need astrocytes—well, *humans* need astrocytes—to regulate the volume of cerebrospinal fluid. The CSF volume drives production of neuroglobin and regulates the amount of oxygen to the brain."

The befuddled pigeon just hunkered farther away from the gutter pipe, so Galen turned his thoughts inward. Neuroglobin breaks down into carbon dioxide, bilirubin, and heme. Heme regulates EIF2. EIF2 produces astrocytes. Astrocytes regulate oxygen, which protects the oligodendrocytes so they can continue to produce myelin. Lack of myelin causes the symptoms of VWM. Galen's brain was swimming. What was the critical point? He taped his sketches together then flapped the drawing like a patchwork quilt and let it float to the floor.

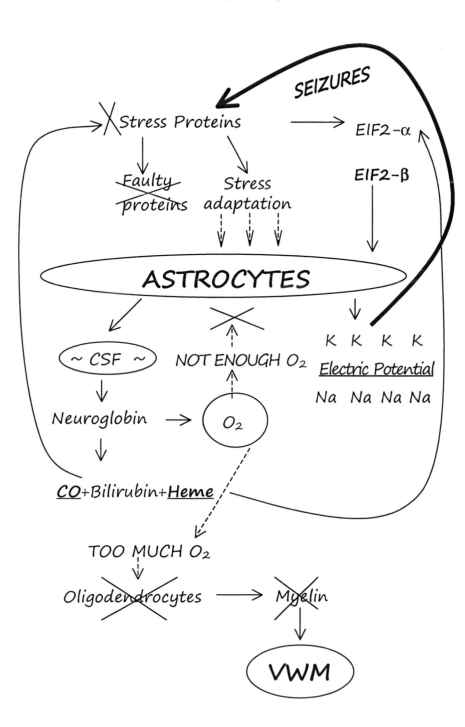

He walked in a circle around the drawing, talking aloud. "Kids with VWM have faulty EIF2, so they have sickly astrocytes, so their oxygen sensor doesn't work right. That could mean two things: too much oxygen, which would disrupt myelin production, or too little oxygen, which would kill astrocytes and make the system even worse at regulating oxygen. A quintessential vicious cycle."

He grabbed the last slice of cold pizza from the kitchen counter and took a bite. Okay, why did the Lexistro monkeys have *more* astrocytes? It had to fit together somehow. He swallowed and threw the crust in the trash then jumped high and slapped one of the exposed pipes running along the ceiling. "Trauma and fever induce stress proteins."

He paced across the apartment. "In VWM, maybe the faulty astrocytes are being carried off by stress proteins. If so, after trauma and fever, there'd be even fewer astrocytes. Which would mean the system would have to work even harder to keep up the myelin. If the myelin is sparse, nerves would be like a stripped wire, so the brain signals wouldn't travel well. That would explain why kids with VWM would have problems walking and talking after an infection."

He stopped in front of the mirror. "Okay, but what about the other symptoms?" His reflection, guileless and keen, offered no response. He returned to the drawing. "Astrocytes affect the balance of sodium and potassium." Galen squatted down and put his left hand on *astrocytes* and his right hand on *electric potential*. "Electrical imbalance can cause seizures." He put his right foot on *seizures*. "Seizures are trauma that induces stress proteins." He swung his left foot to land on *stress proteins*. "Stress proteins cart off astrocytes. Missing astrocytes cause imbalance. Another vicious cycle."

He moved his left hand underneath his leg, toward *heme*. "Without neuroglobin, there's no heme released. Heme regulates EIF2, which produces astrocytes." He reached his right hand toward *EIF2*, lost his balance, and collapsed onto the floor. "So no neuroglobin, no new astrocytes."

Galen flopped onto his back, stretched his arms and legs wide, and lay still with his eyes closed. He inhaled and exhaled, letting the thoughts settle in his mind.

Suddenly, he leapt to the window, startling the pigeon. "Every part of the VWM system is spiraling out of control! Fewer astrocytes are produced than normal, and those that are produced are sick. Every time the kid gets a cold, astrocytes get carted off by stress proteins. And when the kid is well, the good astrocytes are dying off anyway because there isn't enough oxygen. There isn't enough oxygen because the astrocytes aren't working right, so they can't tell the CSF they need more neuroglobin. Without neuroglobin, astrocytes aren't produced."

Galen's heart stopped and his body trembled like the day he first saw 423 under the microscope. If he injected Lexistro into the cerebrospinal fluid, then it would act like neuroglobin to provide the oxygen that would trigger new astrocytes and keep the old ones from dying.

Balanced astrocytes would mean intact electric potential, so no more potassium buildup, thus no more seizures.

Fewer seizures would mean fewer stress proteins, so fewer astrocytes being carted away.

Lexistro would break down into heme that would regulate EIF2 to produce more astrocytes. It would also break down into carbon monoxide to further reduce the stress reaction.

Enough astrocytes would mean oligodendrocytes are released to produce myelin.

Enough myelin would mean signals are traveling easily from the brain to the body.

Lexistro could stop the fatal cycle of VWM.

Galen tore the corner from his diagram and wrote a note to Elizabeth Rose.

19

LEXI SPRAWLED ON the carpet doing her pre-algebra extra credit, the living room so quiet that she imagined the spring frogs in the pond past the field were actually in the living room, lounging under the couch, peeping out homework hints. Her father was reading the newspaper in a nearby easy chair, and her mother was on the couch with a romance novel. After an hour of silence, Roger put down his newspaper and asked, "So what do you want for birthday number nine?"

"A chemistry set!"

"Don't be silly," Linda said quickly. "How about we get your ears pierced?"

Lexi scrunched her nose. "That's gross. Do you know how easy it is to get infected that way?"

"You and your infections. I'm going to stop letting you spend so much time over there."

Lexi went back to her homework. She knew her mother's threat was empty. Lexi spending time at Sera's meant Lexi wasn't the third wheel at home, and that was good for everyone. "You asked," she muttered.

Roger chuckled. "Alexandra, you're a tough one to figure out sometimes."

Lexi didn't answer. It bugged her when he called her by her full name. As if he wasn't even related to her.

"DO YOU EVER think you might be adopted?" Lexi asked. She sat on the second twin bed in Sera's room while Sera tested out Lexi's birthday present, a makeup case containing a dozen colors each of lipstick, nail polish, and eye shadow.

Sera dipped a Q-tip into one of the colors and applied it. Careful not to touch her lips together, she said, "No, I have DNA results." Sera affected a pose and batted her eyelashes. "How do I look?"

"Glamorous, of course. Try this one." Lexi handed Sera a purple nail polish. "Maybe I should get a DNA test, too. Maybe I was switched in the hospital or something. It's like my own parents don't even know me. I mean, this is my mom's idea of a chemistry set. How wacked is that?"

"It's still a cool present. Then again, I'm not a brain like you, so I wouldn't want a real chemistry set anyway." Sera grimaced. "You should put some of it on. We can pretend we're rock stars."

"See, that's a perfect example. I never wanted to play the piano," Lexi said.

"I want to play the harp, but mom says it costs too much."

"I don't know any rock stars who play the harp."

Sera shrugged. "So, I'll be the first."

"Anyway, at least your mom gives you a reason when she says no. When I wanted to join the cross-country team, my mom got all twitchy, and I got piano lessons instead. It doesn't even make sense. I think my own mother doesn't like me. I'm just some dumpy freak she got stuck with."

Sera stopped applying makeup and studied her friend for a long moment. "You're definitely not dumpy." She grabbed Lexi by the hand. "Come on, I haven't done my exercise today."

Elizabeth heard the back door slam and walked over to the kitchen window, holding the phone to her ear. "I can't believe we're even having this discussion. No, the company should *not* settle." She pulled the curtain aside to see the girls running into the yard. "I know I always say that, but this time it's madness. The prosecution's case is that the victim was disabled and couldn't work for two years because insurance wouldn't pay for the fibromyalgia treatment, right? So your counter case is clear: she could have paid for the treatment out-of-pocket, but she also thought it wasn't worth the cost. Both she and the insurance company made the same hard decision. That changes the argument from whether it was the right decision to who's responsible for the consequences."

Elizabeth watched the girls cartwheel across the lawn and start a cheer. She picked up Sera's latest disappointing report card from the counter and sighed. Maybe she had stressed Sera's physical development at the cost of her intellect.

"I want this to go before a jury," she said. "We have to get away from big settlements that encourage law suits that make everyone's premiums go up. And we need to build the repertoire of verdicts in favor of individual responsibility. It's too easy to blame a faceless corporation."

She checked the oven and turned down the temperature. "Yes, it is twisted that we're making money in the process." She laughed into the phone. "Let me tell you about my project . . . ."

SEVERAL WEEKS LATER, while waiting for the jury to return its verdict, Elizabeth met Kevin Jenkins for lunch on a bench outside the courthouse.

She was holding several pages of notepaper scribbled with numbers. "If you had to hire a plumber, and they all charge the same, but one would fix your pipes and also put money in your health savings account for next year, wouldn't you hire that one?"

He bit into his sandwich and nodded, a knowing twinkle in his blue eyes.

"Yes, I'm ranting again," Elizabeth said. "That's what you get for asking me to lunch." She knocked her heel against his dress shoe. "So, what if you were the plumber, and instead of getting two hundred dollars cash, you got a thousand dollars of credit in your health savings account that you could use next year or any time in the future."

"Like funny money at the zoo."

She couldn't help smiling and rolled her eyes at him before she took a drink of lemonade. "Seriously, though, wouldn't that put health care closer to everyone's reach?"

He wiped his smirk away with his napkin, though his eyebrows still danced when he said, "If that were the system, insurance would go back to being catastrophic only, and people would have to decide for themselves which extra tests or high tech scans or new expensive medicines to buy. There wouldn't be anyone to sue. Wouldn't that put you out of business?"

"You're impossible to talk to today." She got up to toss her bottle into a nearby recycling bin. Her beeper went off. She checked it then returned to the bench and put half of her sandwich back in the bag. "Jury's back. See you later."

Kevin grabbed the strap of her purse and she turned back. He said, "It sounds great, but who's going to pay for it?"

"Interest on the seed fund," she said.

20

"HONEY, I'M HO-O-OME!" Eddy shut the front door and walked into the living room.

Joy looked up from her stack of catalogs on the floor. "What's with the Cheshire grin?"

Eddy didn't answer, just continued to smile mysteriously as he moseyed past her to the couch where Abigail was reading. He took her book, closed it, and set it on the coffee table. Eddy winked and took Abigail's hand to tug her off the couch toward the door. He motioned to Joy to follow, his grin widening. The three of them stepped onto the front porch, and Eddy gestured dramatically toward the driveway. "Behold!"

Joy gaped and Abigail stifled a giggle. Eddy's grin collapsed. "It's a Firebird Trans Am."

"Oka-a-y?" Joy cocked her head.

Eddy perked up again. "You just need to see it closer." He bounded off the porch.

Joy whispered loudly, "I'm pretty sure that's not going to help." Abigail giggled.

Eddy whirled around and pointed at them. "I heard that." Abigail covered her mouth with her hands.

In the driveway was a mud-covered pile of red metal with a silver and rust running board, two flat tires, no roof, a cracked dashboard, and used-to-be-gray upholstery. "Is that—" Joy stepped closer and gingerly touched the seat. "Velour?"

"Classic, baby." Eddy stepped sideways and put his arm around Joy. "It's an '85." She rolled her eyes. "You've heard of 1985: REO Speedwagon, Rambo, the *new* Coke."

Joy elbowed him in the stomach, and he pretended to double over in pain. She looked back at the car. "Oh, sweetie, don't sit on that." Abigail had climbed over the door and was grinning at them from the backseat.

"That's my girl," Eddy said. "You want to help me fix this up, kiddo?" Abigail nodded vigorously.

"Does this even run? How did you get it here, anyway? What are you going to do when it rains?"

"Details, details. It's a fixer-upper, so we'll improvise." He gave Abigail a high five.

"Well, hon, there's a fine line between a fixer-upper and a thrower-outer."

EVERY SATURDAY OF the summer, the neighbors could see Eddy's legs disappearing under the car, or his rear pockets sticking out under the hood, and Abigail painting, patching, or polishing. The local automotive store clerk had to smile whenever he saw the two crossing the street—her skipping barely as high as his waist, in her paint-and-grease-stained overalls with the flower embroidery, and him holding her hand, grinning ear to ear.

"What can I do for my two favorite customers today?" the clerk would ask.

The blonde man would say to the girl, "I don't know, what's it's going to be, chief?"

The girl would answer seriously with the fancy mechanic words she had memorized. "Today we're fixing the cat'll-lick-it converter."

On the Saturday after the first week of the school year, a high school student working the ice cream counter at the Snack Shack saw a shiny red Trans Am pull into the lot. A movie star quality couple and a strawberry-haired girl who could only be their daughter were squeezed in the front seat with the convertible top down and the radio blaring. Sweet ride, he thought. They pulled close to the menu board, and the girl hopped out of the car to his window.

"Three *large* chocolate and vanilla twists with rainbow sprinkles *and* cherry dip. *Please.*" She emphasized the plea by standing on her tiptoes.

"You want sprinkles and dip on the same cone?"

"Yes, please." She carefully counted out several dollar bills and change. He brought the first cone out and she ran to the car, took a lick, handed the cone to the woman, and ran back to the counter. He handed her the second cone, and she turned around toward the car. He went to the back room to get more sprinkles.

When he returned to the window, all of the customers were clustered next to the red Trans Am, and neither the man nor the woman were in the car. He saw a rainbow splatter on the ground, and next to it, sticking out from the crowd, was a pink sneaker under a pant leg embroidered with flowers.

An ambulance pulled in, and the crowd backed away. The paramedics loaded the girl onto the stretcher and rolled her into the hatch. He saw the man and woman argue briefly before they both climbed in with the stretcher. The paramedics closed the doors, and the screaming ambulance pulled away.

The other patrons milled about, then one by one got into their cars and left, until the red Trans Am was alone in the parking lot.

21

ABIGAIL WATCHED HER father pace—to the hall checking for the doctor, over to the window, and back to the door. Her mother was sitting by the hospital bed, holding Abigail's hand on top of the blanket. Finally, the doctor came in. He cleared his throat a couple of times, looking toward the bed.

Eddy stopped pacing and started tapping his foot. "It's okay, she can hear."

The doctor said, "I believe Abigail has suffered a small stroke."

"She's nine years old!" Joy said.

"The MRI suggests this may not have been the first."

Eddy stopped tapping his foot, and Joy's grip tightened on Abigail's hand. Abigail saw her parents exchange a look that she couldn't decipher.

"Do you have any family history?"

Eddy answered with a thick voice, "Yes, my sister . . . ." He looked over at Abigail. "Um, went through that. TFI."

The doctor nodded. "Transient forebrain ischemia. I believe Abigail's condition is also ischemic rather than hemorrhagic; her MRI doesn't show any bleeding, but there does appear to be some structural constriction in the blood vessels. You're familiar, then, with the mechanism of failure?"

"Just that when blood can't get to a part of the brain, the oxygen is cut off, and sometimes the cells . . . choke."

The doctor nodded again. "I recommend that we start Abigail on daily aspirin. That should lower her risk by improving the blood flow. You should watch for any decline in mental function, which may be a symptom of additional attacks."

"That's it?" Eddy said. "She had a stroke, and you're going to give her headache medicine?" He turned his back to the doctor. "We're no better off than we were fifteen years ago."

"Eddy, don't," Joy whispered.

"What about Lexistro?"

The doctor seemed surprised. "Lexistro is currently only FDA-approved for single acute treatment, not yet for chronic use. And it's only approved for adults. But there are clinical studies ongoing that are recruiting children, and I believe Abigail would be a perfect candidate—"

"No."

"She'd receive excellent care, returning every two weeks for blood samples and cognitive testing plus some periodic MRI scanning. If you consider—"

"My daughter is not a guinea pig." Eddy's fists were clenched at his sides.

"Maybe we should discuss this in the hall," Joy said. Eddy turned his head to glance back at Abigail and nodded.

Abigail's parents each kissed her on the forehead, then they went into the hall with the doctor, pulling the door closed behind them. She hadn't understood most of the conversation, except that she needed to take medicine and that her brain might stop working. She sat up in the bed and whispered her multiplication table. "And twelve times twelve is a hundred and forty-four." She lay back. There was nothing wrong with her brain.

She heard her father say dully, "I understand, thank you. We'll try the aspirin and hope that's all she needs."

WHEN SHE RETURNED to school, Abigail was the primary topic of the suburban grapevine. A group of kids gathered around her at recess.

"Did it hurt?" the girls asked.

"Was there blood?" the boys asked.

Abigail, sociable like her dad, enjoyed the celebrity. If a person had to have an illness, something spectacular that didn't hurt was a good one to have. She didn't embellish. Just the news of the ambulance ride, the hospital, and the number of needles she'd been given were enough to ensure that she had a group of lunch buddies every day of September and October.

Then came book report day, when her brain disorder became too close for comfort. Abigail was standing in front of the class giving her rendition of *The Witch of Blackbird Pond*, when suddenly she couldn't talk. The classroom narrowed and blackened to a pinpoint, and she thought she would pass out. But she wasn't so lucky. She was fully conscious to experience the world tilting sideways, to feel her head cock to her left shoulder and freeze there, and to see the horrified expressions of her classmates. She tried to leave the room, but when she walked, she lurched to the left. So she stood still while everyone stared, until the teacher had the wherewithal to guide her to the nurse's office.

Abigail was out of school for several days, and when she returned this time, no one wanted to know about what happened and they steered clear of her in the halls.

EDDY HUNCHED OVER his computer in the dark quiet of the early morning. Joy and Abigail were asleep, and he was in the den, staring at a spreadsheet. A desk lamp dimly lit his math scribbled on a notebook.

After the second attack, Eddy had insisted that Abigail be given Lexistro, but he had refused to allow it as part of a study that would require her to be prodded like an animal. The study doctor agreed to prescribe it, not strictly according to the FDA approved usage. The doctor also suggested that Abigail continue to be treated every two to three months indefinitely.

Eddy's insurance refused to pay, citing that she was underage, and the drug was used "off label". Just the one treatment had nearly wiped out his and Joy's discretionary savings. The doctor said Lexistro was likely to be approved within the next year or two for chronic and pediatric use, at which time insurance would consider covering it. Until then, Eddy would have to find $60,000 to pay the treatment costs out-of-pocket.

The spreadsheet contained all of their assets. Joy had gone back to work part-time, which would pay for their groceries and a lean Christmas. The boat was already for sale. They would have to downsize their vehicles. He didn't want to touch the house, and Joy had said the Trans Am was off-limits as well, that it would crush Abigail if he sold it. The only thing left was their retirement. He knew they would take a big tax hit if they dipped into it, and he didn't know how they were going to replace it. But what did it matter compared to his daughter's life?

He should have listened when his father told him to max out his retirement contributions. He scanned the screen again. Well, they'd have enough to get through another year anyway. He clicked off the computer and went to bed.

22

TWIRLING HER PENCIL like a baton, Patricia waited at the conference table for her FDA colleagues. They were scheduled to review the public commentary on her latest draft regulation. Writing regulations wasn't strictly in her job description, but few opposed her uncommon zeal.

Nearly four years ago, she had given up her assignment on Biolex in order to concentrate on regulations, and she was somewhat dismayed when the company's first product received such fast approval. Lexistro seemed to be working out all right, but she still kept a close eye on it.

Since the fibromyalgia experience, the name Patricia Chen had become synonymous with caution. The previous year she had insisted upon additional animal studies for a drug that was poised for clinical trials. The company had protested, but when they conducted the study, one of the monkeys suffered serious side effects, and the company decided to table the drug. Patricia's guilty conscience over fibromyalgia had been assuaged.

The current regulation under review contained two of her most controversial suggestions to date. The first was a requirement for clinical study sponsors to offer sperm and egg cryopreservation to all study participants, in case a drug caused infertility. The second requirement was for all study participants to register with the government and report on their health status for ten years.

Her colleagues finally arrived, including Patricia's biggest rival, who sat across from her. When he opened the meeting, his tone was cordial, but quickly turned personal. "Look, Pat," he said, his forearms resting on the table. "We all appreciate your dedication to safety. Really. The additional animal studies and cracking down on off-label use are admirable. But these latest provisions are a bit extreme, you have to admit."

"No, I don't." She was settled tall in her seat.

"Come on! The public comments are right on target. Your proposals would add millions to the cost of research, which would further increase the cost of prescription drugs, and to what end?"

"To what end?" Patricia asked calmly. "What's the cost of a life?"

"Oh, save the melodrama." He rushed on before she could respond. "Aside from the costs, this is going to make it impossible to recruit for trials, so it will probably double the time for clinical development. It already takes special people to consent to be studied, and now they're going to have to agree to big brother watching them for a decade?"

"We need to know whether these drugs have long-term effects. And not only if companies *happen* to find out about them."

He stood and put his hands on the table and towered toward Patricia. "Who's going to weed through all the data? Government employees? Taxes will have to go up to pay for that. And who's going to decide what's an effect of a drug and what's just normal life? A lot of things can happen to a person in ten years."

She didn't move from her position. "We have to make companies accountable for the side effects of their drugs."

"There are safeguards in place already. Our time is better spent enforcing the existing regulations than adding new ones."

Patricia crossed her arms. "We'll have to agree to disagree."

"We do disagree, but I'm the last word." He sat down. "Those two provisions go, but we'll keep your other suggestions. Doctors will face up to one month in prison for each instance of off-label prescription, and companies will be required to run studies in at least two hundred non-human primates before starting human trials."

Patricia predicted it would be another two or three years before the controversial set of regulations would take effect. But still it had been a good negotiation; she got what she came for.

23

ABIGAIL COULDN'T CONCENTRATE, distracted by the pressure of the stares from the class. Since she had returned to school after the book report incident, avoidance had turned to curiosity and gossip, which had escalated from insensitive to cruel. The teacher asked her in front of everyone how she was feeling, and she heard more than one scoff from the rows behind her. Abigail lowered her head and wished she were invisible.

Later, while she stood in line in the cafeteria, she overheard two of her classmates talking about her. "You know she just did it to get attention." Abigail ate her lunch alone at a table in the corner.

As miserable as lunch was, there was no point in rushing, because the next period was gym. Since Abigail wasn't allowed to do anything physical for a few weeks, she had to record stats on the sideline of the basketball court, exposed to every glare and snicker.

When the last bell finally rang, Abigail was the first out the door. She spent the walk home dreaming up excuses not to go back.

THE TAUNTS HAD been relentless for the last two weeks:

"Hey, smart Alex! How's your Alexdandruff?"

"Lexi isn't sexy! She's an Alexamazon!"

Lexi tried to shrink into her sweatshirt until she could get through the line and find a quiet corner of the cafeteria. Why couldn't she be in the same lunch period as Sera?

Life had been miserable ever since the local newspaper wrote an article on the science fair and singled out Lexi's computer program. She didn't see the big deal; it was just a simple decision model. The user was supposed to enter up to ten outcomes and seven stakeholders then assign a point value from negative three to positive three, like a weighted list of pros and cons for each stakeholder. The program would then figure out the combination of outcomes to maximize the total point value for all the stakeholders. The journalist had said it was remarkably complex programming for a fifth grader, but what had attracted the most attention were Lexi's stakeholders—a lawyer, a pharmaceutical company, an insurance company, a consumer, FDA, Congress, and voters – and her outcomes, which were based on Elizabeth Rose's legal cases.

Lexi and Sera had been role-playing prosecutor and defendant ever since they could understand the snatches of Elizabeth's telephone conversations and closing argument rehearsals. Lexi didn't realize it would turn her into a big old nerd. She should have made a video game.

Lexi was resigned to yet another day of misery when suddenly Sera, all four feet and fifty pounds of her, pushed through the line, followed by three of the most popular cheerleaders in the eighth grade. The cheerleaders started talking loudly.

"Hey, did you hear that a modeling agency saw Lexi's picture in the paper and offered her a contract?"

"I'm not surprised. I would kill to have your hair, Lexi. It's like a Barbie doll!"

"In high school, you'll totally be going out when all the rest of us are stuck doing homework."

"Hey, you and Sera should go to my party Saturday!"

The taunts had stopped and the kids in line and at the closest cafeteria tables were staring.

"Come on, Lexi, you're way too awesome to be eating the same junk as these dorks." Sera pulled her out of line and into the hallway, where they high-fived the cheerleaders. Then the two friends snuck into the theater, where Sera had stashed two bag lunches behind the curtain.

"Did you see their faces when we said you were going to be a model? I almost peed my pants!" Sera said. They sat on the stage and let their legs dangle over the edge.

"And when those cheerleaders invited us to their party? Classic! How did you ever get them to do that?" Lexi said.

"Oh, they're pretty cool. One of them has a little brother who gets picked on, too. Besides, everyone wants a chance to take care of me, like it's their good deed for the year." Lexi was shocked. Sera said, "I'm allowed to use it sometimes, for a good cause."

They both bit into their peanut butter and jelly sandwiches and drank a swig of milk. Lexi said, "I wish my parents didn't sign me up for the sixth grade algebra. Now I have to eat lunch with those terrorists for the rest of the year." Lexi put down her sandwich at the unappetizing thought.

"You can't switch now. My mom just got me into your class."

Lexi threw her lunch bag at Sera. "Are you serious?"

"Yeah, so now we have the same schedule. But you'll have to tutor me, because you know I stink at math!"

24

GALEN TRIED WITHOUT success to avoid looking at the newspaper stands during his morning run. The public outcry was escalating over Congress' lack of action, either to make it legal to buy lower-cost prescription drugs from other countries or to regulate U.S. prices, and the pharmaceutical lobby was being blamed. Nearly half of the states were condoning importation, in violation of FDA regulations.

Biolex was one of the prime targets of venom. Lexistro was now being used routinely, and the company was making millions, so the honeymoon period with the press had ended. Galen had plans for a lower price structure but hadn't been able to implement it because approval of the chronic use indication had been delayed; there weren't enough parents willing to enroll their kids in the study.

Today's headlines were typical:
"CEO Salaries Reach All Time High"
"A Healthy America: At What Cost?"
"No Cure for Congressional Impotence on Drug Bill"

Later that morning, Myesha put her head in the doorway of Galen's office. "What's with the face? Tabloids again? Or is it hate mail this time?"

Galen flipped another page of the newspaper. "It doesn't hurt to ask myself the questions."

"It does when you were born with a guilt complex." Myesha's expression was stern. "Listen to me. There are people out there who might have been paralyzed, or mute, or dead without Lexistro. So whatever they pay us, it's more than a fair exchange."

"That's not the point. The question is, do I have a right to profit from the exchange?"

Amos appeared in the doorway next to Myesha. "People don't go to Fenway for the hot dogs."

Galen was baffled at the comment. Amos let out a huff.

"It's the same as saying the Red Sox are overpaid, when every company that advertises in the ballpark is making money because people's butts are in the stands. Never mind the networks who ransomed commercials during the World Series."

"Baseball isn't exactly life and death," Galen said.

"Fine, then. When people have to choose between food and medicine, no one blames the farmers."

"Farmers aren't rich."

"Well, you and the Easter Bunny will be disappointed to learn that more than one company in the agriculture industry made a profit over a billion dollars last year." Amos threw up his hands. "Oh hell, forget the analogies. You're a fool to apologize for your accomplishments." He spit into a wastebasket and turned to leave.

Galen said, "A lot of people would argue that the families in the stands are getting screwed."

Amos turned back with a glint in his eye. "A lot of people will complain about anything until the money is in their pockets. I just say, did they enjoy the game?" He walked away.

Galen asked Myesha what she thought. She shook her head. "A better question is what does your conscience think? I can't answer that for you, and neither can the Internet forums you surf." She followed Amos down the hall.

Myesha was right. The problem was that Galen's conscience had been stuck in guilt overdrive for years before he ever started making money. He looked toward the bottom drawer of the filing cabinet, where he held his biggest guilt of all.

As much as his professional success was rich, Galen's personal life was stark. He hadn't dated since the divorce. He restricted his mysteries to science, where he could be certain there was an answer. It might take years to figure it out, but two plus three always equals five, and four doesn't get mad at three for that.

He hadn't even kept up a relationship with his best friend. Things were so complicated after the divorce, and when Galen was truthful with himself, he knew that he was jealous of Eddy, for having Joy and Abigail. With a new company starting up, Galen had found many excuses not to visit, and it was disturbingly easy to let the relationship peter out. They hadn't spoke in five years.

When Linda had asked for the divorce, she told him, "Galen, eventually your life is going to come down to your work or Lexi. I'm trying to spare you from that decision. And I'm protecting my daughter from the slow agony of being phased out of her father's life." She was right, because isn't that exactly what he had done to his best friend?

Galen shoved the newspaper off his desk into the trash. Then the phone rang. It was Eddy.

25

GALEN SCANNED THE diner. Something in Eddy's voice had told him the request to meet was more than just a New Year's resolution to reconnect with old friends. Eddy was in a corner booth. As Galen approached, he could see that Eddy had shaved, but badly, his eyes were puffy, and his shaggy hair had more than five years' worth of gray. He stood to greet Galen but didn't look at him directly. They shook hands then sat across from each other in the booth.

Eddy cleared his throat. "Abigail has TFI."

Galen's stomach plunged. Of all the reasons he had imagined for this meeting, his mind hadn't allowed this one. It was happening again, and he still wasn't ready. Why hadn't he insisted Lexistro go immediately to chronic use and pushed harder on the pediatric studies? "When?"

"Sixteen months ago."

Galen drew back and stared at the top of Eddy's head. Why hadn't Eddy told him before? Why was he telling him now?

"I wouldn't have come here if we weren't in a bad way."

Galen leaned forward, wanting to put a hand on Eddy's shoulder. But feeling awkward, he sat back. "Is she . . . ?"

"She's okay; she's getting Lexistro. But our insurance won't cover it." Eddy took a deep breath and let it all out. "It was manageable at first, but then my bonus didn't come through, and we had to sell a few things. We thought it would be approved by now, but it's taking so long. I know that's not your fault. The house was already mortgaged twice, so moving to a smaller place doesn't make sense, and our retirement savings are gone. We tried to get Abby into a study, but she doesn't qualify because she's already tried the drug." He stared hard at the table. "I'm supposed to take care of her, and I can't."

Galen was dumbfounded. He knew his reimbursement department worked with people every day to address these same problems, but he never thought his best friend would become their poster child. "I'll pay for it. Abigail's like my—"

"I don't want your money." For the first time, Eddy looked Galen in the eye.

"But—"

"I mean it. I just want to work out a discount or something. I read that companies can get a tax break for char—" Eddy cleared his throat. "For giving people a break. If Biolex can't do that, then I'll figure out something else. I'll go to my father if I have to, but I won't take it from you."

Galen nodded, ignoring the fallacy.

A WEEK LATER, Galen called Eddy. Eddy told Joy that it was a business call and took the phone onto the porch. "So?"

Galen said, "Your income is too high for our discount program. And with the laws the way they are, our reimbursement department can't even touch off-label use."

Eddy was resigned to the worst. He had heard all this before.

"But I worked it out."

Eddy held his breath.

"You pay what you can of the insurance bill and send a copy to my secretary, and the rest will be taken care of."

Eddy suspected Galen was going to do something illegal, but he didn't want to know the details. Whatever the risk, he had to take it. "Thank you, Galen, really." He almost told Galen to keep in touch, but didn't.

"Anything for a friend."

Eddy hung up the phone and rested his head on the porch pillar. The night was cold, but he was so relieved he didn't trust his legs to take him inside yet. He felt a twinge akin to resentment but put it out of his mind. At that moment, all he wanted was to lean against his house and savor the respite.

ELIZABETH PULLED THE wrinkled scrap of paper from its envelope. She carried it with her everywhere, as a kind of talisman, and it was soft as cotton now. She touched the handwritten return addressee: *Galen Douglas*. The paper held one sentence: *If I can help, I will.*

When she had received the note, she immediately searched the Internet for every snatch of biography she could find and learned all she could about Lexistro. It was a miracle for those patients, and she dared to hope Galen Douglas had a miracle for Sera, too. She had checked the Biolex website regularly for nearly two years, but there was still no sign of progress.

Yet she believed he meant what he wrote. He must have, to stop whatever he was doing and tear off that corner, so urgent to tell her that he couldn't waste time on formality. It was too raw to be insincere. And there was something familiar in his face that she trusted.

26

GALEN'S BREATH MADE white puffs in the air, and his face was red from the biting wind, but he was agitated enough to be warm while he ran the Charles River loop. He had a hard decision to make, and it was no easier after the argument with Amos.

Biolex had been trying to develop a treatment for Huntington's disease, but the Phase II trial results released the week before revealed that although the treatment was safe, it didn't work. That was bad financial news, not only because they had spent forty million dollars on the research to date, but because they would have to continue to fund all of their remaining projects on only Lexistro revenue for the foreseeable future.

Lexistro had been priced so Biolex would have $100 million for research next year. However, Medicare was going to lower the reimbursement rate due to pressure from the citizen lobby, so for all sales to Medicare recipients, now the company would receive barely half of the target price. The majority of stroke patients were on Medicare. Amos told Galen that after costs, even all but eliminating senior management bonuses and cutting profit in half, they would now have only $74 million for research next year.

Galen's options were limited. Biolex had saturated the Lexistro market in the U.S. and was trying to grow sales in other parts of the world, which would address the revenue problem in the long-term. But in the short-term, he had to either raise Lexistro's price for non-government payers or delay internal projects to manage cash flow. Galen was vehemently against raising the price. He had been surprised when Amos agreed, saying it would be bad publicity, if nothing else. After re-prioritizing all of their other internal costs and projects, the remaining option was to delay either Lexistro for VWM or a different product for Alzheimer's disease. Both projects were ready to start clinical trials.

Galen's heart told him to keep VWM, which he argued rationally until Amos began yet another lecture on economics. Galen threatened to sell his shares and resign. Amos gave his usual bullying speech, and Galen had stormed out.

Their argument pounded in Galen's mind as each foot hit the pavement. The Alzheimer's drug would be a new source of revenue. But other companies were already working on Alzheimer's. But they hadn't succeeded yet. But VWM had no other champion. What if Biolex could cure Alzheimer's? What if Biolex could cure VWM? Which disease had more victims?

As he rounded his eighth mile, Galen's temper subsided, leaving a familiar empty sadness. He didn't have the stomach for these decisions. Even so, he knew he would stay on at Biolex. And he would agree to delay VWM.

EDDY HUNG HIS keys on the hook and glanced at the pile of mail on the hall bench. At the top of the pile was an envelope from Biolex. Eddy knew it would contain a copy of his insurance statement marked only with the word "paid". His shoes hit the wall with a loud thump, and he went into the kitchen, leaving the mail.

"Hi hon," Joy said. "You got a letter from Galen."

"I saw."

"Not that one, a personal letter. It's right here." She handed him a neatly opened envelope with a typewritten sheet of paper inside. "You know, we really should invite him to dinner. It's a shame you two lost touch after the divorce." Eddy tossed the letter onto the counter. "Aren't you even going to read it?"

"I already know what it says. How's Abigail? How's Joy? How's life?" Eddy grabbed a pitcher of iced tea, sloshing some of the contents onto the floor. He cursed and banged the pitcher on the table.

"What's wrong with you?" Joy said.

He ripped off a piece of paper towel. "Nothing, it's been a crappy day." Joy gave him a so-what's-new look, to which he didn't respond. He wasn't going to tell her that his boss had turned down his request for a raise, again. It was the same old story: his boss was sorry, the company was tightening the purse strings to meet the new manufacturing regulations, maybe he should have taken the promotion when it was available. He threw the wet towel into the trashcan and slammed the lid shut. "He's just fishing for a thank you."

"He shouldn't have to fish."

"So you're on his side?"

"We're not playing pickup basketball, Eddy. He's spent the last nine months doing something incredibly generous for this family after we didn't talk to him for years. So you have no right to be crashing around here like a spoiled teenager." Joy took the stack of dishes from his hands and turned away.

Eddy grabbed a handful of knives and forks. "He's not doing anything for us; his company is. And to them, we're just a tax write-off against their donations quota."

"When did you become such a cynic? He used to be your best friend."

"People have to choose between medicine or food while he's making millions. You want me to have friends like that?"

"I know he offered to make you partner." Eddy froze. "Linda told me years ago."

Eddy clenched his jaw. "Yes, and I chose to turn him down."

"And now you're mad because he didn't need you anyway. That's why you never mentioned it to me, isn't it?"

Eddy faced her across the table. "I didn't want to advance that way."

"Or at all?"

Eddy threw the forks against a plate. Joy met his glare. The lingering clang of silver hung between them like a force field.

Suddenly, Eddy smiled wide. "Hey, kiddo." Behind Joy, Abigail was walking slowly down the staircase. Joy resumed setting the table. "Got a hug for your old man?"

When she reached the bottom step, Eddy circled his arms around her, lifting her to the floor. "Hi, Dad." They walked together to the dinner table, him with a forced jauntiness and her with a heavy gait.

After a tense dinner, Eddy dropped his and Abigail's plates into the dishwasher. "I'm going for a quick run. Want to go, kiddo?"

"No."

"Okey dokey, smokey."

After Eddy left, Abigail said to her mother, "Why does he do that?"

"He's doing the best he can."

"I hate how he pretends nothing's wrong. Like I'm just a hypochondriac or something."

"You know he doesn't think that."

"Well, that's how he makes me feel." Abigail went back up the stairs to her room before she started to cry for the fourth time that day.

In bed later that night, Joy said hesitantly in the dark, "Eddy, I think you should go with me to the support group."

"I'll pass, thanks."

"Your daughter is miserable, and so are you." Joy clicked on the light. "You don't talk to each other anymore. I think the group would be good for you. For us."

He sat up and leaned back against the headboard. He felt her watching him. He took her hand and smoothed his thumb over the lines of her palm, as familiar to him as his own. She was trying to save all that mattered to him, offering a way out of his anger and isolation. He would be lost without her partnership.

He didn't know why he'd kept Galen's offers from her, especially when they shared everything else. Maybe he'd expected her to reach a different decision, and he didn't want to expose his justifications.

Joy saw a different Galen than Eddy did. She hadn't been there at the beginning. She and Eddy had only started dating when his sister had the first bad stroke that left her disabled and frightened. Galen spent every day, including the last one, helping her with the physical therapy, researching the brain so she would understand what was happening, sleeping in the cot by her bed to protect her from the nightmares, and sharing a bond that left Eddy on the outside looking in.

That's the Galen that Joy had met, the pale knight—composed, devoted, caring, and strong. No wonder she had wanted Linda to meet him. She couldn't see that he'd fallen apart after the funeral. She didn't know his insecurities like Eddy did. And she didn't know Eddy was the champion before Galen came along.

He ran his hand up Joy's arm and drew her close. "I'm sorry I didn't tell you."

THE TOPICS AT his first support group meeting were as touchy-feely as Eddy had dreaded—dealing with anger, helping your kids feel normal, managing marital stress. But he had to admit that some of the suggestions made sense.

He sat on the metal chair in the church basement the second week, expecting more of the same. So he was pleased when the conversation turned to how to get access to medical care and where to find funding, the logistics that plagued Eddy every day.

One woman in clean but threadbare nursing scrubs said, "I know it's illegal, but I—I bought his medicine off the Internet. From France." The woman looked around at the other faces and rushed on. "I just didn't know what else to do. I knew I was going to run out of money. This way it'll stretch farther. I just didn't know what else to do."

Eddy wanted to know how she did it. He had searched the Internet himself but hadn't dared to take a risk that could jeopardize his job and make the situation even worse.

A big man with a southern drawl and expensive shoes said, "Don't you worry, miss. The government may not have the guts to change the law, but they don't have the guts to enforce it, either."

"That's exactly the problem," said one frustrated mother. "We need a state legislature with some backbone. If Congress won't legalize importation, states should." There were several murmurs of agreement.

"This group needs to take action," said the man with the drawl. "We need a candidate in this election who will give us folks a voice. Heck, I'd donate the money to run a campaign if we could find the right person." Several of the fathers looked away, their hands reaching unconsciously to their thin wallet pockets. Eddy thought of Galen, and the usual resentment rose higher, chased by guilt. He needed a way and a reason to get out from under that obligation.

On the ride home, Joy said, "You're awfully quiet."

"What would you think if I ran for state legislature?"

Joy didn't answer right away. He could feel her looking at him, and although it was a clear night, he concentrated hard on the road ahead. Finally, she said, "How long have you been thinking about this?"

"Well, it wasn't until they mentioned it tonight that I consciously considered it. But once someone said it out loud, I knew I'd always wanted it. Does that make sense?"

She was studying him again. "I haven't seen you want something out of your career in a really long time."

He wanted to be irritated, but he knew she was right. "Deep down, I know I can do it."

"I know you can, too."

He pulled into their driveway and switched off the engine. "It would mean we couldn't accept Biolex money for Abigail's treatments anymore."

"Do you think that man tonight would help us?"

Eddy jerked himself out of the car. "I'm not going to jump out of the frying pan into the fire, Joy."

The elderly neighbor who had been sitting with Abigail met them on the porch. They thanked her and went inside, where they resumed the conversation.

"Then how are we going to afford it?" Joy asked.

"We can sell the Trans Am. That'll get us through the end of the year."

Abigail was sitting at the kitchen table doing her homework. "No! You can't sell it, Dad, please!"

"Kiddo, it's important. You wouldn't want to hold onto it if it could help other people, would you?"

She mumbled half-heartedly, "Yes, I would."

"Let's think about this before we decide. There might be another way."

"I've been over the numbers a thousand times, Joy. The only other option is to sell the house and move into a trailer, and how would that look?"

Before Joy could answer, the phone rang. Eddy picked it up. The drawling voice on the other end said, "Hullo there. I didn't know if you folks would be home yet. Glad I caught you."

"Uh, hello." Eddy and Joy exchanged puzzled expressions. "What can I do for you?"

"Well, I saw you listening hard tonight, and I just wanted to tell you, you can't be doing anything squirrelly with your little girl's treatments."

"Excuse me?"

"It isn't safe. Believe me, I know."

Eddy leaned heavily against the counter. "Uh, thank you. I'm not sure—"

"Is there anything I can do to help you folks?"

"Thank you, but we're o—" He stopped. Abigail's tears were spilling onto her homework, and Joy was watching him expectantly. He would be selling out more than just a car if he let his pride answer for him.

"Hullo? You still here?"

"Uh, yes. Sir, what do you know about running a campaign?"

"Hot dog! I had a sense about you. Now, you're a fraternity brother, right?"

"That's right."

"Then you'll have yourself a fund. And you volunteer, don't you?"

"Yeah, with the Boys and Girls Club."

"Then we've got ourselves a campaign."

Eddy felt like he was in a dream, a good one this time. He told Joy, "I'll ask my father for the money."

GALEN SAGGED AGAINST the wall, feeling like a scolded puppy. In his hands was a letter from Eddy. *Thank you for your assistance in this matter.* Galen had read the line a dozen times but still couldn't understand. He knew that it would look bad for a campaign if anyone saw envelopes from Biolex in Eddy's mail, but the cold dismissal felt like more than keeping up appearances.

Helping Abigail had made Galen feel connected to what he still thought of as his real life. Now everything from that life was gone—his marriage, his daughter, and his best friend. All for Biolex. Was it worth it? How many times had he asked that question, and how long would he feel guilty for thinking the answer might be yes?

Abigail was alive. That was the important thing, no matter who paid for it. He prayed that someone was looking out for Lexi the same way.

ELIZABETH POKED A stick of wood into the fire, and Sera and Lexi screamed as a log fell over in a fountain of sparks. Their giggles echoed over the lake.

"This is way better than Girl Scouts," Sera said. She popped another marshmallow into her mouth. "Ow, ow, it's ha." Lexi laughed and Sera kicked dirt at her.

"All right, you two," Elizabeth said. "Did you zip up the windows in the camper?" They nodded.

The three sat quietly contemplating the stars. Elizabeth tried to remember when they had begun their annual Labor Day weekend trip, but her mind was dozing while she listened to the waves lap against the shore.

"You know what would be perfect right now?" Sera said.

"What?" Elizabeth asked, already knowing the answer.

"Harp music."

"Give it a rest," Elizabeth said. She had to suppress a smug smile, because she had already found a harp for Sera in an online auction. And with it, she had found the future for the seed fund, soon to be PHASE—Privatization of Healthcare by Auction for a Sustainable Economy.

27

FOR TWO MONTHS, Monday and Wednesday evenings at the Parker house were spent stuffing and stamping dunes of envelopes at the dining room table. Anyone watching would have seen Abigail occasionally glance toward Eddy when he was pasting flaps, Eddy looking toward his daughter when she was concentrating on folding, and Joy smiling at the tops of their heads while they each smiled down at their tasks. They traveled as a family to flyer the neighborhood, inexperienced and unaware that they were creating photo opportunities and a likeability factor worth more than a year of shaking hands.

For the first time since her book report episode, kids were asking Abigail questions about something other than what she called her "freak-outs". She had changed overnight from Abby Abnormal to the girl whose dad was kind of famous. She wished the campaign could go on forever.

One night in October, Eddy knocked on Abigail's bedroom door. "Hey, kiddo."

Abigail was sitting yoga-style on her lavender bedspread, doing algebra homework. "Hey, Dad, what's up?"

"I was invited to be in the homecoming parade this Saturday."

"You should take the car! You'll look really cool."

"That's what I was thinking. I was also thinking it'd be cool if you rode with me." Eddy held his head to the side, as if waiting for a blow.

Abigail's smile faded and she looked down at her book, shrinking into herself. "You don't want me there."

"Yes I do, kiddo. And I wanted to talk seriously with you about it."

"Because I might have a freak-out, right? I know it'd be really bad, but I can't control—"

"Abby. No." He sat next to her. "This campaign is a family effort, and I'm proud of that. I'm proud of you. This is our opportunity to enjoy what we worked on so hard. I won't do it without you."

"You are *so* melodramatic," she said.

Eddy threw up his hands. "Did a tween-age girl just call *me* melodramatic?" He poked her in the arm.

"Dad, quit it!" She poked him back.

"No, you quit it."

"No, you."

"No, you!" Abigail fell to giggling, and Eddy wrapped his arm around her and pulled her close. "I miss that laugh."

Abigail put her head on his shoulder. "Dad, I don't want to mess stuff up for you."

"You won't."

She looked up. "But what if I have an attack?"

"You won't."

"But what if I do?"

"Then we'll take care of you."

She sighed, much too heavily for an eleven-year-old. "I'll think about it."

Eddy left the room and closed the door. Through it, he said, "Love you, kiddo."

"Love you, Dad." She lay back on the bed and recited her nightly brain check. "Two times two is four, two times three is six . . . ."

The following Saturday, Abigail sat on the back of the convertible between her parents and waved with all her might. At the end of the parade, she turned to Eddy and said, "Let's keep going!"

"You're the boss." Eddy slid into the driver's seat and drove them up to Gloucester to Wingaersheek Beach, where they enjoyed a family picnic and spent the rest of the afternoon splashing around the shore and searching for crabs among the rocks— and schmoozing with future constituents. Abigail didn't see her dad much for the next few weeks during the hard campaigning, but the glow from the day of the parade stayed with her.

ABIGAIL WAS DUE for another dose of Lexistro at the end of October. "Can't we do this like every six months or once a year or something?" she complained while she and her mother waited for the doctor after her MRI. She dreaded the spinal injections more every time, because of the excruciating post-injection headaches and week of queasiness.

"Well, we can ask the doctor," Joy said.

The doctor reviewed Abigail's scan with them. "It's difficult to tell how frequently we need to administer Lexistro. The scan doesn't show any indicators of restricted blood flow, which is good. But I can't stress enough how much we don't know. I'm not sure if we want to alter the regimen if it's working."

"I'm sure," Abigail said. "You would be, too, if you were getting *that*." She pointed at the six-inch needle on the counter next to the exam table.

"Touché," he said. "But even so."

Abigail gave up on the doctor and turned back to her mother. "The election is only two weeks away. Can't we wait just 'til then? I'm fine, and I don't want to feel like puking when Dad wins."

At Joy's obvious indecision, the doctor said, "Why don't you make an appointment for tomorrow and talk it over tonight with Mr. Parker?" Joy smiled gratefully, clearly relieved that the decision wouldn't rest solely on her shoulders.

When Eddy came home that night, Joy explained the situation and what the neurologist had told them. "Kiddo, I don't want to risk you. I appreciate your enthusiasm, but winning isn't going to mean much if you're in the hospital."

"What if I'm real careful not to get excited and stuff? *Please, Dad.*"

"Why don't you go to bed and let Mom and me talk it over?" Abigail ascended the stairs, making a show of her reluctance, but knowing she'd be able to hear them from the register on the floor in the upstairs bathroom. She heard Eddy say, "I just don't know if it's a good idea."

"Nobody does, it seems. And nobody's sure if it's a bad idea, either." Joy's frustration quivered in her voice. "What I do know is that Abigail hasn't wanted anything in such a long time. This campaign means the world to her."

"She has seemed like herself again lately, hasn't she?"

Abigail rolled her eyes at the register. Her dad was pretty oblivious for a people person.

"Joy, I'll be honest, I'm scared as heck to do anything different, just for that reason."

"But we're going to anyway, aren't we?"

"I think we have to."

Abigail suppressed a cheer. No needles for two more weeks, no headaches for two more weeks. Two more weeks to be normal and popular. Then when her dad got elected, everything would be *perfect.*

ON THE NIGHT of the election, Eddy's campaign headquarters was charged with electricity. The exit polls were favorable, and Eddy took a break from his mingling to practice his speech in the coatroom. "Thank you for your confidence in me, and I will keep my campaign promise to make prescription drugs available to everyone who needs them. We will eradicate the suffering of knowing there's a cure for your loved one but not being able to afford it. If that means we have to open the doors to Canada or

Europe or Japan or anywhere else, I will fight to make that legislation happen. Also—"

"I'd like to thank the Academy." Joy stood in the coatroom doorway in a blue velvet dress in the style of June Cleaver. Her auburn hair fell loose around her shoulders.

"Are you mocking me?"

"Why, yes, Mr. Representative. Are you ready?"

"Is no an acceptable answer?" Joy reached over to give him a supportive kiss. They broke apart abruptly. "What the heck is that?" Eddy said. "Do I hear a dog?"

They emerged into the party room where a golden Labrador retriever was eagerly making the rounds, licking everyone within a five-foot radius, as if he were the one running for office. Eddy spied his campaign manager, the dog's owner, and he and Joy crossed the room. "Are you trying to pull a bait and switch on me?" Eddy said.

"Nah, I just thought this place could use a little more chaos." Among the dueling televisions and roar of the excited crowd, there was an occasional bark.

"Mission accomplished." The dog had found Abigail and leaped up for a bear hug. On hind legs, he was taller than she was. Abigail ruffled his ears and grinned widely.

"I thought she could use some company. She's a trooper, but it's a pretty dull place for a kid after the first hour."

"That was really thoughtful of you." Joy put her hand on the campaign manager's arm, and the man blushed.

Abigail ran over to her father, the dog close at her heels. "I'm going to take Buffy to the big room, okay?"

"Sure, but come back in twenty minutes or so. You don't want to miss anything."

"I will. Buffy, get down." Laughing, she pushed the dog away as he tried to lick her ear. He scrambled to jump back up against her hands. "Buffy!"

"What kind of shampoo did you use, essence of cat?" Eddy asked. Abigail ran away from them, the dog following close at her heels. When she stopped to open the lobby door, Buffy jumped up again, and she pushed him down once more before they disappeared into the lobby.

A cheer went up. "What'd I miss?" Eddy turned to one of the television screens and saw the latest results showing him with a considerable lead. He felt several hands clap him on the back, then he was swallowed into the crowd. Over the next hour, the news updates showed similar and better results. Eddy was basking in the frenzy when he felt Joy's hand on his arm. He leaned over so he could hear her.

"Have you seen Abigail?" she asked.

"She took the dog out." He looked at his watch. "They should be back by now." They heard a bark and looked in its direction. Buffy was at the door, but Abigail wasn't with him.

For Eddy, all of the campaign sounds went silent. He and Joy pushed urgently through the crowd and followed Buffy to the lobby, where Abigail was slumped on a couch. To anyone walking by, she was just a kid who had fallen asleep waiting for the adults' party to end. Eddy and Joy knew better. They ran to the couch and knelt to the floor, shook Abigail, stroked her head. "Abigail, wake up. Abby!" Eddy fumbled in his pocket for his telephone and with shaky hands, dialed 9-1-1.

Twenty minutes later, the campaign revelers watched in shock as their new representative rode away in the ambulance.

SERA DELICATELY OPENED her November Christmas gift, a simple envelope that Elizabeth had tucked into the rails of the stairwell. Inside was a piece of a crossword puzzle that read, *HARP & LESSONS.*

Sera jumped up. "Are you *serious*? Where is it?" She whirled around.

"Check your room."

Sera dashed up the stairs.

The year after Sera's symptoms first manifested, Elizabeth had started a tradition of the Twelve Months of Christmas, where she and Sera exchanged simple, homemade gifts on the first

Tuesday of every month. Their only late December celebration was church. Sera looked forward to the creative project each month, and it relieved Elizabeth from the momentousness of each holiday season, thinking about what she might miss next year.

Today Elizabeth's Santa satisfaction was a mixed feeling. She had denied Sera gifts like this for years. They had lived in the same house with its peeling paint for a decade, sat on the same furniture now fraying at the edges, and shopped for clothes only once a year during back-to-school sales. Their only vacations were the camping trips, one state away. All so they could afford a cure. Between the savings and her husband's life insurance, they had close to a million dollars in the bank. But there was no cure. There still wasn't even treatment. So what was the point in saving anymore?

WHEN THE AMBULANCE reached the hospital, Abigail was immediately given Lexistro. By the time she was admitted, she had regained consciousness. When she and Eddy were alone in her room, Abigail started to cry. "It's all my fault."

Eddy squeezed her hand. "Nothing is your fault. Just rest now."

"But I ruined everything."

"What are you talking about? I got to go to the party, but I didn't have to make the speech." He attempted a smile.

"I'm sorry, Dad."

"Kiddo, listen to me. You have nothing to be sorry about. You're okay, and that's what matters."

"Everyone is going to hate me even worse now."

"Nobody hates you. We love you."

Abigail didn't answer and drifted to sleep. Joy came back and handed Eddy a cup of coffee. Her eyes were rimmed red. They stepped out of the room and quietly shut the door behind them. In a nearby waiting room, Eddy dropped heavily into a chair. "It's all my fault. I should never have let her delay that injection."

"We both made the decision. I'm the one who talked to the doctor. I should have asked more questions."

"But he wouldn't have had any more answers. Let's face it, no one knows anything. We're alone in this." They stared at the white wall of the sitting room while their coffee went cold in their hands. "Joy," Eddy said softly, "I thought for a minute it would save money. If there was more time between treatments." He rushed on. "It didn't affect my decision." He paused. "But what if it did?"

Joy didn't answer right away. Eddy was sure he had finally crossed the boundary and shared the one thing their relationship couldn't handle. At last, she whispered, "I thought it, too." The guilt in her eyes mirrored his own. Eddy's political resolve cemented in that moment. No mother should ever have to suffer such choices.

THE NEXT DAY, Eddy sat at Abigail's bedside while they watched television, deliberately avoiding election coverage. Out of the blue, Abigail said, "Dad, if I get medicine from Canada, then what would the kids in Canada use?"

His campaign manager was keeping the press away from their room, but Eddy could hear echoes of them in the hallway. "Canada will get more."

A long silence passed, and Eddy thought Abigail was dozing, so he started to get up from his seat. She spoke again. "Are Canadians rich?"

"Some are, I guess." He strained to hear what was going on outside.

"Are those the people who would pay for my medicine?"

Eddy turned his full attention on her. His eleven-year-old daughter was worrying about who would pay for her medicine. That wasn't right. "Mom and I will get your medicine, kiddo. It'll be okay."

"But what happens if you get it from Canada?"

"It's just an extra step. Canada buys it from the company that makes it, and then we buy it from a person in Canada."

"Like the lemonade stand? When I bought the cookies from the store?"

He had to think before he remembered. "Yeah, like that. Now, get some rest, okay?"

After a few more minutes, she said sleepily, "Dad, some of the kids didn't get any cookies."

28

EDDY COULDN'T CONCENTRATE on the chaplain addressing the freshman class of Massachusetts legislators. His senses were overwhelmed with the vibrations of history in the State House furniture and the smell of legacy and power and dreams in the air. Even in the half-empty committee chamber, the speaker's voice didn't echo; it was absorbed by a crowd of shadows and walls insulated with centuries of ideas and debates.

Before this inaugural day, Eddy had researched who would be ending their committee terms. His networking talents would be put to good use garnering their influence to make him the replacement. For the first time in his professional life, Eddy felt he was right where he was supposed to be.

That night, he burst into the house like a five-year-old after his first trip to Disneyland. Joy was in the kitchen making supper. He kissed her on the cheek, winked at her, and grabbed a handful of carrots and a peeling knife. She raised her eyebrows. "I take it this means you're not having second thoughts about entering politics."

He flashed a roguish grin before he answered seriously, "It's my calling, Joy." He launched into descriptions of the chambers, his potential assignments, each of the other freshman representatives, and his grand plans for carrying out his campaign promises.

She listened and asked questions while she checked on the steaks and began to set the table. Eddy felt like the luckiest guy in the world. His wife was perfect, he had a second income and a new career opportunity, and Abigail was healthy right now. "Oh, hey, you pulled out one too many plates. I'm distracting you with my yammering."

Joy didn't look at him. "No, four is right. We're having company."

"Wow! Abigail's having a friend over?"

"I wish." She hesitated. "It's Galen."

Eddy calmly set the silverware on the table and stepped into Joy's full view. "And you were planning to tell me when?"

She didn't blink. "When the doorbell rang."

They were both startled when the bell did ring. "I guess you planned it well." He walked with deliberate strides toward the entryway.

"Eddy, be angry at me, but don't take it out on him."

Eddy saw the car and driver pull away, and he opened the door with his widest campaign smile. "Buddy, so glad you could make it! Come on in! How have you been? Would you like a drink? We've got Scotch, rum, anything you'd like, a fully stocked bar. I make a mean martini now. We've come a long way. Have a seat."

Galen froze wide-eyed in Eddy's high beams. Joy took his coat and gave him a warm smile. "Would you like a beer?"

Galen exhaled, blinked, and nodded. They moved into the living room and Joy continued to the kitchen.

"So, how's business?" Eddy asked.

"Good. No thanks to me, I think." Galen perched on the edge of the couch. "You can take the mouse out of the lab, but he still squeaks."

Eddy bristled. False modesty.

Joy came in with three frosty mugs of beer. Galen grinned up at her. "How's Abigail?"

Eddy answered. "Good. She's in the seventh grade this year, can you believe it? They grow up so fast." Eddy could see Lexi all over Galen's face, and he mostly regretted his comment.

Joy rescued them from the awkward moment. "So what are you working on now?"

"It's undecided. But I want to hear about politics. That's really something. Really."

Eddy couldn't help feeling proud, and familiarity took over. "I suppose if anyone knew I had a mouthpiece for industry in my house, I'd be tarred and feathered as a traitor."

"You think so?" Galen cocked his head. "Our goals are the same, making medicine available."

"You followed my campaign?"

"Of course."

Abigail walked into the room, and Galen stood. "Oh, you've grown." He sounded disappointed.

Eddy got up and put his arm around her. The three of them avoided eye contact until Joy, already the perfect politician's wife, broke the tension again. "Soup's on." They managed to spend ten minutes cordially passing the food around the dinner table and complimenting Joy on her cooking. She went back to the kitchen to check on the pie, and the only sounds at the dinner table were the munching of lettuce and the occasional clanging of fork against plate.

Eddy finally asked, "Do you think the Pats will win the Superbowl?" Magically, the safe topic carried the conversation forward, and they were able to talk about nothing controversial for the rest of the meal.

When their plates were empty, Galen said, "Joy, that was great. I'm sorry to eat and run."

"Don't apologize. You said you couldn't stay long. But you'll have to come again soon. And take some pie."

"Can't say no to that."

When Galen left, Eddy kissed Joy on the forehead. "Okay, it was a decent evening. Are you happy?"

"Blissfully."

29

Four Years Later

ELIZABETH DRAPED ANOTHER blanket across Sera's feverish body and silently gave thanks for one more night with her little girl. She sat next to the bed in the same rocking chair where she had kept vigil so many nights since Sera was born, ensuring that the covers continued to rise and fall.

Sera had just turned fifteen, outliving all standard projections. She had always bounced back from her bouts of illness to be an otherwise normal kid, full of life and energy, healthy to any passing observer. But Elizabeth couldn't ignore that the bouts were becoming more frequent and lasting a few days longer each time. Then yesterday, the seizure. Elizabeth lived in fear of the changes happening in her daughter's brain that no one could see, and that would lead to a day when Sera couldn't bounce back.

Elizabeth sent a thought out to the universe, a prayer to God and scientists: *Please hurry.*

GALEN SWUNG THROUGH the doorway of Myesha's office. "How are my monkeys?"

She grinned widely. "Mighty fine."

"VWM is a go, then?"

"Yep, we've finally met the requirements. It'll take two weeks to get the documents together, then FDA has thirty days to respond. So we could be treating someone before summer's over."

Galen was elated. It had been a long haul. Three years before, just as the VWM trials finally had funding to commence, a new FDA regulation took effect, requiring two hundred monkeys to be exposed to Lexistro before the clinical trial. Galen thought going back to monkeys would be a ridiculous waste, and voiced as much. Lexistro had already proven safe in tens of thousands of humans who had been given the product for stroke. But his objections fell on deaf ears.

Worse was that the new experiments couldn't just prove safety; the monkeys were required to have some form of VWM and get better. The Biolex science team had spent a frustrating year developing an acceptable non-human primate model for VWM. But Galen swallowed his anger and frustration when the first set of monkey studies showed that Lexistro didn't work as well as they expected. Galen and the science team spent another year working furiously on a new formulation, Lexi-VM. Based on the results to date, no sane FDA reviewer could keep Lexi-VM from clinical trials any longer. The monkeys were cured.

EDDY STRODE THROUGH the halls of the Capitol, his walk full of purpose and power gained in his first few years as a statesman. In his short tenure, he had finessed his way onto the much-coveted health care committee, sponsored bills on tort reform and performance accountability for grant recipients, and relentlessly questioned the rationale and funding strategies for medical research and access programs. Despite these efforts, the cost of health care continued to rise exponentially. So Eddy had narrowed his focus to prescription medications, now a professional as well as personal cause.

Eddy had maintained his corporate job for the past four years along with his public responsibilities, as more than half of the legislators now had to do to make ends meet. Although Eddy was exhausted, he believed it served all constituents well to have regular working people in office.

When he entered the lecture hall where the day's bill-signing event was scheduled to take place, he was met with congenial handshakes and congratulations. Much of Eddy's finesse had been due to his social skills, likeability, and passion, but he knew he also had his genes to thank. Joy often remarked how unfair it was that Eddy grew more handsome and distinguished as he aged. His more ambitious colleagues recognized that it meant Eddy's face would be shown on television often, and he knew some kept him close for that reason alone.

Cameras flashed for several minutes as the governor and the bill sponsors, including Eddy, held their polished poses. When the photography event was over, the governor shook Eddy's hand with an added sound byte. "Congratulations, Mr. Parker. Massachusetts is now the twenty-sixth state to allow global importation of prescription drugs. We have just tipped the scales in a national debate."

Back at his office, Eddy had his aide field a number of calls, but the only one he answered himself was from Senator Kevin Jenkins. In their fifteen-minute conversation, Eddy learned that the Senator was interested in his commitment to driving down the cost of health care. They exchanged ideas on the role of federal versus state governments and how they could make them work better together.

Before they hung up, Senator Jenkins said, "Mr. Parker, although I don't believe that states taking matters into their own hands is the way to handle drug importation, I will concede that my federal colleagues and I have been woefully sedentary on this issue. I hope we can work together to change that in the near future."

"I look forward to the challenge."

Eddy hung up the phone feeling energized. Although they disagreed on how to provide access to health care, Eddy found it refreshing to talk to someone who shared his passion and cooperative spirit. It hadn't taken long after the election for him to become disillusioned with the blatant partisanism in the capitol. He had always assumed the polarization he saw on the news was hyped, or at least the exception rather than the rule. That was his first of many misconceptions.

His worst frustration was the inertia of politics. He had quickly learned how to maneuver around his few unscrupulous colleagues, but the bigger challenges by far were the unyielding stance-takers. He longed for the days of Thomas Jefferson, before compromise became a dirty word. If only others would compromise with him, they could accomplish so much more. The right thing to do was clear: When people need medicine, get it to them. Why argue?

30

"HOW WOULD YOU like to host a back-to-school party with Squirrel 104.7, the Electric Watermelon Band, and a hundred of your closest friends?"

"Hey, everybody, quiet for a sec!" Sera waved her girlfriends back from the radio.

"The competition will be held on August fifteenth, and if our panel of celebrity judges chooses your act as the winner, you'll be ringing in the school year with style. The entry fee is a new package of socks and three canned goods to benefit Restore Dignity. Check out our website for details."

Sera whirled around and jumped onto her bed. "Dolls, we *have* to do this. Can you imagine how *awesome* junior year will be if we get to pick a hundred people to party in person with the EWB?" She hopped around, playing air guitar. Lexi fell to her knees and pretended to be a wild, adoring fan, waving her hands in the air and fake weeping. The three other girls at the slumber party mimicked Lexi, clamoring up at Sera, who was singing at the top of her voice to the song playing on the radio. Sera jumped off the bed and paraded around the room while the other girls followed her in various stages of mock hysteria.

Elizabeth opened the bedroom door. "I'm not even going to ask what you're doing. Pizza's here when you're done." The five girls tumbled down the stairs in fits of laughter and tore into the pepperoni and veggie pizza waiting on the picnic table on the back deck.

"This is *so* not good for my diet," said one of the more willowy girls. Four pairs of eyes landed on her in mid-chew then turned to each other.

Sera took a big bite and said with her mouth full, "It's great for my diet." The others were quick to follow her lead and conversation resumed.

"So, what's our act going to be for the contest?" Lexi said.

The reply was a chorus of bickering from the three other girls while Sera chewed pensively on her second slice of pizza.

"You weren't serious about that, were you? We don't have any talent."

"Shut up. You have, like, fourteen trophies, hello?"

"I don't mean that kind of talent. I mean stuff you can take on the road. You can't exactly swim on stage. Hello?"

"No, but you can dive off the stage," Sera said mysteriously.

The other girls stared at her then looked at Lexi, who shrugged. "We should probably read the rules before we do anything."

Sera jerked her head up. "Good thinking, as usual. HEY, MOM! CAN WE USE YOUR LAPTOP?"

Elizabeth appeared at the sliding glass door. "You don't have to yell; I'm right here."

"Oops, sorry." Sera's voice dropped to a whisper. "Can we use your laptop?"

Elizabeth set her computer on the picnic table. "Wiseacre," she said, pretending to flick Sera's ear. Sera ducked and grinned as she powered up the computer. "Just be careful with that, okay?"

"Yes, Mom," the girls answered in unison.

"You're all wiseacres. But I know where you're sleeping tonight." Elizabeth pointed a warning finger at each of them before she reentered the house.

"Your mom's so cool, Sera."

"My mom wouldn't let us sit on the furniture, never mind use her computer."

"My mom would never let us eat pizza. If we were at my house, right about now we'd be choking back alfalfa sprouts and some tofu sculpture."

"Gross!"

Lexi didn't say anything about her mother. She peered around Sera to the computer screen. "Yikes, it's a *band* contest." She flopped onto a deck chair. "Too bad we don't have a band."

"Not yet, anyway," Sera said, with a mischievous twitch of her eyebrows.

"ABBY, WHY DON'T you take your bike down to the beach or something? It's a beautiful day," Joy said. Abigail, sitting on a pillow on the floor in a dark corner of the den, continued reading. "Aren't you hot? It's ninety degrees outside."

Abigail was dressed in a black turtleneck and black jeans with her red hair tied back in a dark navy bandana. "All the more reason to stay inside," she said.

Joy shrugged in defeat and left the den, closing the door behind her.

"SERA, MAYBE WE should just go to the beach and hang out with everyone else. We're never going to be ready in time," Lexi said, after four more frustrating hours of trying to arrange a cover of a Billy Joel song, a task they were realizing was far beyond their skill set.

"No!"

"Geez, bossy much?"

"Lex, I want this so bad. It's like my aspiration."

Lexi didn't consider a high school band contest to be much of a life goal, but then she knew she would finish high school and go to college. Sera, on the other hand, had always been single-mindedly passionate about whatever idea was in her head at the moment, maybe because every goal might be her last. Lexi didn't like to think about it.

"Hey, Mom!" Sera was halfway out of the room.

Lexi followed her down the stairs. She wasn't as convinced as Sera that they could make a rock band out of a harp, a piano, a lead singer, and two back-up dancers. The five of them had spent a week just trying to decide on a song. They had finally pulled an old CD at random from Elizabeth's collection.

"Mom!" Sera skidded around the corner, almost running into Elizabeth emerging from the office.

"Whoa, where's the fire?"

"Mom, your boss plays in a band at the Spectrum, right?"

"Are you planning to ask him to sneak you and your posse into the club with your fake IDs?" Elizabeth teased.

Sera put her hands on her hips and raised an eyebrow. "Maybe."

Elizabeth squeezed the backs of the girls' necks as she passed between them in the hall. "Yes, he's in a band. Why?"

"We can't get the arrangement right. Would he help us?" Sera followed on Elizabeth's heels.

"I don't know. I'll ask him when I see him on Monday."

"Can't you call him now? Every day counts!"

Elizabeth turned around with an expression that Lexi didn't understand. Apparently, neither did Sera, whose face was still expectant. Suddenly, the larger meaning of her last three words dawned on the two girls. Sera whirled around and stomped up the stairs. Lexi was surprised that Elizabeth looked almost helpless as she stared after her. Lexi didn't know what to do, so she just stood frozen in the hallway. Elizabeth finally noticed her there. "Sweetie, go on back upstairs."

Lexi trudged up to the bedroom. Sera was sitting with her back to the door, leaning her head toward the stereo speakers. "Hey, Lex, I know what we need to do!" Her irritation had apparently dissipated. Lexi was confused, but the pangs of jealousy that she usually felt toward Sera and her mom were quiet for a change. Maybe everyone had parental issues.

Sera thrust a piece of paper at Lexi. "Look at what Mom wrote for her yearbook. I found it in the CD case."

When Lexi finished reading it, she said, "It's perfect."

Sera played the music over a few times, while Lexi took notes on their ideas. An hour later, they heard a knock at the open door. "I thought you girls needed a producer or something? You'd better get a move on; he'll be here in twenty minutes."

Sera flew out of her seat. "That's wild!" She hugged her mother with such force that Elizabeth nearly lost her balance, and Lexi felt one small pang.

WHILE THE GIRLS worked with great mystery in the garage with her law-partner-by-day/rock-star-by-night, Elizabeth shook her head at the phone. Senator Jenkins had just asked her yet again to testify at a hearing for one of his many causes. "Kevin, I appreciate your faith in me, but I've been telling you for years, I have my own cause at home."

"It's become something of a challenge for me, to wear you down. How is your cause doing, by the way?"

"She's well, thanks. She's a teenager," Elizabeth proclaimed. "And your daughter?"

"She's a teenager," he complained. "Are you sure you don't have time? You're eloquent and have much more appeal than I do."

"Oh, don't underestimate yourself." Elizabeth laughed. "Several hundred thousand people did vote you into office."

He chuckled. "So tell me," he said. The tone in his voice had changed. "We've been friends for what, five years now?"

"At least." Elizabeth was perplexed at the sudden shift in the conversation.

"It's a good milestone point, don't you think?"

"Sure . . . ?"

"Would you like to—have dinner—sometime?"

Elizabeth was stunned. She hadn't been on a date since before Sera's diagnosis, not that there hadn't been offers. She had rebuffed Kevin Jenkins early in their friendship, citing Sera as her top priority. She didn't realize he still had feelings for her. She felt slightly guilty, because she had continued to talk and meet with him regularly over the years, not only for the intellectual stimulation but also glad for the male company.

Now that Sera was a teenager and starting to spend more time with her friends, Elizabeth could justify starting a relationship. But something was still holding her back. "Kevin, I don't know . . . ."

"It's okay. I had to give it another try. But don't let's be awkward, because I really do value your opinion. This hasn't been a five-year ploy for a date."

"No, I know." Elizabeth stuttered. "I'm flattered, it's just—I'm sorry."

"Don't worry about it. Listen, I really called to ask what you think of this import mess. We're getting heat from industry, and some are threatening to stop selling to Canada and Japan if we pass a national bill. We're getting heat from the FDA because they can't ensure safety when states make their own rules. We're getting heat from states for denying citizens access to cheaper drugs. And everyone is giving us heat for not taking some kind of federal action. But none of the debate answers the real question of how we make prescription drugs affordable while still promoting research. So what do you think?"

Elizabeth gaped at the phone. "I thought answering yes or no to dinner was hard!" They both released some tense laughter. "I'm no senator, but I think the problem is that all of the players are tripping over each other. Not just about importation. The whole health care system is broken, and everyone is trying to fix their own little part, but they're just ending up like bumper cars that can't get out of the pavilion."

"So you're saying we need the politicians to stop politicizing and provide some direction."

"Sort of, but people other than the politicians have to come to the same conclusion. There isn't one person or group of people to blame. That's what makes it so frustrating." Kevin didn't answer

159

so Elizabeth went on. "If the issue were in the private sector, you'd have a mediated working session where representatives from all sides could put their objectives on the table and argue, negotiate, and compromise—without cameras or Robert's Rules of Order. You could do that. You've already done the hard work of identifying the players. So if you could get them in a room together for even a day, they might just move the fleet forward. Or at least stop spinning in circles."

"Of course! Why haven't I done this already?"

Before she knew it, Elizabeth was helping to organize the event, whether out of guilt or excitement, she wasn't sure.

GALEN LEANED AGAINST the whitewashed railing on the deck of Amos Theriault's beach house while Amos gulped a beer in the wooden chair next to him. The salty air suited the old man, Galen thought. But the plaid, oh, the plaid. Was there anyplace that would fit in?

"I heard you're representing CBE in Washington," Amos said.

CBE, the Coalition of Biotechnology Executives, was established to put a face on the amorphous entity represented by the pharmaceutical lobby, to remind Congress that "the American people" included business owners, no matter the size of the business, and that each was a constituent, a voter, and a taxpayer. The group claimed Galen was a co-founder, but he was sure he had only suggested the idea and would never have chosen to lead it.

"It was Senator Jenkins' choice," Galen said. "I think he figures I'm harmless."

"He's a fool, then."

Uncomfortable with praise, Galen kept talking. "I'm probably just a familiar face, since Lexistro got so much media exposure early on."

"Either way, it was a good choice. Especially with Frank Ellis there."

Galen groaned and bent forward over the railing.

"Shore it up, son. He represents the hard issues that we execs aren't s'posed to talk about."

Galen scoffed. "The way a suicide cult represents organized religion."

"Well, Frank didn't get to be the most influential lobbyist on the Hill by being harmless." Amos reached his scaly, sun spotted arm into the cooler for another beer. "But he does need to get reined in sometimes. That'll be your job."

Galen sprung off the railing. "No! I can't bridle a porcupine. I'm not even good with regular people."

"You're the ace in the hole, son. Frank respects you. You just have to say the word."

"Why should he listen to me?"

"If you don't know, you're a blind fool, too."

EDDY NEARLY BURST from pride when he showed Joy his invitation letter. "I'm not sure how I ended up on the roster. It's a pretty elite group, and I haven't known Kevin Jenkins very long."

"You've been persistent and successful, so why wouldn't he invite you?"

"You have to say that; you're my wife." He hung his jacket in the closet. "It's going to be quite a showdown, I think. There are representatives from every conceivable side of the issue. And this issue is a monster polygon."

"Washington, D.C., huh?"

"Yeah, I'm thinking we should make it a family trip," he said toward Abigail, who was lying on the couch staring at the ceiling.

She answered dully, "Sounds great, Dad."

31

THE DAY OF the band competition, Sera sat rigidly in a chair in the dressing room while her mother applied her makeup and curled her hair. "Why so quiet? Aren't you excited? You've worked awfully hard," Elizabeth said.

"I don't feel good."

Elizabeth forced herself to keep curling. Don't react, just let her be a kid today.

Sera twisted around with an incredulous expression. "D'you know what it is? I think I'm nervous! How cool is that?"

Elizabeth laughed out loud. She would give anything for Sera to be healthy, but her illness had provided a priceless perspective on life. "Well, you are a marvel, my dear." She gave the hair combs one last pat and pushed Sera toward the backstage.

Elizabeth went out to the auditorium, recalling Sera as a little girl. From the time she could walk, as soon as Elizabeth set her down, she was off like a wind-up toy, as if she instinctively knew she had a lot to do and precious little time.

Elizabeth recognized a group of Sera's friends chanting near the front row, including the three girls who had dropped out of the endeavor. Elizabeth wondered what was in store, since Lexi and Sera had been fiercely secretive, holding their practice sessions in every garage on the block except their own, and at such low volumes, some of the elderly neighbors wondered if they were singing at all or just using their instruments as a front for marijuana trafficking. Elizabeth took her seat just as the curtain opened and the battle of the bands began.

After the seventh band on the roster screamed words that Elizabeth couldn't understand, the curtain opened again to the two girls, looking very small on the gaping, dark stage. In an attempt to be futuristic, they were wearing black jeans, glow-in-the-dark pink and green turtlenecks, matching neon lipstick, and plenty of glitter. Sera was seated with her electric harp to her left, and on her right was a percussion synthesizer that she had just learned to operate. The instruments shone under the stage lights, catching the metallic shades in her hair. Lexi was behind an acoustic piano, her blondeness illuminated like a halo. Both girls looked ill. Elizabeth felt butterflies flapping wildly in her own stomach.

The music started with just Sera strumming the harp, and the auditorium hushed. Lexi joined with a delicate but driving piano theme. Sera began to softly half-sing, half-narrate:

We all have a story
Each born with a cross and a crown
Potential to soar free
A curse we fight, that ties us down
Yet we judge one another
For choices we make, beliefs we hold
All seek revelation, discovery of secrets more precious than gold.

Elizabeth recognized the words as her own, and the room got misty as she remembered all of the teenage passion and hope she had poured into her poem on the verge of graduation. The music crescendoed and Lexi's voice took over.

It is our generation
We carry the torch of the truth
That science and miracles are one in the same

We're wiser youth
Self-reliance and angels, reality, dreams—we prize, we need
We wish with eyes open, aspiring to reason, conceding to lead.

Lexi's piano theme took over. Sera turned a rhythmic beat on the synthesizer and strummed the harp, eliciting an ultramodern and mystical harmony. Both girls started to sing.

We must champion the future
Still cherish the past, learn from pain
Relentless is nightfall
So is the dawn, we can't restrain
The past carries forward
Our epoch will be the age that heals
We'll reverse disenchantment, rescue the heroes, live out our ideals.

Elizabeth's heart hurt. The lights dimmed, and the piano and harp faded into silence. The stage was black and the girls were still. The crowd roared in wild applause.

32

ON THEIR FIRST night in Washington, the Parker family was invited to a dinner at Senator Jenkins' house in Georgetown. "Would anyone like a drink?" he asked when they arrived. He led them down the steps of the foyer and through the crowded living room, alive with hubbub in the glow from a stone fireplace flickering off the red brick walls. A mission-style table was covered with punch bowls. "We're chemical free tonight, for the kids," the Senator explained.

A blond girl about Abigail's age approached them. Senator Jenkins eyed her casual jeans with a stern look. She ignored him and stuck her hand out. "Hi, I'm Darcy." Abigail smiled self-consciously and reached out to return the handshake, but suddenly the girl waved heartily at someone behind Abigail. "Sera, over here!"

Abigail pulled her hand back and turned to see, bounding toward them, a petite girl in a sapphire blue party dress. She was followed more demurely by a woman Abigail guessed was her mother. Senator Jenkins looked very glad to see the woman and put his palm on her back as he introduced her to Abigail's parents. "Meet Elizabeth Rose, the mastermind behind this affair."

As the adult conversation turned to the impending symposium and the guest list, Abigail's attention was drawn back to Sera, who was saying to her, "What are you doing tomorrow?"

At Abigail's confused expression, Darcy Jenkins said, "Sera's throwing an awesome party tomorrow night. Electric Watermelon is going to be there!"

"There's going to be a hundred people! Wanna come?"

Abigail could think of nothing she would less like to do, but to her shock and horror, her parents stopped mid-sentence of their conversation to accept for her. Abigail recoiled into her turtleneck. "I wouldn't want to be rude."

"I'm *inviting* you," Sera said. "Besides, Darcy's boyfriend isn't going."

Darcy rolled her eyes. "Come on, it'll be fun," she said.

Abigail did not agree. She looked at her parents, their eyes pleading to her as if they were the teenagers. She couldn't think of a good way out, so she sighed inwardly and said, almost choking on the words, "Yeah. Sure. It'll be fun."

While the Parkers' attention was turned toward the party, Kevin's finger continued to trail down the list of conference attendees. When it landed on Galen Douglas' name and Elizabeth saw his RSVP status for the party, she felt a pang of disappointment. Kevin said, "I can't say I'm surprised he isn't coming tonight. It's no secret that he doesn't like crowds. I guess every great man has his eccentricity." Then he folded up the confidential list and put it away.

33

AS ELIZABETH WALKED through the U.S. Capitol toward the parking garage, she pondered the meeting about to start. She felt that it had the potential to be monumental. Part of her wished she could stay for it, but she had higher priorities, set long ago when she promised not to miss anything important in her daughter's life if she lived to be a teenager. So, she couldn't miss any of the preparations for Sera's big party tonight, both their aspirations achieved. Lost in her thoughts, Elizabeth didn't see Eddy Parker rushing toward her until they collided.

Eddy dropped the tiny building map that had been distracting his attention. He apologized and crouched down to retrieve it. When he stood up, Elizabeth Rose smiled widely at him. "Oh, hi. We met last night, right?" She gestured toward the map. "It's a little bigger than the state house, isn't it?" When he didn't answer, she said, "Well, good luck today." He smiled back briefly, feeling a rare flash of insecurity. She was right; this was the big time. Why was he invited? He put the question from his mind and picked up his pace toward the committee chamber.

As Galen waited in the committee chamber for the event to start, he was uncharacteristically interested in the people trickling through the door, wondering how they might shape his company's future.

Frank Ellis approached. "So this rep from Massachusetts, you know him right? He's on our side?"

"I didn't say that."

"But he'll follow you?" Frank said.

"He's not a follower. He'll do what gets health care to the most people."

Frank scowled. "Are you sure that's his only agenda?"

"I told you, he'll be here for the right reasons."

Eddy burst through the doorway, looking flustered. If Galen had been thinking like a CEO seeing a politician, he might have stayed put. Instead, he was thinking like a fraternity boy seeing his buddy when he shot across the room to the doorway. "Ed!"

Eddy glanced right and left, visibly agitated. "I didn't know you were going to be here." He turned his shoulder to getaway position. "We should really find our seats."

Galen became conscious of his suit, his arms too tight in the dress shirt and jacket sleeves, and his dress pants constricting his breathing. He longed to be in sweats, running across campus. "Oh, sure, later." He swallowed his next words when Eddy darted away.

Eddy looked around to see who had been watching the exchange. He was relieved that no eyes were turned in his direction and also that he wasn't one of the last to arrive. Only a couple of people were seated at the U-shaped table marked with thirty place cards and outfitted with microphones for each of the faction representatives. At one end of the table, a slide was projected onto a screen: *Health Care Cross-Objective Working Group*. Eddy found his marked place and sat.

He took a deep breath to calm his racing pulse and thought about the greeting by Galen. He had no idea Galen knew Senator Jenkins. Now it all made sense why Eddy, just a junior representative, had been invited to such an event. He was expected to toe the line. His pulse raced faster. Galen was calling in a favor.

The rest of the participants made their way to their seats, and Senator Jenkins summoned the meeting to order. "I'm sure many of you are thinking, like I am, that this type of symposium is long overdue. I would like to thank everyone for their pre-work, which you can see on the pages before you as well as the placards at the front of the room." He gestured toward several printed hard-back posters full of bulleted text. The biggest board contained a list of health care objectives that the attendees had all been given in advance: Affordability, Availability, Control, Discovery, Profit, Quality, and Safety.

"The symposium staff compiled all of the solutions you submitted to meet these high-level objectives and split them into their component proposals, which are randomly distributed on these posters. Today, representatives will each have five minutes to present to the working group the combination of proposals they submitted. The rest of the day will be an informal discussion on the pros and cons of each proposal. Our objective for the day is to narrow these lists to a set that can feasibly be negotiated on a bigger stage." He introduced the professionally accredited mediator who was to run the session and address any disputes regarding the record.

The mediator nodded and took the microphone. "You'll notice that there are no cameras or press in this room. You're here to solve problems that aren't easily solvable, and it's to that end that we have made this a closed-door discussion, so you can take the gloves off without repercussion. I encourage you to put all of your issues on the table and warn you that the discussion may get heated. That said, let's begin."

Each representative in turn made his or her presentation. When Frank Ellis rose to speak, he sent several references in Eddy's direction, each beginning with, "I'm sure the statesman from Massachusetts would agree that . . . ."

Galen was sure Eddy didn't agree at all, and each reference made him cringe. He tried to signal his apologies across the table, but Eddy didn't turn in his direction.

Eddy could feel Galen's eyes on him, which added to the ire that had been building while Frank Ellis spoke. He would not let those two manipulate him. There was only one more speaker before Eddy, so he focused on composing himself. When it was

Eddy's turn to speak, he calmly unveiled the five-point plan he had been working on for the past year.

"Point one. No one should have to spend more than twenty percent of their income on health care if their disease is chronic or life threatening. The government is here for the common good, and it's good for everyone if people continue to have a reliable income, so they don't burden other parts of the system. The government would pick up the tab for anything over twenty percent. Therefore, prices need to be reasonable, to limit taxes.

"Point two. We need to regulate individual income of pharmaceutical executives in order to lower prescription drug prices. It's a perversion of capitalism to allow anyone to profit from another's misfortune, and the rate of executive compensation now is unseemly.

"Point three. We need to require insurance companies, including Medicare, to pay for a new drug within its first year after FDA approval. People who pay insurance premiums should be able to get what they need.

"Point four. We need a federal law to open the borders to prescription medication as part of a global free trade agreement. This will create real competition with Canada and Europe and Japan and other countries to drive down U.S. prices.

"Point five. All pharmaceutical companies should put seventy-five percent of the profits from government reimbursement back into research and development. This will allow the government dollars to achieve results at the level of private industry, it will ensure that industry is not profiting from taxpayers, and it will stimulate the discovery of new treatments." The room had become increasingly charged during Eddy's presentation, indicating a lively debate to follow.

By eleven a.m., each of the representatives had spoken, and there were over fifty proposals up for discussion. The mediator guided the attendees through each. Some proposals were immediately dismissed as too controversial. Others were considered for only a few minutes before the moderator halted discussion and marked the point as one for the larger stage.

When they broke for lunch, Eddy cornered Galen in an alcove outside the men's washroom. "I don't appreciate what you're trying to do. I'm nobody's puppet." At the guilty expression on Galen's face, Eddy turned on his heel and marched back to the committee room.

Galen gaped after Eddy. Surely he didn't think Galen agreed with Frank Ellis' asinine commentary. Galen felt guilty that he had allowed the comments to continue as long as they had. He tried to catch Eddy to explain the situation, but it was clear that Eddy was avoiding him until lunch was over.

One of Eddy's points was the first up for discussion after the lunch break, and Galen's stomach churned when the mediator displayed it on the screen:

REGULATE INCOME OF PHARMA EXECUTIVES

Unfortunately, Frank Ellis was first to speak. "The pharmaceutical executives I represent would like to know whether the regulation of income would take into account the negative salary the executive incurred while building his business?" Galen wanted to crawl under the table. Frank went on. "We would also like a definition of 'seemly'."

Eddy said glibly, "A good rule of thumb is if there are families going hungry to buy your medicine, then you're probably making too much."

Ellis replied, equally glib, "So, should executives be as poor as the poorest person in the state? In the country? Should they live on the streets themselves? That's the only way to ensure that they're not making *any* money off others."

Galen could tell that most people in the room were feeling abrasions, so he tried to soften the message. "I think Mr. Ellis is saying that a significant profit is a necessary incentive, because the risk of investing in drug development is significant."

"Pharma has been peddling that story for years," said one exasperated insurance company executive. "No one is saying that you shouldn't make *anything*. Just keep it within reason."

Eddy said, "Money is a poor incentive in any case. The proper driver should be public service." Galen was perplexed and annoyed by his holier-than-thou attitude.

"Aha!" said Frank, slapping his hand on the table. "Then executives should be as poor as statesmen! Tell me, Mr. Parker, do you work for free? Have you given up one of your cars to pay for your neighbor's medicine? If not, then I submit that *you* are making money off your constituents' misfortune of having to pay taxes. In fact, I believe that my colleague, Mr. Douglas, is one of those constituents. What is your service to him?"

Galen trembled from the effort of restraint; he wanted to tackle Frank Ellis. True to form, the man had gone a step too far. He could feel the anger shooting from Eddy, who, for the first time during the session, was glaring directly at him.

Eddy's nerves were as raw as stripped wire. His electric bile turned briefly from Galen to the mediator, who crossed the controversial point off the list and moved to the next proposal. Eddy saw Galen pass Frank Ellis a note, and there were several furiously scribbled exchanges, then Ellis left the room. Eddy had calmed down somewhat by the time the mediator projected his next point an hour later:

LIMIT COSTS TO 20% INCOME IF LIFE-THREATENING

A representative from Louisiana said, "Most of my constituents don't have even twenty percent to pay out-of-pocket. You have to go by need."

One senator argued, "What we need is for government to be less involved, not more. If taxes were lower, then maybe people could actually afford to pay for their own drugs."

An insurance company representative said, "This has to be a state decision. Forty thousand dollars in a state like Montana is middle class, so 20% is doable, when the same amount is practically poverty in urban California. There is no national solution."

Eddy nodded to him in respect. The mediator crossed the proposal off the list and displayed the next one, also Eddy's:

COVERAGE REQUIRED WITHIN 1 YR OF APPROVAL

The same insurance exec refuted this point. "If the pharmaceutical industry knew insurance companies *had* to reimburse their new drugs, then we would lose all negotiating power. What company can profit honestly under those conditions?"

An economics professor said, "If regular insurance companies start going out of business, it will create a world where insurance is a luxury that only the richest—perhaps the pharmaceutical executives—could afford." The jab at the executives elicited a chuckle that broke some of the tension in the room. "Everyone else would be forced to pay out-of-pocket. It would be a catastrophe for the economy."

"It would finally bankrupt Medicare," said a government official.

The mediator crossed it off the list.

Eddy was depressed that the proposals he had thought out so carefully were being discarded. He felt a little better when he noticed that only a tenth of the proposals discussed thus far were still up for consideration. He was further heartened by the response to his next point:

ALL PROFITS FROM GOVERNMENT BACK TO R&D

The senator most opposed to Eddy's previous point said, "I would agree wholeheartedly if it were more like fifty percent, or if there were a tax break in addition. We want to stimulate new discovery, but we need to maintain incentives, too. I think at the heart of it, this is a great idea, and I would support this if it went to the Senate for a vote."

A representative of the citizen lobby said, "This would take care of some of the executive compensation issues, too. Profits can't all be spent on executive bonuses if a certain portion are required to be committed to R&D—or dare I say, *earmarked?*" The legislators in the room smirked at the reference to their

173

never-ending struggle with pork barrel spending. "There will always be companies that try to get around it, but for the most part, it could work."

Galen nearly stood at his chair and craned his neck to make his point to all of the attendees. "This could be the jackpot idea. Medicare could be funded to reimburse at the same price as private insurance, so we could actually charge less to private payers and still have enough for more research!"

"You want to charge even more to Medicare? Are you really that greedy?" Eddy said.

Galen drew his eyebrows together and squinted across the table. "It's practically net zero for government, so why do you care? The public gets back in research what their taxes lay out in reimbursement. Medicare can stop squeezing industry, so—"

"So you can make more money." Eddy folded his arms and sat back hard in his chair.

"No!" Galen threw his hands in the air. "So we can charge less to private insurance!"

A member of the citizen lobby said thoughtfully, "It would take the Medicare double-whammy off the middle class and youth. Right now, the latter are paying taxes for Medicare, even though it'll be bankrupt before they can benefit from it. And the former are paying high premiums because private insurance is overcompensating for Medicare's insufficient rates. So your proposal together with higher reimbursement rates is a win-win."

Eddy said, "Raising prices is an industry choice. Let's be honest about who's administering the whammies."

"It's business, Ed! What has made you so blind?"

"Disillusionment, I guess."

The rest of the participants watched their exchange with curiosity. The mediator left the proposal up for consideration and called for a break. This time, Galen cornered Eddy. "What is going on?"

"I'm not toeing any line for you, I don't care what our past is. So stop trying to make a fool of me in there."

Galen gritted his teeth, his confusion overcome by anger. "Who's trying?" He walked away.

Eddy's most controversial point was raised at 4:30 p.m., when all of the participants' tempers were tested to their limit:

INCLUDE PRESCRIPTION MEDS UNDER NAFTA

The governor of a border state said, "Canada and Mexico and the Midwest states did so great under the North American Free Trade Agreement, I'm sure the whole world wants to jump right on board."

For the first time since her presentation that morning, Patricia Chen spoke. "The FDA's job is to make sure the drugs on the market are safe. Under this proposal, FDA may as well be disbanded, because we can't control the quality of products from outside the U.S. It would be a medical train wreck."

"This proposal is leaving other countries to do our dirty work," said a representative of the coalition for government reform. "The United States government needs to step up and regulate prices if it wants them regulated."

A policy professor agreed. "Each time another state allows importation, and the federal government does nothing, it endangers people and ruins businesses, and it makes our legal system weak and meaningless."

Eddy defended his proposals. "All citizens should have access to health care. Plain and simple."

"Who do you mean by *all* citizens?" Senator Jenkins asked quietly. "What about those who have no treatment?" He paused and his eyes scanned the faces around the table. "What is their access if prices go so low companies can't afford or have no incentive to spend money to discover new drugs? And what about access for Canadians if U.S. pharma stops selling to Canada?"

"With all due respect, Senator," Eddy said, sounding sincere, "if it were truly an open border, then U.S. companies couldn't choose not to sell to Canada or anywhere else."

Galen was exasperated. "You can't force companies to sell a product any more than you can force them to start a company in the first place. And no one is going to open a business if there's no flexibility to profit. You know what it takes—the risk, the *price*. You *know*." Galen half-pleaded, half-glared at Eddy across the table.

Eddy glared back. "And you know how your pricing impacts families. It's my job to ensure that my constituents aren't put in that position." He turned to the rest of the participants. "Look, people are going outside the U.S. anyway. They're getting their kids' drugs off the Internet. We don't have a snowball's chance in hell at protecting people from a black market like that. But parents do it because they have no choice. *Devoted* parents will do whatever it takes for their kids."

The last comment was unmistakably directed toward Galen. He responded in kind. "People need to stop relying on government to solve their problems. They should have savings rather than bigger houses—and boats."

Neither man could remember when he had ever been so angry.

34

THE PARTY WAS every bit as horrible as she expected, Abigail thought as she stood near the speakers at the edge of the dance club floor. She was trying simultaneously to appear entranced by the band and to plug her ears to keep from going deaf. Darcy Jenkins and her friend who had given them a ride had immediately squealed hello to someone and vanished, leaving Abigail in the spot where she'd been standing for the past hour. Abigail thought there weren't enough black clothes in the Mall of America to make her and this night disappear.

She tried to be philosophical about it, like her post-traumatic stress shrink was teaching her. She had been fine ever since she started receiving the Lexistro every two months, so she didn't have to worry about having a freak-out now. No one here knew her history, so she could be anyone she wanted to be. She looked around the room packed with kids her age, dancing to the music, laughing with their friends, and flirting. She could just walk up to the bar, get a soda, and see what happened. She could pick out a stranger and just start talking. She could just go out on the floor and start dancing. She had spent years mastering the art of being invisible, so no one would even see her. Why not just do it? But she was rooted to her spot.

She saw someone point to two girls across the room, and Abigail recognized one of them as Darcy Jenkins' friend, Sera. She watched the two girls with envy. They had everything she had ever wanted; they were confident and popular enough to invite a hundred people to a party. Abigail wondered if she had thrown the same party, would anyone have accepted the invitation?

Sera was petite and colorful and sparkly, as if she knew she deserved to be noticed. Her tall friend with the blonde hair was quietly beautiful and probably didn't even realize it. What made them friends? Maybe they just complemented each other. Abigail wasn't a complement to anyone, with her freak-out tendencies and red hair that escaped from every hat she tried to hide it under.

At the thought, her hand flew to her head. She had noticed when she came in that no one else was wearing a hat, so for the first time conscious of fashion, she had put hers in the coatroom. She regretted it as she tried to smooth the hated waves around her ears and shoulders. Then, to her horror, the blonde girl looked straight at her.

"Who's that girl?" Lexi asked Sera.

"Which one? There are a lot of people here I don't know. Isn't it wild?"

"The one over by the speakers."

Sera looked where Lexi was nodding. "Oh, hey, I met her last night. I wish I had her hair. It's like a fountain of pennies. Poetic, huh?" Lexi rolled her eyes. "I always thought I should have been a redhead. Don't you think that would have suited me better?"

"And give you an excuse for being a spaz? I don't think so."

"You're funny," Sera said flatly. "We should go say hi."

Sera grabbed Lexi by the bracelet, and they made their way over to the speakers. "Hi!"

"Uh—um—h-hi," Abigail replied.

"You don't look so good," Lexi said, then she clapped her hand over her mouth. "I didn't mean you don't look—I wasn't being rude, you were just kind of . . . well . . . in shock or something."

Abigail smiled despite herself and took a deep breath. "This is an awesome party."

Sera perked up. "We won it in a band contest!"

Abigail provided the expected amazement. "Cool." There was a long pause and a lot of looking around until Abigail finally spoke again. "My name's Abigail."

The blonde girl smiled warmly. "I'm Lexi. What school do you go to?"

"I live in Boston," Abigail said.

"I always wanted to go to Boston," Sera said.

"No, you didn't," Lexi told her.

"Well, I always wanted to go somewhere. Boston counts."

Abigail laughed out loud. She stopped abruptly, feeling like she had just shouted into a megaphone and got hit with a spotlight. But the other girls were grinning at her, so she grinned back.

Lexi said, "I want to go to Harvard."

"Me, too!" Abigail replied.

The band stopped playing, and the Squirrel 104.7 disc jockey stepped up to the microphone. "Electric Watermelon would like to invite our contest winners to join them on stage for their next song." Lexi and Sera linked arms and jumped up and down. Sera impulsively linked her other arm with Abigail's and made a move toward the stage.

Abigail was paralyzed. She would rather get beheaded than get on that stage with all of those eyes on her. It would be just as bad, though, to protest and make a scene. She worried that if she let her panic rise, she might even have a freak-out in front of all of these strangers and the two coolest girls she had ever met, and then her life would just be over. But the sparkly girl wouldn't let go of her arm, so Abigail moved numbly with them up to the stage, willing herself to breathe normally. Make sure your brain gets enough oxygen, she thought.

The band had started to play loudly and gestured them to sing along. Three more girls joined them on stage, laughing and shouting the lyrics. When Lexi and Sera started singing, Abigail didn't want to look like a bump on a log, so she sang, too. The guitar player stepped forward next to her and played a riff. It was surreal, all those kids looking at her like she was the rock star. The six girls shouted into the microphones and danced around with the band, and Abigail thought she was having another of her dreams where she had friends. When the music ended, all of the girls high-fived each other and tumbled off the stage into a crowd of kids. Abigail had never been happier in her whole life.

A group accosted her to ask what it had been like up there, and she was answering them animatedly when Darcy Jenkins grabbed her by the elbow. "We have to go. My friend had a fight with her boyfriend," she shouted into Abigail's ear.

"Oh, no." She looked around for Lexi and Sera. "I have to say goodbye."

"She already called her mom to pick us up, and my friend's mom isn't all that nice. Come on!" Darcy yanked Abigail toward the door.

The group of kids who were calling to her, "See you later!" As she was dragged outside, Abigail waved with all her might.

On the side of the room opposite the door, Sera and Lexi were describing their stage experience to a select group of classmates and strangers. The party attendees had been painstakingly chosen after hours of debate rivaling the most elaborate wedding reception plans. They had only invited forty-nine classmates and allowed them each to bring a friend, which made it a mixed crowd. It had also allowed them to finagle an invitation to Sera's big crush, Danny, without much ado. Sera looked over to where Danny was standing, in the corner farthest from the band. He looked like he'd rather be doing anything else.

"Sera, just go up and talk to him already!" said one of the girls.

"Chicken," said another.

"I'm never chicken." Sera put her hands on her hips. "I'd go over there in a second, but that would defeat the purpose. He has to come to me if he wants to go out with me. I read *The Rules*."

"You're trying to get a date, not snag a husband," Lexi said. Sera rolled her eyes.

BACK AT THE hotel suite, Joy and Eddy were sitting on the sofa watching the news. "The big showdown on Capitol Hill today was the meeting of health care leaders from around the country. It was expected to be interesting, but no one anticipated the fireworks between the CEO of Biolex and a junior representative from Massachusetts. Channel Five reporters caught an exchange between the two during a break from the closed-door session." On the screen was a picture of Eddy and Galen staring each other down in the alcove.

"Oh, Ed," Joy said. "After all you've done to build your reputation."

"Yeah, it was pretty ugly." Eddy sighed.

"So call him."

Eddy stood and grabbed his glass off the side table. "He tried to use me professionally. Friends don't do that." He clinked ice cubes loudly into the glass.

"You might have jumped to the wrong conclusion. You didn't know he was going to be there; maybe he didn't know you'd be there, either."

Eddy shut the micro fridge. "He knew."

The suite door opened, almost hitting Eddy. "Hey there, kiddo! You're home early. Did you have a good time?"

To her parents' shock, Abigail grinned.

35

ELIZABETH CLICKED OFF the news channel, which had just completed a recap of the Parker-Douglas debate. When she had first seen Galen Douglas on the list of attendees for the event, she wasn't surprised that Kevin Jenkins had singled him out. Of all of the CEOs Elizabeth had contacted in the early stages of Sera's disease, he was the only one who hadn't offered condolences and empty stock sentiments. She still believed there was sincerity in his response, but she had long since stopped expecting signs of progress.

She watched the coverage of the debate with interest. She had researched Eddy Parker's short legislative history, and although she didn't agree with most of his health policy proposals, she was impressed that he had carried the flags she had had to drop years ago—to rationalize the medical malpractice laws and to ensure that Medicare and NIH tax dollars are used efficiently and get results in the current decade. Being a good lawyer required her to be a good study of people, so she wasn't surprised that there were sparks between the two men, both being as intensely committed as they were.

Resurrecting an old habit, Elizabeth slid her laptop across the coffee table and navigated to the Biolex website. There were the usual biographies about the executive officers and their educational backgrounds, a company timeline, and a description of Lexistro. It really was a miracle product, she thought again. At the bottom of the page was an inset entitled "Future therapeutic areas of interest". She started to read the list, which included Huntington's chorea, Alzheimer's disease, and—she froze at the next words—*leukoencephalopathy with vanishing white matter*.

Elizabeth's hands were shaking as she dialed Kevin Jenkins' number.

"Elizabeth, how nice to hear from you!"

"When are you meeting with Galen Douglas?"

"Hello to you, too."

"I'm sorry, I—I—"

"I'm just joshing you. He's meeting me in my DC office on Friday afternoon. We've been trying to get together for a while, but I have so little time when I'm in Massa—"

"Could I join you? I'm sorry to impose."

"Of course, you're always welcome. But you've been turning down these meetings for years. Why the sudden change of heart?"

For some reason, she didn't want to tell him the truth. "Just . . . curiosity."

When Elizabeth hung up the phone, she called up the stairs, "Sera!" Sera appeared on the landing. "You're still staying over at Lexi's Friday, right?"

"Sure, why? You got a hot date?" Sera winked.

"Do you ever turn it off?" Elizabeth said with mock perturbation.

"What, my charm? No, lucky for you, it's open twenty-four-seven."

Elizabeth shook her head and turned away, relieved to have dodged further questions. She didn't want to get either of their hopes up yet.

On Friday, Elizabeth rode the train into the city and took a cab to the Capitol. Her insides were jelly when she knocked at the Senator's door. One of his aides looked up and smiled. "Hi, Mrs. Rose. Come on in. Senator Jenkins is running late as usual, but please have a seat." She turned to where the aide was gesturing, and a man stood up from the cluster of chairs.

"Galen Douglas," he said in a voice as deep as a vat of molten chocolate. He extended his hand to Elizabeth.

His hand was warm and soft. Like his aura, she thought. Maybe he felt familiar because he had been in her thoughts for so many years. Maybe she was searching his eyes to confirm his soul worthy of answering a prayer. Maybe she imagined his strength enveloping her because she had already shifted her heavy hopes onto his broad shoulders.

"Elizabeth Rose. Pleased to meet you."

Her hand was delicate and cool. For Galen, it was as if the ever-present fog had evaporated, and he was reflected in the black glass of her eyes. Like the faint scent of her name, she exuded a mixture of femininity and strength that he could feel so surely that he had to fight an alien urge to embrace her. He wanted to hold tight to this comprehension, this bit of human insight that was so elusive to him.

"The pleasure is mine," he said.

Kevin Jenkins burst through the door, apologizing for his tardiness. Elizabeth released Galen's hand, startled. The three moved to the inner office and talked for the next hour about the results of the working group, the proposals under consideration, and next steps. Elizabeth sat next to Galen, sensing him so intensely she couldn't look at him. She was acutely aware of Kevin's usual manner of showing her off like a prized possession. She was so uncomfortable she didn't know what words she spoke, merely forced herself to appear normal.

After an hour, the aide stepped into the doorway and tapped his watch at the Senator. Kevin stood. "Well, Mr. Douglas, I know you have a schedule, so I won't keep you. Elizabeth, if you could stay a minute longer?"

They all exchanged handshakes, and Galen left. Elizabeth fidgeted while Kevin reached into his briefcase and pulled out an envelope embossed with the White House seal. "These are President's Box tickets for a Celtic Symphony at the Kennedy Center tomorrow night. I hope you and Sera are free. I thought it might be a treat for her. There'll be harps."

Elizabeth was so embarrassed she couldn't speak.

"It's a token of my thanks for all of your work over the past year, because I know you don't have a lot of time to spare."

Tears sprung to her eyes. What was happening to her today? She held the envelope in both trembling hands and thanked him sincerely.

She felt guilty then, for rushing out of the office and down the hall after Galen. He had stopped and was fishing through his briefcase. When she was a few feet away, she said, "Mr. Douglas?"

He looked up, surprised.

She blurted, "My daughter is fifteen. She has VWM." His face expressed an odd pain, different from the usual sympathy she received upon this revelation. It occurred to her that his reaction was more to Sera's being fifteen than her having VWM. She filed it away as a curiosity and went on. "I wrote to you a long time ago, and I noticed on your website that Biolex is researching VWM, and I wondered . . . ." She let her desperate hope finish the question.

Galen's eyes darted rapidly back and forth at hers. Peripherally, she took in the beginning traces of gray at his temples, the neat hairline around his ears, and the sinewy muscles along his neck, which hinted at the runner's physique underneath. Finally he said, "It *is* you."

All sound was suspended in the marbled hallway as recognition washed over them both. After a long moment, Galen reached into his pocket then handed her a business card. "I have to catch a plane, but—"

Elizabeth snapped to attention. "Oh, I'm sorry to keep you."

"No, no, please. You can call me at the office or—" He took the business card back and scribbled a number on it. "This is my cell phone. I—I travel a lot." He handed her the card again.

"That's so generous, thank you. Is there a good day?"

"Any day. I would be happy." They locked eyes again.

"Well, I know you have to catch a plane . . . ."

He jerked to look at his watch. "Yes, I'm sorry."

She handed him her business card but immediately regretted it. "If you ever—need legal services." Legal services? Oh, brother. To her immense relief, he laughed, and they smiled freely at each other.

He nodded and started to hurry away but turned back. "There's a clinical trial. In Boston."

Her eyes misted again, and she whispered, "Thank you." As she watched him walk down the hall, she wondered at the sadness in his eyes, too.

36

ABIGAIL OPENED THE refrigerator, looking for a snack. It was nearly seven o'clock, but Eddy wasn't home yet. Her mother was leaning on the counter watching the little television under the cupboard, occasionally stirring the simmering chili.

"We're going to eat pretty soon," Joy said.

Abigail sighed and shut the refrigerator door, empty-handed. She and Joy turned to the television when it showed the familiar picture of Eddy and Galen in heated discussion.

"When asked about the reelection of Mr. Parker, Biolex spokesmen declined to comment. Parker's daughter has been receiving treatments with Lexistro, the company's cash cow, since his dramatic first election when she was rushed to the hospital after suffering a stroke." On the screen was a clip of Abigail being wheeled into the ambulance with Eddy looking on in anguish. It was the same clip that had been shown a hundred times in the weeks after the election.

Abigail was stunned that anyone would dredge up what she had worked so hard to put behind her. She felt her mother's hand on her arm. "Don't worry about it, hon." Abigail jerked her arm away and returned to her room, her only safe haven.

LEXI LAY ON her bed, staring at a postcard. *I miss you.* It was from Boston, addressed to her, and postmarked twelve years ago.

The card had fallen out of one of her mother's old romance novels that Sera and Lexi had snuck from the attic. At Sera's urging, Lexi had shown it to her mother.

"Where did you ever find that?" Linda had asked.

"Who is it from?"

"What were you doing in the attic?"

"Who is it from?"

Pause.

"It's from your father. He was in Boston on a business trip when you were little."

"She was totally lying!" Lexi told Sera later. "The only traveling *Roger* ever does for his job is riding up and down the elevator."

Lexi hadn't stopped thinking about it since. She looked again at the picture of the Citgo sign above Fenway Park and the lights reflected off the Charles River, sensing that she was holding a ticking bomb. She took a deep breath and rolled off the bed, sticking the postcard into her book. She was determined to raise the issue with her mother again at the first opportunity.

Lexi could hear the television as she descended the stairs. "As Channel Five News reported earlier this week, Mr. Parker and Mr. Douglas were roommates at Harvard University and had apparently been friends until their infamous meeting last September. Many suggest that the root of the rift may be the cost of treatments for Parker's daughter, who is a regular recipient of the profit-maker for Douglas' company, L—"

The television clicked off. "Is that you, Lexi?"

Lexi walked into the living room. "Yeah, Mom." She plopped down cross-legged on the couch and opened her book. She couldn't concentrate. It was a perfect time to bring up the postcard again. She just had to ask nonchalantly, not let on that it was a big deal. Just say it.

Fifteen minutes later, Linda broke the silence. "Listen, your dad and I are planning a trip for next summer. We thought it would be nice to look at some colleges before you start your applications."

A family vacation? What a concept, Lexi thought. All she said was, "Uh huh."

"So, are there any colleges that you want to see?"

"The usual." Lexi knew it was irritating her mother, but she kept reading. She was desperate to go to Harvard, but hadn't mentioned it, afraid her parents had something else in mind. Now she was doubly determined not to mention it until the Boston mystery was solved.

"Lexi, would you look at me? Don't you care where you're going to spend four years of your life?"

"I don't know. Whatever," Lexi said.

Linda exploded. "Would you get your nose out of that book and make up your mind? You're just like—" Linda cut herself off with an exasperated huff.

Lexi put her book down and stared at her mother. "I'm just like who?"

Linda didn't flinch. "Just make up your mind, for once."

"For once? I've told you what I want plenty of times, but it's never the right answer, so what's the point? You're going to tell me what to think, anyway!"

"All your life I've only tried to do what was best for you. Those decisions aren't easy, and I've never been appreciated for it, not by anyone!"

"Okay, then how's this for a decision: I want to go to Boston."

Linda stormed out of the room. Lexi's triumph was short-lived, overwhelmed by the ever-ready guilt.

37

EDDY WATCHED GALEN fidget with a paperclip while they sat side-by-side at the desk across from the host, preparing for the live interview to air. The two men hadn't spoken to each other since their face-off on Capitol Hill four months ago. Eddy's campaign manager thought this television show would be a good start to the new legislative session, either to stir up the debate for publicity or to put it to rest. Eddy suspected Galen's advisors had convinced him of the same, and that he was regretting the decision as much as Eddy was.

Even if he wanted to talk to Galen, he wouldn't know what to say, so Eddy distracted himself by marveling at the life-size photomural of the show's host. He couldn't be more than twenty-five, but his Howdy Doody similarities together with his talent for stirring controversy translated well into television ratings.

Howdy leaned forward over the desk, and the interview began. There was an introduction of the two men, some light-hearted bantering about Harvard with the Yale-educated host, then a general recap of the purpose of the meeting on Capitol Hill. It was a cordial beginning but quickly jumped to the hard questions. "Mr. Parker, I'm intrigued by your recent press release regarding a proposal to limit executive compensation in the health care sector. Mr. Douglas, what do you think of Mr. Parker's proposal and its potential effect on the economy? I believe it was Abraham Lincoln who said, 'That some should be rich, shows that others may become rich, and hence is just encouragement to industry and enterprise.'"

Eddy looked sideways at Galen, who wasn't moving to speak. So he said, "My point is that we need to foster a society where well-off people give back."

"Based on the tax code, a person who makes $72,000 or higher might be considered well off, isn't that right?" the host asked, his freckles dancing with anticipation.

"It depends on where you live. Here in New York City, probably not."

"Interesting. Is $73,000 well-off in New York?"

Eddy assumed a tolerant smile. "No."

"Seventy-four? Seventy-five? Seventy-six? When do you get there?"

Eddy forced the smile to stay on his face. "Point taken, thank you. It's a sliding scale, and the tax code is somewhat arbitrary."

"Shall we use $100,000? Six-figure salaries are generally accepted milestones." Eddy shrugged noncommittally.

"Okay, average school debt for a dentist is $250,000. With loans having a payback period of ten years, that's $25,000 per year just in debt payments. After taxes. In salary pre-tax, that translates to more like $35,000. So take that off the $100,000, and his take-home salary is effectively only $65,000, which we've already established is not well-off." The self-satisfied host waited for a response.

"Do you want to be a dentist?" Eddy asked, as a distraction. *When you grow up* was implied. He saw from the corner of his eye that Galen was suppressing a smirk. Eddy wasn't sure whose discomfort was causing the amusement.

Howdy ignored Eddy's comment and turned to Galen. "What do you think of Mr. Parker's proposal?"

Eddy was surprised to hear Galen's response. "I don't think on a given day my presence is worth ten to twenty times more than anyone else in my company."

The host raised his red eyebrows and leaned even farther over the table. "Don't you devote more time to it?"

Galen shrugged and cocked his head dismissively. "So I work eighty hours a week instead of forty. That's two times, not ten."

"Don't you think you have a bigger impact on the company?"

"That's a different question."

Eddy was amused that the host had his head poised, expecting Galen to keep talking. Of course, he didn't. Finally the host said, "What do you mean?"

"Bonuses are the reward for impact. That's why they shouldn't be limited. If the company performs great, then the people who made it happen should share the profit."

"There's an incentive system, and then there's bribery," Eddy said convivially, trying to make his point without seeming antagonistic. Galen stared straight ahead and didn't respond.

The host was barely seated, he was straining so far forward. "Isn't there a lot of pressure in your position, Mr. Douglas? It isn't just about skill set, is it? Not many people can do what you do, or even want to. So isn't supply and demand what drives up compensation?"

Galen sat back and crossed his arms. "I don't know what other people think."

The host gave up on Galen and turned toward Eddy. "Would an executive who took a million dollar bonus be rich?" Eddy's jaw worked back and forth under tightly closed lips. "What if his company went under, and he had a million dollars of debt to pay off? Or what if he made a big investment and it didn't pan out? What if executives only saved their money and didn't invest at all, or only made safe investments? Wouldn't that hurt the economy? What if he's sixty by the time he takes the bonus, and the company never does that well again, so it's the last bonus he ever gets? If he lives another twenty-five years, that million is going to be worth less than $50,000 per year. Now is he rich?"

Eddy could hardly bring himself to answer the smug little Boy Scout. Finally he said, "That's a lot of ifs."

"Ifs are the measure of risk," Galen said. "That's one down-side to a free country; there are no guarantees."

Eddy turned to face Galen. "Especially in a free country, everyone should be guaranteed health care." He thought the host's suspenders might snap.

Over the remaining half hour, the conversation declined from cordial to markedly impersonal, until both men were facing forward and speaking directly to the host, addressing each other only in the third person.

"Mr. Parker's solution is to regulate away profits, regardless of the economy."

"Mr. Douglas thinks the economy is all that matters and that the ends justify the means."

"Mr. Parker's policies are short-sighted."

"Mr. Douglas doesn't distinguish between policy proposals and business proposals."

"In a capitalist society, they're inextricable, for better or for worse."

The host jumped on the opening. "Mr. Parker, you used the word 'bribery' before. Does the argument between you two have something to do with using business to steer policy? People are interested in what could cause such a disagreement between friends."

Eddy said, "There is nothing newsworthy about our disagreement. I'd bet less than half of your audience has regular contact with their college roommates. The difference with us is that we happened to cross paths again, on opposite sides of the fence."

"This is a little more than a simple drifting apart though, gentlemen. Are you sure this has nothing to do with your daughter, Mr. Parker?"

Eddy's heart pumped blood thick and hot. "I can't deny that I have been more than angry at the repeated displays of my daughter's picture on the news." He stared a warning at the host and thought he sensed Galen doing the same.

"We have no intention of sharing her picture tonight. I'm simply asking whether the rift had anything to do with Biolex providing money for her treatment."

Galen and Eddy snapped their heads toward each other in question and accusation. The host, like a lion before a big meal, asked, "What's the matter, gentlemen? Did you think that your kickbacks were better hidden?"

"They weren't kickbacks," Galen and Eddy answered in unison.

"So you're saying, Mr. Douglas, that you weren't hoping you could use the charity to your advantage?" Eddy bristled at the "c" word. "And you expect us to believe, Mr. Parker, that you didn't think you would be asked for anything in exchange, that this was a gift out of the kindness of the big corporate heart?"

Before Galen could answer, Eddy said, "Companies get tax breaks for such 'gifts'. That's the exchange. That is all."

The host went in for the kill. "Through our sources, we know that for more than a year, you sent your insurance bills to Biolex and that you received quarterly mail from Biolex in return. And we know you couldn't have paid the full bill from your own income, which is public knowledge. Yet there has been no evidence that Biolex has received a tax benefit for any of that."

Galen more than once took in a breath as if about to speak, giving the impression of a fish out of water. Finally, Eddy said, his face burning, "I don't know anything about company accounting practices. I only know that it wasn't a political situation. At least not to me."

• Galen's leg bounced like a jackhammer. "This is exactly why I don't watch the news. You've distorted the situation into a corporate scandal, when it was just a friend doing a friend a favor."

"So then, Mr. Parker, you did agree to do favors for Biolex."

"No, I did not." Eddy's eyes were wide with the effort of restraint.

"But what were they expecting to receive, if not the tax break?"

"What Biolex expected is immaterial; I'm not for sale."

"I didn't expect anything," Galen said.

Eddy turned to him, forgetting they were on live television. "Drop the naive act. It doesn't suit you anymore. We both know you showed up in Washington thinking you had me in your pocket."

"Why are you so quick to believe that?"

"What else am I supposed to believe? It's like they're all saying, company money has strings." The studio was silent for a full fifteen seconds while the cameras rolled on.

Then Galen said quietly, "It wasn't company money," and the show ended.

EDDY AND GALEN delayed their argument until they were waiting for the valet in the parking garage, then Eddy couldn't hold it in any longer. "It wasn't company money?"

Galen said, "Look, I know you didn't want my personal help, but Biolex couldn't do anything legally. And I couldn't just say 'sorry' and do nothing. Besides, no one was supposed to know."

"And yet, somehow they found out. How is that?" Eddy saw Galen's anger ignite.

"The press can find out anything if they have reason to look. And no one would have had the reason if you hadn't assumed the worst of me."

"If you hadn't lied to me, I wouldn't have had to assume anything. You humiliated me." The valet pulled up with the rental car and handed the keys to Eddy. Eddy got in the car and slammed the door.

Galen said, "The ironic thing is that Biolex could have been yours anyway."

Eddy revved the engine. "Galen, we were never going to be partners. Get over it."

38

IN THE WAKE of the confrontation with Eddy, Galen contrived a reason to go to Washington, DC and invited Elizabeth Rose to dinner. He figured he might as well get the next rejection out of the way while he was still numb. But Elizabeth had accepted his invitation.

He watched her walking purposefully toward the Thai restaurant where they had agreed to meet. She was wearing a skirt, which so few women did now, especially in February. He admired her confidence—and her legs. Galen wondered again whether it was right to feel attracted to a mother who wanted him to save her daughter's life.

Elizabeth saw him and gave a small wave as she approached his table. They exchanged a few pleasantries, and she mentioned the live interview. "Was that host as much of a twerp in person as he was on television?"

"More."

"Too bad. For once, he had respectable guests with actual principles and a legitimate difference of opinion on something that matters. It could have been a good show."

"Then no one would've watched it."

Her eyes smiled from behind the menu. Like sunrise. Usually about now, Galen would be starting to sweat, knowing there was an elephant to acknowledge but not knowing how or when or if to bring it up, not wanting to be insensitive and talk about something else, but not wanting to be awkward and talk about nothing at all, until he was trapped in a vortex of insecurity. But with her, he felt calm. Somehow he knew she would mention it when she was ready.

So they talked about Senator Jenkins and incentive systems and the cases she had worked on. Galen was sorry they would have to stop talking long enough to eat.

After they were served, Elizabeth's aspect turned solemn, and she said, "I contacted the investigator at Massachusetts General Hospital. He told me that Sera couldn't participate in the study until she turns sixteen."

Galen's heart sank. He knew the girl was only fifteen; it was Lexi's age. Before he could apologize, Elizabeth reached a hand out and said quickly, "I didn't mean that as an accusation. I just thought it was strange, since most kids with VWM don't make it to sixteen, or ten, even. Unless you know something else?"

She asked it with a hungry expression that pained Galen to answer. "We had to start the trial in the older ones first. Until we can meet the new requirements for kids under twelve." He had never wanted more acutely to find exactly the right words. But all he could think to say was, "The average prognosis is still nine years, but that means some of the kids live into their twenties."

Elizabeth nodded, as if used to disappointment. "You'd think the FDA would make it easier to get treatments to children, not harder." She shook her head. "No, I keep forgetting that I'm only seeing this from one point of view. But it does seem to be taking longer and longer, doesn't it?"

Galen's back started to bow like it hadn't done in years. She needed him to respond, but he didn't know how. Then she looked up, into his eyes, searching. And he felt certainty. He said, "We're all trying to protect them."

"Yes." She kept her eyes on him. "All I've ever tried to do is protect my daughter. But I couldn't." She blinked rapidly and turned her head away. Galen felt an upsurge of guilt and longing.

He had failed so much more than she ever could in that depart-ment.

He waited while Elizabeth composed herself. "I'm sorry. I don't usually get emotional," she said.

"You have every right to be."

"Well, it doesn't make for very good dinner conversation." She smiled dismissively.

He talked for a long while about starting his company and how being a CEO was the hardest job in the world for someone who doesn't understand people. But he understood her, and he talked more than he had ever done, because he could sense that she needed time to settle her thoughts.

He had forgotten what it could be like with another person. For the past two decades, when he connected with anyone, it was fitting brains like puzzle pieces—dovetailing ideas, matching edges of humor, and putting thoughts together to figure out a problem. But he felt Elizabeth as a continuation of his own mind, and feelings and thoughts without shape flowed back and forth between them. He recognized when she was ready to talk again, so he eased the conversation to her, and she began to tell him about her health service exchange business. He was amazed to realize he had handled the conversation flawlessly, as though he had always known how to do it.

"We're only piloting it in one community right now," she was saying. "People have been banking health care credit for about two years now, through an Internet auction. I got the idea years ago, but it took a while to launch, since I know very little about computers. My daughter's friend built the website, and I don't understand a bit of it."

Galen admired her for feeling pride in someone else's child.

"So for example, last month, someone posted a service of two hours of cleaning toilets, and someone else posted two hours of investment planning, and someone else posted two hours of portrait painting. Companies and individuals have bid on those services, and they pay for them directly to PHASE. Whenever anyone buys services through the auction, the provider banks health care credit at the rate of a hundred dollars for each hour of service, regardless of the end price. They just have to wait a year to use the credit."

She was leaning toward him so close that he absorbed her passion as she talked. "It works, because in that year, the capital funds produce the hundred dollars of interest. All we have to do is cap the amount of services bought and sold, according to the capital at the start of the year. The buyer also benefits on the sale, because one third of any money paid for a service is banked for the buyer, or they can donate it to someone else's bank. Another third becomes part of the capital funds. The rest is used for profit and administration of reimbursements.

"We have a very strict list of what can and can't be reimbursed. Right now, it's mostly co-pays and new drugs that insurance doesn't cover. But when the fund gets more established, we can cover bigger problems, like long-term care, or maintenance of income during rehabilitation. And since no one at the fund is an elected official, we don't have to worry about getting re-elected, so we can actually enforce our own rules!"

She smiled widely at him then dropped her eyelids and turned away. "I'm sorry, I have a tendency to ramble on this topic."

"I like to hear ideas."

She looked at him curiously, and he felt her in his mind. He wanted to prove his sincerity, to make her see that he never said what he didn't mean. He scribbled on a napkin:

$1,000,000 seed X 0.06 = $60,000 interest
$\qquad\qquad\qquad\qquad\quad$ = $60,000 credit avail.
$60,000/$100 per hr credit = 600 hrs service allowed
(600 hrs X ave auction price) X 1/3 = add'l capital

He said, "If I understand, with a million dollars of seed capital at six percent interest, that would be sixty thousand dollars you could pay out that year. At a credit rate of a hundred dollars per hour of service, you could allow six hundred hours of service to be auctioned. And the increase every year thereafter depends on how much was added to the capital the year before."

"You *were* listening." She beamed at him. "So you see the possibilities. If we got as big as one hundred million in capital funds, then six hundred thousand hours of services could be exchanged. That would be six million dollars in *earned* health care coverage!"

He believed anything was possible, as long as she had her hand on his.

She pulled back and gestured in the air. "My dream is that eventually, everything outside of catastrophic health insurance would operate through PHASE. When it works, it'll be like a flying citadel, a whole system that would span across industries and break the ropes that tie health coverage to jobs and government and put it back into personal control. The trick is getting it off the ground."

Then she laughed. Galen liked the sound of it. "You probably think I'm crazy, trying to change the behemoth health care system on a few hours a week and my measly legal coffer."

"Something tells me you can do it," he said. They regarded each other with admiration, in comfortable silence.

The meal ended far too soon for Galen. It was the closest he had come to a date since his divorce. A decade. Hard to believe. Was he imagining it, or was her expression mirroring his thoughts?

He walked her to Union Station, and when the boarding of her train was announced, they awkwardly shook hands. Before Elizabeth exited to the tracks, Galen said quickly, "If you have more questions, feel free to call." She smiled back at him then disappeared through the gate. He agonized the whole trip home about whether he sounded as desperate as he felt.

39

LEXI TOOK TWO dollars from the boy standing in front of the concession counter and slid him an index card and an envelope. "Write a note on the card and the name on the envelope."

He eyed her suspiciously. "You're not going to read it, are you?"

She battered her eyelashes mischievously until he appeared to reconsider. "Chill," she said. "No one's going to read it. Just seal the envelope and put it in here." She pointed to a two-foot cardboard box decorated with hearts, flowers, and pink tissue paper, and bearing a sign: *Valentine's Day Rose Sale Sponsored by the MHS Jazz Band and Johnson's Florist Shop.*

The boy leaned over the counter and curled his arm around his head to shield the index card as he hastily scribbled a message. Lexi couldn't help peeking when he dropped the envelope into the box. She gasped. "Sera?"

"Shhh!" The boy spun his head around with a horrified expression. "You can't tell her!"

"Did you sign the card?" Lexi whispered.

"You won't tell, right?"

"You didn't sign the card? What's the point in that?"

"Lexi, come on."

"I won't say anything if you buy another one and sign it this time."

"No way."

"Alright, then." Lexi crossed her arms.

"What does that mean?"

"She's my best friend. I'm obligated to tell her."

"I knew I shouldn't have done this." He looked right and left and back, his body tense with indecision.

"At least write a clue."

"Girls," he said as he grabbed another index card, scribbled his initials, and dropped it into the box. He slapped two more dollars on the counter and hurried away.

When her shift was over, Lexi met Sera at their usual lunch table. Lexi whistled a tune toward the ceiling as she sat down.

"What's that all about?" Sera asked.

"Maybe I know a certain someone might be getting a rose from a certain other someone."

Sera dropped her tray on the table and straddled the bench next to Lexi. "Who?"

"Can't tell."

"I'm your best friend!"

"I promised."

Valentine's Day was the following Friday, and Sera badgered Lexi relentlessly all week. She sent a text message while the biology teacher wasn't looking: *Tommy C?* Lexi stared forward, as if in close attention to the lesson. *MMM?* No response. *Tommy A?* Lexi made a sour face.

The next day, Sera passed a series of notes in trigonometry class: *Does he have brown hair? Is he tall? Is he in this class?*

Lexi tried to hide her smile from the teachers when she slid a piece of paper back. *Shouldn't you be concentrating on trig? Remember, you stink at math!*

ON THE MORNING of February 14, Elizabeth knocked on Sera's bedroom door. "Day off from school today. I got calls from two moms whose kids are staying home sick." She closed the door and went downstairs.

Sera flew out of her room. "No!" She trampled down the steps. "Mom, not today!"

"Watch it, you're going to slip."

"It's Valentine's Day!"

"People do get sick on Valentine's Day, you know."

"This is important. I *have* to go to school today."

Elizabeth turned around and narrowed her twinkling eyes. "What do you *have* to do that's so important?"

Sera blushed. "Never mind."

Elizabeth smiled as she continued toward the kitchen. "Whatever it is can wait until Monday, if it's that important."

"You're missing the point!"

Elizabeth looked at Sera sternly. "I think you're the one missing the point. You're forgetting that if you get sick, that's truly serious."

"How can I forget? You remind me every single day!" Sera stormed back up the stairs. "I'm going to school," she announced and slammed her door.

Elizabeth was taken aback by the uncharacteristic rebellion. She followed Sera to her room. The door was unlocked, and Sera was sitting on her bed, as if waiting for the confrontation. "I care about you," Elizabeth said. "That's why you have to stay home."

"I haven't been sick in a long time. And I'm not going to get sick today."

"We can't risk it, sweetie."

"You mean *you* can't risk it. I can't believe you're going to ruin this for me."

Elizabeth was hurt. "What have I ever ruined for you?"

"Nothing, just every happy, carefree thought I ever had. You always have to remind me I'm sick. 'Sera don't slip.' 'Sera don't inhale.' 'Sera don't sit; there might be cooties.' You think I don't see you checking me over every morning?"

Elizabeth put her hand to her face, as if she had been slapped. "I'm trying to keep you safe."

Sera flounced off the bed and into the closet. "Maybe sometimes I don't care about being safe. Maybe sometimes I'd rather just go to school and get a rose from a boy and forget for once that I'm going to die."

Tears sprang to Elizabeth's eyes, her reactions so uncontrollable these days. She left the room quietly and returned to the kitchen. A half-hour later, Sera appeared, dressed for school in a carefully carefree look, not too new jeans, a red velour hoodie, and a ponytail. She sat at the table where Elizabeth was halfheartedly reading the paper. Sera pulled the entertainment section toward herself and wrote in the daily crossword.

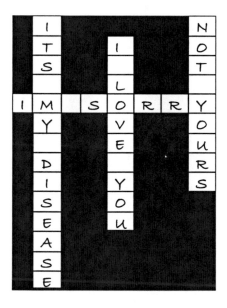

Sera grabbed her backpack and left. Elizabeth felt betrayed, not only by Sera but also by her own illusions. All these years, she believed they had been suffering the condition together, but Elizabeth now realized she and her daughter had separate burdens. Only Sera would face death. Elizabeth had to accept that her life would not end when Sera left her, and that once again, she would have to find the strength to go on. Elizabeth dropped her head to the table, overwhelmed by loneliness.

SERA AND LEXI stood in their usual spot in the lobby after school. Sera was still blushed from the rose she had been carrying since lunch. She had guessed the initials right away.

"I can't believe Danny finally likes me!" she said for the twentieth time that afternoon.

"Well, he does, so get over it already," Lexi said, slightly green. Danny walked toward them. Sera's pink deepened. Lexi turned a shade more jealous, so she told Sera she would see her tomorrow and headed for home.

Danny was watching the ground. "Hi."

"Hi," Sera said.

"Do you like your flower?"

"Yeah."

He kicked a pebble off the sidewalk. "Do you want me to walk you home?"

She couldn't speak, so she just nodded. The conversation eased a little on the cold trip home, the walk making the silences seem less awkward. Two hundred yards from the house, Danny caught Sera's mittened hand. In Sera's driveway, he turned suddenly and kissed her. She was so surprised to feel someone else's lips against hers that she didn't have time to react before he was out of the dooryard.

Sera entered the house apprehensively. Her mother was busy chopping vegetables. "I take it by that silly grin, you had a good Valentine's Day."

Sera's grin widened. "You saw us through the window, didn't you?"

"I wasn't spying, honest." Elizabeth crossed her heart with the paring knife. "So, how was it?"

"It happened so fast. I'm not sure if I liked it or not." Sera raised her palms and shrugged impishly. "Guess I'll just have to try it again." She bounded up the stairs to flop on her bed and re-live the moment.

Danny wasn't in school Monday. Sera's stomach felt fluttery all day, and she didn't know whether she was sick, in love, or worried that she'd have to admit her mother was right. But the next day Danny was back, and Sera felt fine, and life was good again.

40

EDDY WAITED OUTSIDE the committee room at the Capitol building. It was the third time he had been invited to Washington, DC
since his reelection to the Massachusetts legislature. He scanned
the papers in his hand, checking again that he had all of his
notes. He was meeting with the national health care committee to
finalize a bill to allow European as well as Canadian imports of
pharmaceuticals to the U.S., a bill modeled on the state law he
had passed in his first term. He had an unprecedented level of
national influence for a state representative, and he begrudgingly
had to thank his public feud with Galen. The media's obsession
was free publicity, an advantage that congressmen on both sides
of the aisle wanted to share with Eddy.

The huge chamber door opened, and an aide waved him in.
One senator said loudly, "There's our David," which raised a
chuckle from the other members. Eddy cringed. An animated
political cartoon had been making its rounds on the Internet—a
tiny Eddy in a Royal Canadian Mounted Police uniform, sitting
on a tiny horse, shooting rocks with a slingshot across the border.
On the other side of the border was a towering giant of an office
building, with the advertisement on its roof for *BioGoliath, Inc.*

Eddy distributed his papers and told the committee about the
revisions he had made to the talking points against the opposi-

tion. He sometimes felt like a glorified secretary in this process. But it was glorifying all the same.

The senators grilled Eddy on his talking points. "What happens if a pharmaceutical company pulls out of sales to other countries?"

Eddy pointed to page seven of the bill. "The U.S. Government won't reimburse for a drug unless the company can prove that it's selling the same volume per capita of the drug in Canada and all of the other countries listed in the bill where the drug is sold. So if they limit sales outside the U.S., they limit sales inside the U.S."

"What about safety?" another senator asked, flipping through the eighty-page document.

"Individuals will have to declare any pharmaceuticals they're importing," Eddy said. "Anything not from an approved country will be confiscated. The FDA will also track a percentage of declared imports to ensure they're from an accredited pharmacy. One hundred percent of bulk imports to U.S. pharmacies will be tracked, which will also serve to equalize the price of drugs across borders, just like any commodities market."

Several senators scoffed. "What will keep pharma from raising prices all over? That won't make the U.S. very popular."

Eddy had done his homework. "A company can try to raise prices, but in countries where the government regulates reimbursement, that government will just refuse to pay. So if the company wants to sell the product, it'll have to keep the price low. This will regulate U.S. prices without us having to fight internally over it. In return for doing our dirty work, so to speak, what this bill gives other countries is assurance that treatments will continue to be available to that country. Currently, the two largest drug companies in North America are ready to pull sales out of Canada and the U.K. within the year. This bill will be the only thing that would stop them."

"It's a sound bill, Mr. Parker. And I think we have the votes to make it happen."

On his way to the airport after the meeting, Eddy gazed through the window of the cab. The blossoming cherry trees mirrored his life. The party leader had just asked Eddy to consider throwing his hat in the ring to be a United States Senator.

41

SERA AND ELIZABETH were eating dinner together, Elizabeth reading her briefs and Sera reading her literature homework, when Sera's fork clattered to her plate. Elizabeth jerked her head up. "Are you okay?"

Sera answered with a little too much irritation. "It's just a piece of silverware, mom. Chill."

After dinner, Sera went out with Danny, leaving Elizabeth to wash the dishes. Elizabeth acknowledged that she hadn't been a great mother when it came to assigning chores. She picked up Sera's literature book from the table and took it upstairs. She rarely went into Sera's room, allowing her personal space, so when she opened the door to lay the textbook on the dresser, she was shocked to see that the cherished harp was in the far corner of room, piled with a week's worth of discarded clothing. Elizabeth hoped Sera had only given up music in favor of spending time with her boyfriend, because she knew if it meant Sera had lost finger dexterity, another spell was imminent.

LEXI SAT AT the cafeteria table before the morning bell, surrounded by a group of friends. Sera had been out of school for a week, and though Lexi would never admit it out loud, she had enjoyed herself more than a little. Sera's big personality cast such a shadow that Lexi sometimes found it emancipating—an SAT word, she thought with satisfaction—to feel popular all on her own. But it was hard to stay jealous when she remembered the reason Sera wasn't there. At those times, Lexi couldn't help thinking about the pain she would feel when she had to miss Sera for real.

Sera and Danny walked through the door to the cafeteria, and the group of girls surrounding Lexi rushed over to them to share the latest news. "Did Lexi tell you? You're never going to believe . . . ." Lexi felt like a press agent who was good enough for an interview until the celebrity showed up. Then Sera left Danny behind and pushed slowly through the girls to sit next to Lexi, and Lexi berated herself again. It's wrong to be jealous of your best friend.

"I'M GOING TO do it with Danny," Sera said nonchalantly while she and Lexi studied, each stretched on a twin bed in Sera's room.

Lexi sprung to a sitting position. "Are you serious? Why? Where?"

"I don't know. In his dad's car, I think. It's kind of like my Sweet Sixteen present." Sera rolled to her side to look at Lexi. "What do you mean, why? Don't you wonder what it's like?"

"Sure. But his dad's car is kind of—well, it's not romantic." Lexi hesitated. "And you're not, like, in love with Danny, right?"

Sera shrugged. "What if this is the closest I'll get? Danny's going to soccer camp when school gets out, so it's kind of now or never. And I don't want to die a virgin."

Coming from anyone else, this would have sounded melodramatic. Lexi didn't know what to say, so they just went back to studying. After a few minutes, Lexi giggled. "It's probably better than dying with crabs."

Sera threw a notebook at her. "That's gross."

DANNY DROVE OFF the main road onto a dirt trail, and the radio turned to static. He slowed to a stop then turned off the engine. He and Sera stared ahead to where the trail dissolved into the dark, until Sera finally said, "Let's put on some music or something."

Danny quickly hit the radio button. "All you can get out here is country. That okay?" Sera shrugged.

They listened to a couple of songs and part of a third before he finally reached over and took Sera's hand. Then he leaned over to kiss her. He continued to kiss her as he adjusted his position in his seat. Sera's attention kept drifting to the voice from the speakers, singing of options and approaching The End.

She closed her eyes and kissed Danny back hard. He moved closer and reached his arm across her stomach. The voice sang of all Sera could do with the time she had left.

She squeezed her eyes tighter and turned toward Danny and put her free hand on his shoulder. The singer was relentless, reminding her that today might be her last tomorrow, questioning how she would spend eternity, and admonishing her for squandering the gift of life.

Sera pushed Danny away. "I don't want to do this." She looked around her seat for her purse then opened the door and stumbled out.

"Wait, what's wrong?"

She looked back at him meaningfully as the voice sang the refrain. Danny gaped at Sera in horror. He scrambled to find the off button as she limped briskly away from the car. When she reached the road, she twirled around with her arms open wide and dropped her head back to see the stars spinning above her. She yelled at the top of her voice, "I want to live like I'M GOING TO LIVE!"

42

"HEY, BOSS, ISN'T this your old company?" Myesha slid the newspaper across the cafeteria table toward Galen. The two colleagues were working over the weekend to revise their marketing and development plans in response to a prolonged slump in revenue.

"You know it bugs me when you call me that."

"That's why I do it, *boss*."

Galen grabbed the paper from her in mock irritation. He let out a low whistle. "Wow, the industry must be in really bad shape for MFG to be laying off. The father of my—someone I used to know worked there for over thirty years. That's the kind of loyalty I want our company to show its employees."

Myesha didn't meet his eye.

EDDY WARMED HIS hands on a coffee cup, closed his eyes, and breathed deeply. He looked forward to these weekends visiting his parents, when he could start the day on the back deck of his childhood home, away from the sometimes overwhelming publicity of the last several months.

His father grunted. Eddy opened his eyes and lolled his head in that direction. "Look who's on the front page." The bottom right corner cover story was about the drug import bill that had been unanimously passed by both houses of Congress. Eddy's name was mentioned as a proponent of the bill, along with a description of his current proposal to require fifty percent of profits from drug sales from government payers to be used for research. It appeared to have enough support to pass into law. The article declared Eddy the winner in the Douglas-Parker Debate.

His father was reading the other corner cover story. "It's a good thing you got out of the business when you did, boy. And your run for senator better pan out, because MFG is laying off two thousand people. Can you believe that? There are guys who've been working there for thirty years, and I can guarantee they'll be the first to go. They should have retired with me. There's just no loyalty anymore."

Abigail stood in the doorway with her mouth open before she asked abruptly how many eggs they wanted. Eddy had the feeling it wasn't what she had intended to say, and as he watched her retreat into the house, his contentment was replaced by a vague unsettled feeling.

In the kitchen, Abigail chopped vegetables for the omelettes. She had wanted to tell her grandfather that it was better for the economy for two thousand employees to find new jobs than for all twenty thousand employees to earn lower wages or for the company to go out of business. Although he would disagree, he would entertain any discussion with his only grandchild.

Abigail had wanted to be an economist for as long as she could remember. It was just one more thing for the kids at school to tease her about, but her grandparents encouraged her. They even gave her a biography of Alan Greenspan, which was now dog-eared from good use. Abigail loved that Greenspan used to play clarinet in a swing band. She wondered what her secret gem would be when she became famous. Maybe she would go on the late night shows and surprise everyone with a rock star performance. She smiled inside at the image.

The party in Washington the previous fall had lit a spark that shone small, but bright, in the darkness of her adolescence. It was for protection of that spark that she couldn't talk about economics with her father. If he disagreed—or worse, disapproved—it might deplete the meager reserve of confidence she had been squirreling away. Abigail looked forward to college more every day; just one more year to endure, then she'd be free of the people who knew too much, and she could become . . . herself. She could erase her fear of people and draw in her best friend, whomever that might be.

Of course, her father's best friendship from college hadn't turned out so great. Abigail frowned and chopped her frustration into a green pepper. She was convinced her father's troubles with Mr. Douglas were because of her. All the news shows said as much. But he wouldn't admit it.

She had done her own research and was intrigued by their relationship for the same reason she loved economics; it was a collision of math and psychology. She wanted desperately for them to work it out, because it was a complicated friendship, but perfectly . . . synergistic. She thought smugly, I'm going to rock the SATs.

"What are you smiling about?" her mother asked as she descended the stairs toward the kitchen.

"Hey, Mom, I know Dad doesn't want us to talk about Mr. Douglas, but do you agree with him?"

"At least let me get a cup of coffee before the inquisition!" Joy laughed. Abigail shrugged and dumped her vegetables into the frying pan then started dicing potatoes for the hash. Joy took a few sips of coffee before she grabbed another paring knife and sat across from Abigail. "Now, what are you philosophizing about?"

"Do you think Dad's plans on health care and stuff are right and everyone else is wrong?"

"Well, hon, it's not that simple."

"That's the way he sees it."

"Your father is a good man. You should be proud of what he's trying to do."

"Oh, I am! Don't get me wrong; I think Dad's the greatest." She gestured for emphasis and inadvertently flung a piece of

215

potato at her mother, who wiped her eye dramatically. "Oops, sorry." Abigail grinned, not as rare these days. "I just wonder what you think. Not about Dad, but about his politics."

Joy answered slowly. "They're not separate, you know. Your dad is passionate about his proposals because he is a dad. So I can't talk about one and not the other."

Dissatisfied, Abigail threw the potato skins into the sink and flicked the switch on the garbage disposal. Her parents had been telling her for years not to take things so personally. She suspected that her father could use the same advice.

43

SERA AND LEXI perched on the windowsill in Lexi's room, listening for their friend's car coming to pick them up for the movies. A breeze blew the pink lace curtains around Sera's face, and they laughed as she tried to untangle herself. "When is your mom going to let you change these, anyway? They are so not you," Sera said.

"I'm used to them. Kind of like my parents—I've lived with them this long, why change now?" Lexi poked Sera with her toe. "So when are you going to tell me about last night, anyway?"

"Later."

"That's what you said the first four times I asked. Just tell me yes or no, at least."

"Okay, no. So quit bugging me." Sera grabbed a leaf from the tree outside the window.

"But you and Danny did go to Gideon's Trail, right?"

"Lexi!"

"Fine!"

Lexi sulked half-playfully until Sera said, "I'm just kind of confused."

Lexi sat up and put her feet on the floor. "What did he do?"

"Heel, Fido. I stopped it, all right? I realized that I want to live. And that makes me sad."

Lexi shimmied back onto the windowsill. "Now, I'm confused."

Sera gazed up at the clear black sky and breathed deeply of the fragrance of freshly cut grass. "I've always tried to experience everything I could because I knew I would die young, you know? But last night I realized the experience I wanted was love, like you said. And that isn't something you can go after; it kind of comes to you, I think. So it makes me sad that I might not be around when it gets here."

Lexi nodded, listening attentively. Sera confided, "It's more than that, though. I read about this experimental medicine for my disease, and I haven't told Mom about it. I'm afraid that if I start believing I'm going to live, I won't enjoy life as much."

At Lexi's uncomprehending expression, Sera tried to explain further. "When every day is a bonus, you notice each little bit of it. When I wake up and can feel my toes all warm in the blanket and wiggle them just by thinking about it, I know it's going to be a good day. I'm happy just because I can zip my jeans, and tie my shoes, and paint my fingernails, and brush my teeth. Not just that I can squeeze the toothpaste and hold the toothbrush, but that I can feel the weird way the air gets cold afterwards.

"I'm not like you. I don't care about why. It's hard for me to read or study, because it's like I'm spending my precious time on someone else's experiences. Instead, I could be using every muscle in my body to dance or sing or play music or smile or twirl or just stretch. Because tomorrow I might not be able to tell my brain to do any of that. You know how good it feels to stretch?"

Both girls raised their arms above their heads and did their best cat imitations. They laughed a little to diffuse the intensity, then Lexi said, "But I still don't get it. Wouldn't it make you happy if you could get better so you could keep on feeling that stuff?"

Sera shrugged. "But I might stop noticing it as much. It's like, if you're a lizard in the desert and you go around all day with sand in your mouth and it's been dry forever and ever, then a single drop of rain is going to taste really sweet and refreshing, like heaven. But if you plant that lizard near the lake, he won't notice a single drop of rain, because he's going to be worried about drowning."

Lexi nodded slowly. "Sometimes I spend half the day obsessing about my future, because I feel like I'm supposed to do something really awesome with it, since there's nothing in my way. I guess it's the difference between sprinting from the house to the corner and running a marathon. In a sprint, you can see the corner, and you just run as fast as you can. But in a marathon, you're not just training to run faster, but longer and smarter, and you have to keep track of where you're going, too. Not that I've ever run a marathon, but you know what I mean."

Sera pointed emphatically with both forefingers. "I know exactly what you mean. I've spent my whole life as a sprinter, and now I think I want to try a marathon, but I still like to sprint!"

Lexi wrinkled her nose. "So basically, the only thing we know for sure is that neither of us is going to have sex anytime soon."

They laughed at each other's misfortune. Suddenly, Sera sat up. "Did you hear a car? Is that our ride?" They craned their necks out the window.

"I can't tell. I think it's just Mom and Dad."

In the still night, they heard the engine idle and a man's voice saying, "It's going to crush her."

"You don't know that."

"Why now? Where has he been all these years?"

"It's a trust fund. The contract was put in place a long time ago."

They heard the car door slam and Linda's heels clicking up to the house.

"You're telling me you didn't know about it?"

"No, I didn't. But you're going to believe what you want."

"You can't tell her, dammit; she's my daughter!"

"That's the point, Roger. She's not."

The car engine revved and pulled away from the house. Sera looked over at Lexi, who was white as shock.

"HEY KIDDO, I'M going for a run. Do you want to come?" Eddy said. Abigail was already dressed for it. She closed her pencil in her trigonometry book, and they jogged down the hill toward the beach. Eddy slowed when they came to the rocks where he, Joy, and Abigail had spent hours climbing after they had first moved years ago, before the dark specter of stroke had descended upon them.

Abigail thought her father was reading her mind. It did seem like the world was finally coming back around for her. They abandoned the run to climb the rocks together, and Abigail felt the security of her early childhood surround her.

It was still pre-season, so Abigail and Eddy had the beach to themselves. They climbed down and walked along the shoreline. "How's school?" Eddy said.

"Tolerable. Have you passed any good bills lately?"

Eddy laughed. "Lots of them. Funny thing, though—the cost of health care keeps going up."

Abigail hesitated before she said, "It's probably because your bills lower the cost to consumers."

"That is the general idea."

"There's this girl in my class who just had a baby, and she said it only cost her fifteen dollars. One co-pay and the rest was free."

"A girl in your class just had a baby? We should have sent you to private school."

"Don't be a snob, Dad." He elbowed her in the side with a wink. Her feet splashed at the edge of the water as they walked along. "I've been thinking about it, and I figure it's kind of like buying pizza, right? If you only have to pay a dollar no matter what kind you get, and your parents are going to pay the rest, are you going to order cheese pizza or the works? If everybody paid for pizza like that, the pizza shop would be stupid to keep making the cheap stuff." She shook a piece of seaweed off her foot. "It's the same thing if you keep lowering the cost to consumers; they're just going to want more and better health care."

"Interesting idea, kiddo. But it's a little more complicated than buying pizza."

Abigail stopped walking and stared after him. "I know it's not that simple. It's called an analogy." She turned and ran back up the beach.

Abigail's words hit Eddy like a spitball. He immediately regretted patronizing her, but he just couldn't bring himself to have that conversation. Not with her. He started running as hard as he could, in the opposite direction of Abigail, and away from one of the greatest fears shared by fathers—that their little girls will stop seeing them as heroes.

"YOU KNOW," SAID Lexi, lying in her usual spot on the spare bed in Sera's room, "everybody says that parents getting divorced is hard on the kids because the kids blame themselves or get angry or depressed or develop some kind of complex. I think that's all a crock."

"Probably." Sera erased a hole into her page of math homework.

"Take me, for example. Until two weeks ago, I didn't even know my real parents got divorced, but I was screwed up way before that." She flipped over on her back with her genetics textbook on her stomach. "You know, I wasn't really surprised to find out my dad isn't my real dad. Isn't that weird? And it's like Mom knew. I showed her that postcard again and told her what I heard, and she just said, 'Well, now you know, and he's going to pay for college. End of discussion.' That's just not normal." She kicked at something in the air. "It ticks me off that she still won't tell me who he is or what happened. I just want to yell at her and tell her it's not fair that she kept it from me and who is she to make that kind of decision and why didn't he want me? I want to know if I'm anything like him, and if Dad—Roger is ever coming back. It just sucks that even now that it's out in the open, we still can't talk. It's like we never learned how, you know?"

"At least you have a father. Two, actually," Sera said, absent-mindedly.

Lexi threw a green pillow at her. "We're talking about *my* misery for once. Don't be so self-centered." Sera's jaw dropped in a half-hearted attempt at indignation, then she rolled her eyes. "Fine, go on with your misery."

"Thank you. As I was saying, I think what really screws up kids isn't the divorce at all. They're doomed from the minute they're conceived by two people who can't stand each other. It's fine for the parents, because they can get divorced and move on. But kids like me have two sets of DNA inside that are at war all the time. A kid from divorced parents can't win; half of her can't get along with her mother, and half of her can't get along with her father, and she's chronically annoyed at herself. Damage doesn't get more permanent than that."

Sera shrugged. "Makes sense to me." She got up to adjust the air conditioning, passing by the picture of her own father.

"The real tragedy is that the parents ever got together in the first place. People need to be a lot more careful about who they make babies with." Lexi clasped her hands behind her head. "It's actually kind of a relief that I found out, because now all my angst makes sense."

Sera flew across the room and landed next to Lexi, nearly knocking her off the bed. "I know what I'm supposed to do with my life!"

"Were you even listening to me at all?"

"Shut up, I'm *serious*! We were meant to be friends, because I'm supposed to help you find your real dad."

THE NEXT SATURDAY, as soon as Linda left the house for her weekly appointment at the nail salon, Sera and Lexi dropped the magazines they were pretending to read and raced up to the attic. They flipped through every yellowing book on every shelf, hoping for another postcard to fall out, any clue to Lexi's father. But all that fell out were old receipts and advertisements for eharlequin.com. They used a paper clip to pick the lock on a rusty filing cabinet, hoping to find Lexi's birth certificate, but found only a decade of tax returns. They rummaged through shoebox after shoebox of photographs, but there were none of her parents before they moved to Virginia.

They did find a dozen pieces of paper tucked in a trunk full of outdated clothing. The pages were filled with childish drawings of airplanes and the numbers four, two, and three. When she saw them, Lexi felt a twinge in her heart.

The girls snuck down to the basement office and tried to pick the locks on the desk, hoping to find information about the trust fund accountants. But they heard Linda return and had to scurry back to Lexi's room before they got caught. Linda had made it clear that the subjects of Boston and her father were off limits, which fed Lexi's growing resentment.

The girls searched the Internet and amassed a list of government offices in the Boston area to contact for Lexi's birth certificate. Lexi complained that it would be more tedious than finding a misplaced semicolon in a million lines of computer code, but Sera had insisted, so she reluctantly agreed. Lexi was less enthusiastic about the detective work, burdened by the ever-present question of why she was looking for her father and not the other way around.

The night they were talking on the phone about how they would split the Boston calls between them, Lexi could tell that Sera wasn't processing her words well. The next day during study hall, Sera's writing was wobbly and slow. So, after school when Sera brought up the search, Lexi said, "Let's just drop it. There has to be a reason that he gave me up, and I don't think I want to know what it is. He probably forgot about me anyway."

44

*EDDY IS CLINGING to a piece of wood in a frigid ocean, and some-
one is shouting, "Save my daughter!" In the dark to the left, a girl
is fighting to stay afloat. To the right, a half-dozen other victims
are thrashing in the water. "The raft! Get us the raft!" A raft is
floating in front of him. He is the only one who can reach it. But if
he saves the others, the girl will drown.*

Eddy jerked awake and checked on Abigail, sleeping peacefully in the next room. When he went back to bed, the dream
returned.

*This time the girl in the water is Abigail. The others are
swimming toward the raft, but there is another lifeboat in reach
behind them. "Please, take that one!" he shouts, waving them away
with one hand and paddling with the other. "I have to save my
child." He reaches the raft first, rows toward his daughter, pulls
her in. He hugs her tightly as the raft rotates lazily next to the
abandoned driftwood.*

*It is too quiet. He looks up and sees six pairs of eyes in the dis-
tance, sinking into the water. The waves slap an accusation
against the raft: a-leak-a-leak-a-leak. He paddles frantically
toward them. "I didn't know! I didn't know . . . ."*

45

THREE DAYS BEFORE Sera's sixteenth birthday, Elizabeth stood at the bottom of the stairs, all nerves. "Sera, sweetie, could you come down for a minute? I need to talk to you."

"I didn't do it!" came the response. Elizabeth smiled in spite of her apprehension. Her daughter was tapped into some secret well of strength, and she was as fearless and lively as ever. Sera crept down the stairs, holding the railing—like a two-year-old or a ninety-year-old, Elizabeth couldn't decide. Either way, it was wrong.

Elizabeth didn't try to help, just stepped back as Sera made it to the bottom and said, "What's up?" They walked together to the couch.

"Do you know what a clinical trial is?" Elizabeth asked. Sera was quiet for a long minute then nodded. "I've been talking with a man who owns a company in Boston."

"Boston?" Sera blurted.

Elizabeth was confused by the response, but went on. "There's a doctor in Boston working with the company, and he's looking for people with VWM to try a new treatment." Sera didn't say anything. "I know what you're thinking, and the actual guinea pigs got better. But this is your decision. I'm not trying to talk you into anything."

Sera looked away, as if ashamed. "I want to do it, but I'm afraid."

Elizabeth was confused. Sera had never been afraid of dying. What had changed, and where had she been while it happened? "Sweetie, you won't be the first person to take the drug. A lot of people use something like it already to help with strokes."

"That's not what scares me. What's the worst that could happen; I'd get a terminal illness?" She smiled weakly and turned her eyes back to her mother. "I'm afraid that it'll *work*."

Elizabeth was stunned, at Sera's words and at her own reaction. She felt a white flash of anger, hotter than she'd felt when her husband was taken from her, hotter than when Sera's symptoms manifested despite Elizabeth's belief in miracles. She'd been plenty angry at God in her life, but she wasn't prepared for this fury toward her own daughter. She was enraged with abandonment. She wanted to yell: *What is wrong with you? Don't you love me?*

Tears formed in Sera's eyes as she watched her mother's speechless response. Elizabeth's anger drowned under a swell of love and understanding. She hugged Sera tightly. "Fear of the future is the plight of us mere mortals," she said. She felt Sera let out a sob. They were in this together after all.

SERA TOLD LEXI later, "When I heard the drug was called *Lexi*-VM, I had to do it. Everything happens for a reason."

"Okay, but don't blame it on me if it works and you have to go to college and actually study for a change." They laughed, sharing a future for the first time.

SERA AND ELIZABETH walked through the gray lobby of the Department of Neurology at Massachusetts General Hospital after their first study visit. Elizabeth's briefcase held the signed informed consent document that confirmed Sera's participation.

"Some birthday present, huh?" Elizabeth said.

Sera was concentrating on the slippery polished floor, but she smiled, still quick with a comeback. "I suppose the gift of life is better than a minibike."

The study doctor had warned them before they came to Boston that the recent sharp decline in Sera's condition might mean she was too sick to qualify for the trial. Elizabeth's blood had been on a slow boil ever since. To have waited so long and come so close . . . . Elizabeth put the thought out of her mind. She had used up all of her what-ifs years ago. It hadn't brought her husband back, and it wouldn't make the future any easier to bear.

Thoughts of her husband brought thoughts of Galen, and Elizabeth felt a pang of guilt. She was experiencing so many emotions these days, some she hadn't felt in over a decade. But now was not the time to lose focus. They passed by the wheelchairs, not stopping. Elizabeth told herself that Sera would have resented her suggesting they borrow one, but she knew deep down that it was herself who wasn't prepared. Even after sixteen years of expecting the worst, she couldn't admit her daughter wouldn't bounce back this time.

While they stood at the curb waiting for a taxi, Sera pointed out the landscaping in front of the building. "Let's just look at the flowers for a minute." She sat on a bench. Sera had never once in her life shown an interest in foliage, but Elizabeth played along and sat beside her.

"What does this man want to have dinner with us for, anyway?" Sera asked.

"He's been working on the treatment your whole life, so I thought it would be nice for you two to meet."

"It's kind of creepy that you've talked about me."

"We haven't talked about you at all. In fact, he doesn't even know you exist. Your participation in the evening is going to come as quite a surprise."

Sera rolled her eyes at her mother's sarcasm. A cab pulled up to the front of the hospital to take them the three blocks to the restaurant. When they arrived, Galen opened the door of the cab, and Elizabeth took Sera's arm to help her out.

Sera thought her mother and Mr. Douglas acted awfully glad to see each other for such recent acquaintances. She was a little jealous, she was surprised to admit, but mostly pleased that her mom might actually get a life of her own. So when conversation started out feeling stilted and awkward, Sera mustered all of her strength to be lively and charming, and dinner quickly progressed to a comfortable state.

Then her mother dropped curry in her lap. Sera sighed. No wonder the woman hadn't had a date in thirteen years. When Elizabeth left for the bathroom to clean up, Sera turned to Galen to divert his attention. "So, tell it to me straight. Is this stuff going to work?"

Shock was plain on Galen's face. "Well . . . uh . . . ."

"You don't have to sugar coat it for me. I can handle it. Just ask my best friend. Her name is Lexi. That's why I had to do this trial, you know. Anyway, it's my mom who needs protecting, and since she's out of the room, I just want to know what you think. Part of me wants it to work, and part of me doesn't, so you can't go wrong with either answer."

She was caught off guard at the admiration in his expression. There was also something else, like she was a new member at a clubhouse and he wanted to share the club secrets. He looked her straight in the eye. "Just between you and me, I wouldn't have had the guts to meet you if I didn't think you'd get better."

Sera dropped her lashes. She had only meant to distract him from her mother's faux pas, but she was astonished to feel relief and some elation at his response. She wanted to live. She didn't dare to want it, but she wanted it all the same. When she had composed herself enough to look up again, although she had never experienced it before, she knew she was meeting a fatherly gaze. It was nice.

SERA RECEIVED TREATMENTS every four weeks for the rest of the year, and each time Elizabeth and Sera met with Galen—as a friend, forgetting he was the CEO of the company that produced the treatment on which so much depended. First they just had dinner, then later when Sera was feeling and ambulating better, they met at the Boston Common to play tourist or see a show or go to a museum.

On these overnight trips, Galen visited late into the evening to talk with Elizabeth in the living room of the hotel suite where she and Sera were staying. Their conversations roamed from practical to hypothetical to political to spiritual.

Galen tried to explain to Elizabeth why he had chosen to study neuroscience. "I used to think it would help me understand people. Like the brain was a cable box, and if I could see inside and follow the wires, I would be able to predict responses and avoid getting shocked."

"Sounds about as feasible as an autopsy on an angel."

"That's why I only *used* to think it!"

Elizabeth said, "I wish everyone understood that much about people, that their minds don't work like robots. It's absurd how little experience we expect our elected officials to have, if they are likeable. As if good people can't make bad decisions."

"At Biolex, we decide in advance what we care about, and the finance folks make a model that traces the money. Then whenever I have to make a decision, the chain of events is laid out before me, so I'm really choosing between the outcomes. Obviously, things don't always work out exactly like the model, but it's better than if they left it to me to figure it out on my own in the heat of the moment; then we'd sure have a mess."

"That's what frustrates me," Elizabeth said. "We have the technological capability of taking out much of the hand waving from government decisions. It would require Congress to work together to develop a chain of events for the model, but at least with an algorithm that shows the potential consequences of a given decision, they could be conscious of the trade-offs they're making. Maybe they would make the same decisions in either case, but at least they couldn't say later that they were misled."

The only topic off-limits for Elizabeth and Galen was their feelings for each other. They stayed just on the edge of the magnetic circle and were careful not to touch, because it might break their restraint. They had a tacit understanding that Sera was the only priority, for both of them.

Galen and Sera had quickly forged a bond, as though she had been practicing all her life to have a father, and he had been waiting all his life to be one. She insisted on calling him "Mr. Douglas", until it became a joke between them. He helped her with her math homework in the absence of Lexi, whom she mentioned often. Eventually Galen stopped associating the name with his own daughter and in his heart, adopted Sera.

So, each time he saw Sera and saw that she was growing stronger, he grew younger. Soon, all of the years since the summers at the beach with Eddy and his sister seemed like just a day. He secretly promised the caramel-haired girl who had started it all that he would get it right this time, that he would save Sera. He was giddy with the chance to start over.

Sera told Lexi after one visit, "Yesterday, we ate outside in the park, and this frog jumped onto his sandwich during lunch. Mr. Douglas didn't even flinch. He just said to it, 'You're late. We started without you. I saved you some roast beef.' And he fed the frog tomatoes straight out of his sandwich. Then we fed it coleslaw and brownies, and it ate them, too. All the time he's talking to the frog like it was an invited guest. It was so silly, but I was laughing so hard I almost peed my pants!"

Sera had tried to figure out a way to find Lexi's birth certificate while she was in Boston, but she never had a moment away from Elizabeth and Galen, not that she minded. After the last treatment, Sera told Lexi that Galen was going to extend the trial so she could keep taking the Lexi-VM. She was most excited that the trips to Boston would continue. "I think having a kind of dad is as good as the medicine, anyway," she told Lexi.

Sera tried to be considerate of Lexi's parental problems. "How are things with your mom, anyway?" she often asked.

Lexi always waved her off. "We're civil. I'd rather think about leaving for college. Did you sign up for the SATs yet?"

46

GALEN PACED ACROSS his office while Myesha stood helplessly with the fax in her hands. "What do you mean, FDA rejected the extension study? These kids are getting better!"

"It's just on hold pending a few additions," Myesha said, unconvincingly.

"Just a few," Galen said with disgust. "Like chest x-rays, EKGs, and full body scans every other day. There's no scientific reason to think that Lexistro affects vital organs. It's a witch hunt."

"They just want more data to be sure Lexi-VM is safe. These are kids we're treating," Myesha said.

Galen was exasperated. "What more proof do they need, aside from the million people who've been taking Lexistro for almost a decade? Aside from the monkeys that are swinging from their bars in the labs? Why the hell is Dr. Steinberg so jumpy all of a sudden?"

Myesha said, "About that . . . ." Galen stopped pacing. "Steinberg isn't on our case anymore. The official story is that he retired. Anyway, we've been assigned a new reviewer, Patricia Chen."

"Never heard of her." Galen resumed his track from the fax machine to the window, around the desk, and back to the fax.

Myesha stifled a nervous laugh. "Actually, you have. She was the one who originally approved our investigational new drug application. And she's fairly well known in neuro. She's been spearheading a lot of the new regulations since the fibromyalgia hysteria."

"Oh, she's the one, is she? Well, can somebody please tell her to stop living in the past?" Galen kicked the bottom drawer of the filing cabinet. "The right hand doesn't know what the left is doing down there! Washington is trying so damned hard to lower prescription drug costs—from the import bill, to squeezing us with Medicare, to a hundred Chihuahua bills in between—then they make decisions like this and increase the cost of drug development for nothing!" He yanked open the office door, and Myesha stepped back. "Just do what she wants. I'm sick of fighting."

Before he could leave, Myesha said, "One more thing." She took a deep breath. "She wants to add a stopping rule to suspend treatments if there's a death."

"What?" Galen whirled around and slammed the door. "These kids have a terminal illness!" He grabbed the fax from Myesha's hands. "Suspending treatment will only kill them sooner."

"She's just being cautious," Myesha said, trying to be the voice of reason.

"Well, while she's farting around being cautious, we're losing time!" Galen slapped the fax on his desk and stormed out.

THE EXTRA TESTS were added, the extension study was approved, and after three months, Sera began receiving treatments again. In a phone call one night, Elizabeth confided to Galen that it was none too soon. "If I ever wondered whether Lexi-VM worked, I have no doubt now. She was losing motor control at a scary speed during the hold, but she's stable now. How long can she keep on it?"

Galen assured her the study was designed to last until Lexistro could legally be prescribed for VWM.

47

A FEW WEEKS before the election, polls showed Eddy with a twenty percent lead over his opponent. He was a shoo-in for the Senate, until the maker of the best-selling blood pressure medication in the world announced a plan to stop selling product in the U.S., blaming Eddy's global import law that had been depressing domestic industry sales since it took effect nearly a year before.

"Greedy bastards," Eddy muttered at the television, after the twelfth broadcast of the announcement that night.

"Actually," said Abigail, who was sitting on the couch next to her father, "it's probably better for the economy if the boycott succeeds and prices stay high."

"How can you say that?" Eddy peered into her eyes as if searching for remnants of a soul inside a body that had been invaded by aliens.

She blinked. "I'm not saying it's right or wrong; it's just true. If the price of a drug goes down, then the company can't afford to hire as many people or produce as much, so there is less money being spent in the economy and less being produced. Plus the government gets less taxes, both from normal sales and income taxes, and from the percentage of revenue they would have got on the drug sales."

"Is that what they're teaching these days in college prep economics?"

"Dad, don't patronize me. I have a brain of my own. And if I go to Harvard next year, then pretty soon I'll be as smart as you." She elbowed him playfully. "You should be happy to have a conversation with me before that happens."

Eddy clicked off the television with a dramatic sigh. "Oh, wise daughter, what would you like to converse about?"

This was her opening. "Do you ever notice that the people who are supposed to be helped by a law never seem to get the great deal that everyone expected?"

"Why does this feel like a trick question?"

She said, "It seems to me that everyone gets a little poorer when the government tries to shift money from the haves to the have-nots. I know you don't like my pizza analogies, but it's like if someone has a supreme pizza and someone else has nothing and a third person comes in and wrestles a piece from the first guy to give to the second. While they're ripping the slice between them, the cheese and pepperoni are going to fall off and the toppings are going to get trampled in the struggle. So by the time the second guy gets the pizza, it's just crust and sauce, and all the good stuff is mashed in the floor."

"Are you trying to explain dead weight loss to me?" Eddy said.

"How do you know about DWL?"

"I did take economics in college. Once upon a time, I was almost as smart as you." He poked her in the arm.

"Then why do you pass so many bills that try to shift wealth to the consumer when you know that those kinds of laws hurt the wealth of the country as a whole?"

"Number one, I don't think that's necessarily the case; there are a lot of other factors than just pepperoni and cheese."

Abigail bristled at the dismissal. "And number two?"

"Do you think I should just let the haves keep getting richer while the have-nots get poorer?"

The look of disappointment on her father's face tightened the anxiety in Abigail's chest, but she steeled her nerves also, to continue the discussion. "I'm not arguing policy or morality, Dad. I'm saying we have this dynamic capitalist economy, but it seems like you and the other legislators spend all your effort working against it. You're always arguing about how much money to take from people when you should be figuring out ways to work the market so people *give* their pizza away."

"People don't work like that, kiddo."

Abigail sprung off the couch and threw herself into a chair across the room.

"What are you all flouncy about?" Eddy asked.

"It really ticks me off sometimes when you call me 'kiddo'. I'm not stupid." She grabbed a throw pillow and hugged it to her.

"Come on, Abby, you know I don't think you're stupid. But you also don't know everything. I wish everyone was as generous as you, but they aren't."

"It's not about being generous! It's about coming up with a system that *creates* wealth, not the one we have that steals a dollar from one guy to give fifty cents to another."

"No one is stealing anything. Taxes are the price of freedom. That is the way our infrastructure was built."

"Well, maybe it needs to change." Abigail threw the pillow to the floor. "Maybe the fossils who are supposed to be representing us need to shake off the dust and get a little creative instead of adding more of the same problems to what's been piling up for a century. I can't wait until I can vote."

Eddy pulled back as if she'd hit him. "You think I'm a fossil?"

Abigail felt sick to see through her father's armor. She exhaled heavily. "No, Dad. I just . . . ." Part of her wanted to throw her arms around him, apologize, and tell him she didn't mean any of it and that she thought he was the best dad in the world. The rest of her stayed rooted to the chair. She looked down at her lap and fidgeted with the armchair cover. "I feel weird about laws that take other people's money to pay for my medicine. And your new bill to help generics get on the market quicker doesn't seem right, either; it's like the generics get to profit off someone else's hard work."

She looked up. Eddy was gaping at her. She resumed her fidgeting until she couldn't stand the silence any longer. "I know you and Mr. Douglas used to be friends. And I know whatever happened was really personal. Sometimes I get the sense that your bills are more to spite him than anything else. Or like you're looking for someone to blame, because it's easier than tackling a void."

He wasn't looking in her direction, and his face started to flush. "You don't know what you're talking about."

"So explain it to me," she said. "It almost seems like you want to be a senator just so you can make sure businessmen don't make more money. I don't understand that. Why would it matter if some people have more than others, if there was a way for everyone to have enough?"

"In a caring society, people who have a lot have a responsibility to help those with less. And never is *everyone* going to have enough."

"But they could! What if we had a system that would let people trade whatever talent or work they can, to get something they need, like medicine?"

"Number one, the barter system is inefficient. And number two, a lot of people won't have anything to exchange. Government exists to protect those people."

It was Abigail's turn to gape at Eddy. She must have heard wrong. "Are you saying some people have nothing to offer the world? That's an awful thing to think."

Eddy stood abruptly and left the room. Abigail's heart fell. She knew this conversation wouldn't end well, so why had she even started it? She thought of asking her mother how to make it right, but didn't. She was afraid the suggestion would be to apologize, and Abigail wasn't sorry.

While she rocked in the chair trying to figure out what to do, Eddy returned, wheeling an enormous suitcase. "You want to know why I'm running for office?" He yanked open the suitcase zipper and dumped the contents. A pile of envelopes spilled over the coffee table.

Abigail stared for a moment then slid off the chair onto the floor and picked up one of the envelopes. She read it to herself. *Thank you, Mr. Parker, you've saved my mother's life. She can now afford her medicine. You are truly a representative of the people.* She looked up at Eddy, who was standing over her. "Do they all say this?" she asked.

"I started in politics for you, but I've kept with it for these people. They need us."

She read through several more letters as he watched. Eddy's face was stone. Abigail knew that must be his legislator face, and she felt a growing irritation at the realization that these letters were supposed to end the conversation. She felt a perverse need to get the last word. "Dad, I never doubted that you were doing good, but are you doing the *common* good? Especially as a federal senator, aren't you supposed to do things that benefit the whole country? Like building bridges and stopping epidemics and homeland security and big stuff like that. Isn't that what you always told me?"

"You're suggesting I forget people are individuals."

"Maybe you have to. It's like economics; it's about the big picture. If economists start looking at the individual pieces, they're more like accountants. Just like if you start helping some constituents more than others, you're more like a lobbyist. They're both important, but they're different jobs."

Eddy crossed his arms. "You may find this hard to believe, but I'm well-informed when I make my choices about who to help."

"That's my point! I don't think you should be making choices like that at all! You're supposed to care about *everyone*, and only doing stuff that benefits *everyone*. If you can only help one group at the expense of the other, then you're doing it wrong."

"Well, Abigail, when you get an education, choose a career, and find a job, then we can talk about who's responsible for what." He started to scoop up the envelopes and put them back in the suitcase.

Abigail gathered a few of the letters. "I know I'm only seventeen, okay, Dad? But I have a right to an opinion. And I'm just saying if you can't stop taking everything so personally, then maybe being a senator isn't the right job for you."

"Maybe so." Eddy grabbed the envelopes from her hand and shoved them in the suitcase, slamming it shut. Abigail watched him wheel it away and knew the conversation was over.

EDDY SPENT SEVERAL hours in his woodshop reading each letter then shredding it. When he was finished, he gathered the three-foot pile of stationery confetti and put the mass back in the suitcase.

48

"SO, WHY SHOULD we let you into Harvard?" asked the middle-aged alumnus who was interviewing Lexi for her early decision application.

"I made a video game that's on the Internet." His eyebrows flew up, so she knew she at least had his attention—good or bad, she wasn't sure. She pulled her laptop from its case and almost panicked, because she didn't know where to put it. She and Sera's mother had practiced at the kitchen table, but Lexi was now sitting in a cramped office with her knees bumping the front of the interviewer's desk.

She mustered her confidence and decided to put the computer on top of a pile of papers, then she launched into her speech. "The players are people from different parts of the health care system. Each round, there's a decision the players have to make, like do we pass this legislation or do we pay for that treatment, and each of the decisions is worth a certain amount of points to each of the players. The game ends when the total points across all the players have reached a maximum, which is different every time. Whoever has the most points when the game is over wins, but the catch is that each round, if you make a decision that maximizes *your* points but decreases the *total* points, then you lose a turn. So all the players are competing, but they have to work together, too."

The interviewer looked back and forth between her and the screen with a weird expression. She dropped her head, and her long, blonde hair fell to hide her face. "I know it's not that great. I mean there aren't many graphics, and the website is really just one that I built for my friend's mom. Plus, the game is kind of hard to win, because you can't really maximize the common points without giving up your own points. I'd fix that in a different version, maybe develop a quest so players have to create their own health care system or something."

He still hadn't said a word and was hitting the buttons on the computer, moving from screen to screen.

"Was it stupid to show you this in my interview?"

He started. "Stupid? Definitely not."

49

ELIZABETH AND SERA were preparing for their trip to Boston for her fourth treatment under the extension study, when they received a telephone call. Elizabeth said, "Okay, thank you. Please let me know if things change." She hung up the phone and leaned against the kitchen counter.

Sera shuffled in. "Ready?"

"Sweetie, the appointment was cancelled. One of the other kids died, so they have to stop the study for a while."

Sera sat down heavily. "I don't understand, Mom. Don't they know we're all going to die? Why can't we just keep getting the medicine in the meantime?"

"Those are just the rules right now."

"Well, the rules suck!" Sera, uncharacteristically petulant, left the room.

GALEN, MYESHA, AND the Biolex safety officer collected from the study doctors as much medical history as possible on the deceased patient. They pulled it together within three days, and when it was submitted, Galen called Elizabeth.

"Now we wait for FDA's response," he said.

"Can I ask your opinion on something?" she said. "It seems to me that this illness depends so much on maintaining a steady system, I'm wondering if it might be making Sera worse to be on treatment, then off treatment, then on again?"

Galen didn't want to answer. When he did, he spoke slowly. "I wish I could say no." He rushed on. "But this death was clearly not caused by the Lexi-VM. None of the participating doctors even suggested it. So if we can get FDA to look at the data sooner rather than later, hopefully it'll be a seamless transition for Sera."

PATRICIA, LIKE ALL FDA reviewers, was overloaded with work. The regulations passed in the previous decade, many of them her own proposals, had more than doubled the amount of documentation in a typical new drug application. When the global import law went into effect, making FDA responsible for monitoring imports at every U.S. border and postal customs, the workload exploded. But the agency hadn't been allowed to hire more people, since Congress refused to raise taxes going into an election year.

Patricia didn't reduce effort on her assignments. She worked late into most nights so she could study every piece of data twice for all of her studies. Nothing dangerous was going to get by on her watch.

So, it was two months before she had a chance to review the Lexistro/Lexi-VM package. She read the comments from the treating physician: *The outcome was expected in the course of the disease for this patient. If anything, death was delayed since beginning treatment.* She dismissed the doctor's comments as potential conflict of interest, blind enthusiasm, and unfounded bias. She reviewed the data from the stroke studies. On day seventy-three, she sent a fax to Biolex.

MYESHA WAS ALMOST afraid to show Galen the fax. His response was as bad as she had anticipated. "She wants *antibody* data? We did antibody testing in stroke studies, and not one patient developed rejection to the neuroglobin. Since then, millions of people have taken Lexistro repeatedly, and none have exhibited even a hint of the signs or symptoms that this kid had. No one in his right mind believes that antibodies are the cause of this! The kid had a goddamn terminal illness!"

A conference call was held among Patricia, her supervisor, Myesha, Galen, and the clinical and science directors at Biolex. Galen's anger deflated as it became clear that none of them were going to change their positions. After the call, he sat dejectedly at the conference table. He asked the science director, "How long is it going to take to get the antibody assays running again?"

"Three weeks, at best."

Galen sighed and turned to the clinical director. "And to write a protocol to collect the blood?"

"We can write it in a couple of weeks. But it'll take a month to get through the institutional review boards. After that, once the patients are scheduled, it'll probably be a couple more months before we have the samples in house and analyzed."

Galen put his head in his hands and asked Myesha, "How long for the FDA package?"

She said in a low voice, "Nine days from when the analysis is available."

"So we're looking at next year."

"I'm afraid so."

Galen called Elizabeth to explain the situation. For a long while, neither spoke. Then he said, "You could try to find a neurologist who will prescribe Lexistro off label."

"What does that mean?" Elizabeth asked.

"Lexistro is officially FDA-approved for stroke. But physicians sometimes prescribe medications for unapproved indications if they have reason to think it would work. It's always been frowned upon and now could result in jail time for the physician—and for me, if anyone knew I was suggesting it to you. It isn't exactly the same formulation as the Lexi-VM Sera was getting in the study, but it's something."

"Okay, we'll try that, thank you so much."

"Please don't thank me." Galen paused, not sure whether to continue. "It's expensive. Do you—I mean, can I help . . . ?"

"We're okay. We've been saving for just this purpose." Another long pause. Elizabeth finished quietly, "Thank you for offering. It means a lot."

Elizabeth took Sera to a half-dozen neurologists, including the study doctor, former legal clients, and strangers from the phone book. They all gave the same response: FDA had increased the penalties for off-label use, and no one wanted to risk his license or freedom on Sera.

After multiple seizures, Sera had to stay home from school for most of December. She missed the winter carnival dance, semester finals, and the SATs.

50

GALEN'S TEAM HAD hustled to pull together the requested materials, and a response was expected from FDA at the beginning of January. On January 5, Myesha knocked on Galen's door.

"Good news?" he asked.

Galen's tired but hopeful countenance almost made Myesha turn around and leave the room. She forced herself to move forward and sit down. "Galen, you know that the current lot of Lexi-VM expires in February."

"I didn't, but I'm sure manufacturing is on top of it and will make more before we need it."

"Well, that's the problem." When Myesha exhaled, her assessment of the situation tumbled out. "We've been selling Lexistro barely above break-even for the past year, inside and outside the U.S. Our stock is down, because generics are ready to hit the market as soon as the patent runs out. Or sooner, if the Parker bill passes. I don't know if the board will approve the cost of additional manufacturing for the clinical trial, because I'm not sure that there's a market for Lexi-VM anymore. In fact, there's talk of selling out Lexistro—and by that I mean Biolex—entirely."

Galen's mouth was the only muscle moving when he said, "We will continue to manufacture Lexi-VM, if I have to pay for it myself with every last penny I own. End of discussion." He leaned forward and put his hands on the desk. "Now, tell it to me straight. What do you mean by 'selling out'? Why would anyone want to buy us if the profit potential is so bleak?"

Myesha turned away from Galen's intense gaze. She got up and leaned against the wall near the door. "Galen, a lot of companies are going to narrow distribution by pulling out of government sales entirely and jacking up prices to private insurance."

"When we started this company, we agreed we wouldn't do that. Getting the drug to the most people is as important as profit. That's still the company credo."

"I know, but the analysts have been predicting for a long time that with the political and regulatory climates as they are, as long as Biolex continues with that strategy, we'll have little to no growth with Lexistro. Wall Street knows that as long as Galen Douglas is in charge, the strategy won't change. That's why our stock is down."

"So you're telling me that I'm poison to my own company?"

"It depends on what you consider success for Biolex. If someone took over who's willing to sell Lexistro at the optimal price, which is much higher but with only a few less buyers, there's still a lot of profit potential in the time left on the patent."

Galen said, "So by 'selling out', you meant 'selling out from under'?"

"Frankly, yes."

Galen stood and kicked his seat back. "The damned board has disagreed with my strategies for years. They were just waiting for this opportunity."

"Galen, this isn't about the board. It's about your investors. Investors expect a big return for their risk, or they go elsewhere. And I'm not just talking about the fat cats on Wall Street. Your investors are also little old ladies with mutual funds that have a share in Biolex."

"So you're saying there's no win-win here. If the stock goes down, the little old ladies lose. If the company is sold, middle-class sick people who buy Lexistro lose. If Biolex fails, everyone loses." Galen looked toward the bottom draw of the filing cabinet.

"Galen, you can't blame yourself, either. Sometimes economics is just like the weather, and there is no bad guy." They were quiet for a few minutes. Then Myesha said, "Could I make a suggestion?"

"Of course."

"If you're the one to find the buyer, then you could sell on your own terms."

So, Galen dusted off his business presentation skills and set on the road to find a buyer for the baby he had raised. He felt like he was walking out to the edge of the platform at the Olympic high dive, all eyes on him—some well wishers and some hoping he would hit his head on the way down. The air in every conference room was crowded with thoughts he couldn't parse. He vowed that any sale would include the VWM development and all of the Biolex staff who wanted to stay. Amos told him the stipulation was a deal-breaker, but he adamantly refused to sell them piecemeal, insisting that they both were essential components of the company. By the end of February, he had been turned down by thirteen potential buyers.

Galen had received approval from the Biolex board to produce one small lot of Lexi-VM, so the extension study was continuing at least for another month. He sat down with Myesha to discuss budget options. "Galen, we've been in this together for a long time, so I have to be honest. We need to lay off some people."

"But I've promised that as long as they delivered on their goals, they would have a job."

"If the company goes under, we'll all be out of a job."

By March, the deed was done. Galen spoke face-to-face with each person he had to let go to explain the situation and why they were chosen. He doubled their severance out of his own bank account, though he refused to tell anyone but his payroll manager. To Galen, the process was like pulling out his own fingernails one by one.

The temporary improvement to the Biolex bottom line produced a new round of interested buyers. Myesha accepted an opportunity to spearhead a new generics start-up; she would leave as soon as Biolex was sold. Meanwhile, Galen was financing with his own money another round of manufacturing for the VWM extension trial and the first pivotal study that could bring them to market and change the financial outlook.

SERA HAD GONE to bed early after her March infusion, and Galen and Elizabeth were in the living room of their hotel suite on Boston Common. He slumped in the armchair while Elizabeth curled against the arm of the couch, watching him. "I've been reading about what's happening with your company. How are you doing?"

"I'm going to find a buyer, I will."

"I read that you're using your own money for the study. Is that true?"

"You do what you have to do. Speaking of which, how's Sera doing? She covers so well, I can't tell."

"She gets disoriented, and her muscle control is patchy, especially when she's tired, and she tires easily. But thankfully, she hasn't had any seizures this month, her cognition is intact, and she's catching up on college planning with the rest of her class."

"No doubt with this best friend, Lexi, she's always talking about."

Elizabeth smiled. "They're inseparable, as you've probably guessed."

"She's lucky. I hope that my daughter, Lexi, has a friend so good." It was the first time he had mentioned that he had a daughter.

"She turns seventeen this year, doesn't she?"

51

EDDY WAS RELUCTANT to sleep. The dreams had been coming more frequently lately, and he was too beleaguered in the waking hours to fight all night as well. Since he'd been sworn into office as Senator Parker, his position with the newspapers had steadily declined. His repertoire of laws—including the global import bill, increase in FDA reviews, easier markets for generics, and government sales dollars toward research—was being touted a colossal failure. Several companies had pulled out of North American sales, quoting a loss on every treatment produced, and the media needed a bad guy.

Constituents continued to write to him until the letters were just a jumble in his mind: get our medicine back I can't afford it I don't have any medicine you should resign. He didn't know what to do anymore. He stared at the ceiling while Joy breathed evenly beside him, until his eyelids finally gave in, and he drifted slowly to dream.

He's in the raft with Abigail, rowing as fast as he can toward the drowning figures. There isn't time to cross the dark distance, but he won't give up. He hears a small cry in the water they have just passed. He turns around, and there is Lexi, two hundred yards away. "Please don't leave me, Mr. Parker!" Abigail is frantic. "Daddy, save her!" He looks desperately ahead and now, instead of six, there are thirty children crying, "Senator Parker, help us! Please!"

Eddy jerked awake and got up to wash his face with cold water. He went to his workshop and sat on the floor in the dark with his arms wrapped around the suitcase of shredded letters. Were these the voices that Galen always heard, why he had always seemed paralyzed and pulled apart? Had Eddy been living obliviously through a waking nightmare, his whole life caught in the middle of two impossible situations?

Eddy had never felt so insecure. He wasn't alone in his mind anymore. How could all these voices and choices be moral and legitimate and correct at the same time? His head was spinning, and he didn't know which way was right.

52

WHEN GALEN HAD exhausted every option he could think of to sell his company, he returned to Amos Theriault for advice. The old guy had long ago retired, but he was as feisty as ever.

"You're wasting your time looking for a buyout." They sat on Amos' heated porch that extended over the rocks, surrounded by the Atlantic Ocean. Snow was falling hard, and the gray waves scrambled over each other to get to shore, chased home by the nor'easter. Galen opened his mouth to speak. Amos cut him off. "You wanted my advice, so listen up. You have three years left on your patent, yes?"

Galen nodded impatiently.

"So anyone who bought you out now would have to pay enough to satisfy your current investors and also shell out tens of millions for the second pivotal clinical study for VWM. By the time that's over, there's no time left on the Lexistro patent. Congress has been paving the way for generics to take over the market—stroke and VWM—so any money that's going to be made has to be made before the patent runs out. There's no way anyone can make enough in two years to recoup those costs, let alone turn a profit."

Galen didn't believe it.

"Do the math, son. There just aren't that many kids with this disease. Even if ninety percent of the world's population used the drug, the company would still have to charge three quarters of a million dollars for a year's worth of treatments just to break even. Not many insurance companies now would reimburse that, let alone governments, and it would break a charity bank for a patient to ask for it. So it wouldn't even be ethical for a company to put Lexi-VM out there."

"Of course it would. Because at least it would be out there. They have nothing right now, nothing!"

"No company with any sense is going to make the kind of investment you're asking for a drug no one can afford."

"But Lexistro works!"

"I'm not denying that the drug works. I'm saying the numbers don't work. And you're wasting precious patent time arguing with me about it."

The men locked stares. Galen was the first to blink. But he wasn't ready to concede defeat. So they sat, lost inside their own heads, while the wind howled at the windows and the sky darkened.

Amos was the first to speak. "You made up your mind before you got here." Galen tried to protest, but Amos talked over him. "You just argue with me so that I'll bully you into doing exactly what you knew you needed to do in the first place. It's something broken about you, son; you think you need people to tell you what to do. Especially that damned Eddy Parker."

"Hold on, Amos. He was a good friend to me once."

"That's a crock of bull. The best friend he ever was to you was the day he kicked you to the curb. At least then you had to stand up on your own."

Galen wanted to be angry, but somehow he couldn't.

Amos went on. "He thinks he's better than you and everyone else. Thinks it's up to him to take care of the world, and he's doing a damn poor job of it and screwing your company and those kids in the process. He's just like your father was; it's no wonder you were so yoked by him. All them politicians wanting to expand government are just the same; they put the fear of the free market into people, make them think they're weak and powerless against it and that they need the 'better' people like the Eddy Parkers to take care of them. Then they double-back it by painting everyone who prospers in the free market as evil, just in case any of the poor people get ideas. It's job security for the politicians."

Galen had stopped listening midway through the tirade, and his beer was dripping onto the deck, tilted sideways out of his limp hand. "You knew my father?"

THE SNOW FELL harder and the nor'easter gained intensity, rattling the windowpanes while Amos told his story. "It was way back. I'd been working the woods in West Virginia for about seven years when he showed up. Was going to teach us all how to read. Well, I'd been to college, and I'd already spent most of fifteen years in the business world, buttoned into a suit, making money but feeling like a round peg in a square hole. Working in the woods is a damn site harder than a desk job, but I chose it. Then here's this condescending city kid trying to make me think it wasn't good enough.

"He was a perfect match for the evangelist who came along right after, and they started having an affair, and unfortunate for my town, they decided to stay. That's when I decided to leave. Course I'd made up my mind by then to do business on my own terms."

Galen didn't know whether to agree with the characterization or feel angry on his father's behalf. So he just gaped.

"He kept talking about this Galen kid who was so smart and was going to do such great things. I thought, what the hell is he doing here if he has a son back there? That never really sat right with me. So, when your name showed up on the clearinghouse short list, I had to go see for myself if you were the kid. I could tell from the first presentation, because there were two things just like him: you work hard, and you sure believe in what you're working on. But you had a hell of a lot more humility. Maybe too much, but that's how I knew you'd make it."

"Is he still . . . ?"

"Don't know. I never went back."

Galen was sure the off-hand mention of his father was no mistake. Amos wanted him to know. But why now? "Your point is that I'm the one who sacrificed for Lexi-VM, so it's my decision, and I have to trust myself to make it. Everyone else be damned."

Amos gave a hint of a smile. "Put together your regulatory package and go to the FDA with your new drug application."

"We haven't even finished the Phase Three trial."

"Wake up and hear what I'm shouting to you. Unless you win the megabucks, the trial isn't going to happen, and your company is going to go under. But you have a good set of monkey data, a robust Phase Two study in VWM, and a load of stroke data. So you go with that right now. Maybe you get a no. But maybe you just get slapped with a post-marketing commitment for another study. At that point, you'll have a drug that's on the market for an indication in children. That's a real selling point. You know I'm right. Now leave me alone, I need a nap."

GALEN SPENT A sleepless night mulling over all that Amos had said. He wasn't even curious what had become of his father. In the back of his mind, he knew he had lost interest long ago, as soon as he realized his father wasn't coming back. He assumed Lexi had moved on the same way.

Amos was right; Galen already knew what to do. The next day, Galen approached his remaining staff with a plan. They pleaded with the FDA for priority status for Lexi-VM, rather than the typical eighteen months or longer time frame for review. They were granted a conference call ninety days from receipt of the application.

The Biolex team worked feverishly to compile and format the volumes upon volumes of electronic data and study reports and supporting articles. They held numerous practice sessions in preparation for the big call and made arrangements for the lead investigator and other important players to be present. By that time, it was July, and there had been no manufacturing for four months. Galen's personal investments were depleted, and all clinical trials were on hold indefinitely.

53

As Patricia Chen walked down the hall of the FDA, a colleague approached her. "Pat, you know time is running out on the Genentech file."

"I have forty-five days, and it is in only day forty-three. You know how I work." She kept on walking.

Another colleague called out from his office. "Pat, can we discuss—"

"Can't talk right now." She walked faster.

An assistant was posted outside her door. "Pat?"

"I know. I *know*. Just give me a little breathing space, please. I have a call." She pushed into her office and closed the door. The phone rang. This call with Biolex was not going to be pretty, but Patricia had insisted on doing it alone. She checked that each of the appropriate piles of information was in place on her desk and tried to smooth the atypical wrinkles from her button-down shirt before she answered.

Patricia summarized for the Biolex team the discussion among members of the new drug application committee who had reviewed the Lexi-VM package. Patricia emphasized the negative risks. Biolex agreed but emphasized the positive. She stated that Biolex would be required to conduct several additional post-marketing studies, and they accepted without argument. Overall, the conversation was similar to the hundreds of other new drug conference calls Patricia had held over the years, until she revealed that the main reason for hesitation from the review committee was the recent death, and Galen Douglas said something that she knew was against the company's script.

"Ma'am, with all due respect, this is a terminal illness. So every day you spend analyzing one kid, another ten are closer to dying. Please consider that."

Patricia hung up. She did consider it. She had considered it every day of the last twenty-odd years since she finished medical school. It was always the same trade-offs with these neurodegenerative illnesses. Twenty years. And what did she have to show for it?

When she had first come to FDA, things seemed so simple. But she had become less sure of every decision and every action every day since the fibromyalgia outcome. Suddenly, she was overwhelmed with exhaustion. She had been fighting for so long, and she just couldn't do it anymore.

Maybe she would retire. A cabin in the Smoky Mountains would be nice, and a garden. Yes, plants were the answer. She could just water them and put them in the sunlight, and they would either grow or they wouldn't. In any case, they couldn't complain.

AS SOON AS Galen got the response from the FDA, amidst the popping corks and cheers from Myesha and the meager skeleton staff in the office, Galen called Elizabeth. "We did it! We got the approval!"

Galen heard her sobbing. He waited for her to let the hope materialize. He knew that it was a lot to take in, after they had all been through so much. After eighteen years, to now have a treatment—it was a lot for Galen, so he couldn't imagine what Elizabeth was feeling.

After several long minutes, Elizabeth whispered, "She's gone."

54

WHEN GALEN ARRIVED early at the funeral home, Elizabeth was alone, leaning against a dark doorway. He had never seen her anything but confident and composed, even when she was crying. He wanted to absorb it all and protect her from the sorrow. He put aside his feelings of failure and approached her and touched her on the shoulder. When she looked up, her eyes held such gratitude and sadness that, for the first time, he wrapped his arms around her. She surrendered against him.

After a few minutes, she disengaged and looked up at him. "Thank you for being here." He just smiled sadly. When her eyes flickered toward the door behind him, he stepped back. She held his hand in her left as she reached out her right hand toward the door. "Lexi, sweetie."

Galen felt the blood drain out of his head as the girl approached them. Lexi, fighting tears, walked into Elizabeth's outstretched arm and hugged her tightly. Elizabeth kissed the top of her head. "I'm so glad you decided to come." Lexi nodded then sniffed and backed away. "I want you to meet Mr. Douglas."

Lexi and Galen stared at each other for an inordinately long time. Elizabeth looked curiously back and forth between them, until Galen finally cleared his throat. "Hi."

"Hi," Lexi answered in a small voice.

At that moment, Linda appeared in the door. She froze, her eyes locked on Galen. Galen returned a glare full of smoldering anger. Elizabeth's eyes were on Lexi. Lexi looked from Linda to Galen and back, and back again. Her face transformed slowly from perplexity to realization to wider-and-wider-eyed disbelief.

The four of them were suspended in the surreal moment until the funeral director invited them to the chapel to start the memorial service. They resumed motion and seated themselves, with Linda and an aisle between Galen and Lexi.

During the service, Lexi snuck looks past her mother toward her father. Sera wouldn't have cared what the stranger up front was saying, either; she would have been all over this new development. *Are you serious? You mean I've known your dad this whole time? That's wild!* Lexi smiled to herself, hearing the words as clearly as if Sera were sitting next to her. *I told you there's no such thing as a coincidence. We were meant to be friends, and that's a fact.*

After the service, Galen saw Linda rush Lexi to the outside aisle while he was detained at the center in the mob around Elizabeth. By the time he reached the back of the chapel, Linda and Lexi were gone. It was just as well; he needed time to think about what to do.

He milled around the memorial table in the lobby. The table was covered with souvenirs provided by Sera's friends, who surrounded the table, chattering remember-whens. In the middle of the table was a poster, on which someone had carefully transcribed an excerpt from Sera's college application:

> My personal heroes are my mom, who chose to suffer so she could love me; my best friend, Lexi, who will change the world one day; and Mr. Douglas, who has already saved a million people but wants to save me, too. Heroes are brave and self-sacrificing. But above all, no matter how it might end up, the best thing about heroes is they care enough to try. Heroes are just angels in disguise.

Galen kept a protective watch over Elizabeth while, with gracious poise, she greeted the stream of people, including Sera's teachers and friends, Senator Jenkins, and Elizabeth's coworkers. A distinguished white-haired gentleman squeezed Elizabeth's hand in both of his and said, "I must apologize for my wife. First our son, and now our granddaughter. It was just too much for her." Galen knew Elizabeth's own parents had moved to England when she went to college, and they no longer traveled, so he felt gratitude toward her father-in-law; it couldn't be easy for him to be here, either. Elizabeth hugged him tightly, and her composure broke for a split second before she pulled back. He kissed her hand and left. Friend after friend embraced her, asking, "Are you okay? Do you need anything?" Elizabeth waved them off with a courage and self-reliance that made Galen want to protect her all the more.

He retired to a distant corner until Elizabeth walked the final guests to the exit and closed the door. She leaned her head against the jamb and expelled the sigh of a thousand grieving mothers.

Galen put a gentle hand on her shoulder. He felt a weak shudder. "You're still here," she whispered.

"You're not okay."

Galen drove Elizabeth home and sat her at the kitchen table while he made tea. She told him she had refused to allow her friends to hold a reception, thinking she would be better off alone after the funeral. But she was wrong, and she thanked him again for being there.

When he sat down across from her, he glanced through the window to the house next door. He could feel Elizabeth's eyes on him as he took a sip. She said, "They moved here around Thanksgiving. The girls were three." He blinked rapidly, remembering vividly that desperate year when Lexi disappeared from his life. "I have something you might want to see." Elizabeth got up from the table, and Galen followed her into the living room.

While she searched the drawers beneath the china cupboard, he took in the feminine and homey surroundings, learning about

Elizabeth and Sera through the things they chose to display, from the clumsily glued seashell lampshade on a side table to the World's Largest Crossword Puzzle on the wall.

Elizabeth held up an embroidered cloth patch and an ash-ended branch. "This isn't what I was looking for, but these sticks are from the brief Girl Scout escapade. Our girls weren't quite disciplined enough for an organization. The marshmallow roasting was about all that caught on."

Galen followed Elizabeth through every room of the house, finding more memorabilia, each with a cathartic story, unveiling to Galen his daughter's lifetime friendship. He absorbed every detail through all five senses, the pictures of Lexi in his mind developing from the black and white detective photos into an entire childhood.

Occasionally, Elizabeth paused like she was bracing herself. She explained that her memories of Sera were like a beautiful sandcastle that was so solid she could live inside it, until a wave of realization melted the castle, and Sera died all over. It never took long for the memories to rebuild, then dissolve again. Once, Elizabeth sank to the floor with her head on her knees. Galen sat beside her, sharing his strength until the tsunami receded.

In Elizabeth's room, Galen noticed two pictures on her dresser, the first he had seen in the house. One was of a man about thirty years old, and one was of Sera and Elizabeth in front of Massachusetts General Hospital. Elizabeth told him that she didn't take pictures of Sera growing up, because it ruined their carefree moments, reminding them that memories would be all that was left before long enough. They took a picture the day Sera entered the study, on her sixteenth birthday, because Elizabeth thought it would be her last.

Guilt swept over Galen, and he wanted to run from the house. What right did he have to be here when he couldn't save her?

Elizabeth looked at him curiously then said, with a hint of surprise, "You blame yourself." When he didn't look at her, she said, "Don't." She stepped closer, hesitantly putting a hand on his arm. She leaned in until he met her intense gaze. "She had a seventeenth birthday. You gave us that."

The final room they explored was Sera's. Galen didn't look around as he had in the other rooms, but instead kept his eyes on Elizabeth, who was breathing deliberately with squared shoulders. She knelt to the floor and slid out a trunk from under the bed. Elizabeth paused over every item inside, each revealing what Sera had treasured. She gingerly lifted out a t-shirt. Standing behind her, Galen recognized it from the photograph: *#1 Dad To Be*. Elizabeth hugged the shirt to herself then folded it neatly and set it aside. When Elizabeth pulled out a soft, tattered piece of yellow construction paper, she said, "This is it." She pushed up from her knees and handed it to Galen.

On the paper was a crayon drawing of three stick people, holding hands. Also in the picture were a smiling sun, birds, and a rainbow. The stick figures were labeled in childish handwriting: *Lexi, Mommy, Me.*

Galen traced a finger over the yellow crayon hair on Lexi's head, her pink hands linked with Elizabeth's, her smile, and the title at the top of the page: *My Family*. He wanted to crawl into that picture, wrap his arms around the three stick people, and live there happily ever after. He held the drawing for what seemed like all the years he had lost, then he handed it back to Elizabeth, tears pricking at his eyes.

She knelt again and placed the page at the top of the pile and started to lower the trunk lid, then paused. She stayed that way for several minutes, until, with trembling hands, she pulled out the paper again. Galen stood awkwardly with his arms to his sides while Elizabeth put the paper on his chest and placed one of his hands on the drawing, holding her fingers on top of his. She said with unconcealed emotion, "This is yours."

THE MOON WAS full by the time Galen stood on the porch to leave. His eyes flickered to the house next door, watching the lights turn off one by one as the occupants moved upstairs for bed. Elizabeth, standing in the open doorway, said, "You should go over."

"Tomorrow." He gently touched his palm to her face. She put a hand on his forearm and closed her eyes. They stood like that for a long while, a promise between them.

On hthe way back to his hotel, Galen imagined confronting Linda and letting loose the anger he had pent up for fourteen years. But by the time he reached his room, he was feeling the old familiar paralysis of indecision, thinking about what such a confrontation might do to Lexi or to his potential relationship with her.

He loosened his tie and collapsed onto the bed, wondering back on his life, over all he might have done differently to have kept his daughter. Should he have given up on 423? It couldn't save Sera, so what was the point? If he had been more attentive, would Linda not have resented him so much? If so, today he might still be working nine to five and helping Lexi with her college preparations. He might be helping her follow in his footsteps to Harvard. But now he didn't even know if she got into college; none of the stories Elizabeth shared with him reached into the future.

He was still lying there with his shoes on when a light knock came at the door. He opened it to Lexi, whose hands were shoved deep in the pockets of her jeans. He stood in the doorway and stared at her as she stared at the floor.

Lexi spoke first, toward the carpet. "I asked Mrs. Rose where you were staying."

Galen nodded, still watching her.

A few more moments passed.

"Mom doesn't know I'm here."

Galen willed himself to speak. He cleared his throat. "Um. Well. So. Do you want to come in?"

She shrugged and he backed away, farther into the room. She took a wide step over the threshold but remained close to the open door. It saddened Galen that she felt the need to be cautious.

"Sera told me about you. I mean I didn't know it was *you*. But she told me you were nice. And about the frog."

Galen smiled at the memory. Another long silence passed.

"Do you believe in angels?" she asked.

"I do now."

Lexi looked up. His heart broke at the anguish on his daughter's face, a shadow from years before. When he trusted his voice again, he said, "She told me about you, too. I always hoped you had a best friend half as good as her Lexi."

Lexi's hands were still in her pockets, and she bowed her head lower so her blonde curls fell forward. But she couldn't hide the tears streaming down her face. Galen couldn't bear to see her in pain, but he didn't know what to do. He felt an utter failure.

Then he remembered the nights when she had cried herself awake in her crib. He had only to take her in his arms, and she was content. She had known him instinctively. He stepped toward her and wordlessly touched his hand to her cheek.

She pulled her arms from her pockets and wrapped them around him. "You didn't forget me."

He hugged her tightly, determined not to be the first to let go.

55

THERE WERE TWO headlines in the Boston papers eighteen years
to the day when Lexistro was granted its patent:
"Merck Acquires Biolex"
"Parker Resigns from Senate"

56

LEXI RAN ACROSS Harvard Yard to tackle Galen and Elizabeth with a bear hug.

"So, how does it feel to have a full year of higher education under your belt?" Galen asked his daughter.

"All I can say is thank goodness it's finally summer, and let's eat!"

They crossed Massachusetts Avenue to the sandwich shop and staked a table outside where they could experience Harvard Square. When introductory conversation had reached a lull, Lexi said, "Do you think that everyone tries to do what they think is right?"

Galen was surprised at the question. "I'd like to think so."

"And that even when people mean well, they can still end up hurting someone?"

He glanced over at Elizabeth, who was looking as perplexed as he felt. "Heavy conversation for a sunny day, isn't it?" he said.

"I'm just asking whether you would forgive someone if they did something that you disagreed with, if their heart was in the right place."

Galen paused then leaned over the table to look Lexi in the eye. "I know it's hard for you to believe, but I have truly forgiven your mother. We were both trying to do what was best for you in bad circumstances. So if you accept me, you have to accept her, too."

Lexi looked back at him curiously. Abruptly, she stood. "I want to introduce you to a friend of mine." Lexi gestured to a girl standing against the building a few feet away. "This is Abigail."

But Galen already recognized her; her features had grown into the best of her mother and father. Galen was shocked to his feet and embraced the girl. Lexi registered no surprise.

When they were all seated again, Galen, who couldn't pull his eyes away from Abigail, said, "How do you two know each other?"

"We met once during high school," Lexi said. "At Sera's party." She looked over at Elizabeth, whose eyes glistened. "We kind of recognized each other at orientation, then with the news and everything else, we started talking and putting all the twos and twos together. We really are long lost friends!"

"We've been hanging out all year but just didn't know how to tell you, because of the way things are with you and my dad."

Galen looked back and forth from one girl to the other, expecting them to fade away as a dream. "You don't know how happy it makes me that you two are friends. Really," he said. Elizabeth slid her hand into his.

Abigail glanced at her watch and gave Lexi a meaningful look. Lexi hurried on. "She helped me on version two of the video game. The one you have on phasehealth.com." Abigail suddenly waved to someone behind Galen. He turned around and saw Eddy and Joy walking toward them from the subway station.

He turned back quickly and stared hard at the umbrella pole, trying to fight the heat rising under his collar. It seemed like hours before they reached the table. Abigail stood to greet her parents. When they turned toward Galen and Elizabeth, Eddy's face morphed from shock to a barely suppressed anger. Elizabeth's face was frozen hard. Joy's gaze went from Eddy to Galen to Elizabeth and landed to rest on Lexi. They were all silent.

Finally, Abigail pulled two chairs away from the adjoining table and placed them under her parents. She cleared her throat. "So, Dad and Mom, you know Mr. Douglas, and you probably remember Lexi, and this is Elizabeth Rose. You met at Senator Jenkins' house." It was clear to Galen that Eddy and Joy also immediately recognized the name from the papers, which had sensationalized Sera's death in connection with the immediate takeover of Biolex.

"I'm so sorry for your loss," Joy said, mother to mother. Elizabeth's face softened, and she nodded thanks.

Eddy said to Galen, "And yours. Your company, I mean."

Galen held back a scoff and said, "We sold out on good terms. So what are you doing these days?" He couldn't resist the jab at Eddy's abrupt departure from public life.

Abigail said quickly, "So that's why we wanted to bring you guys together." She looked to Lexi for help.

Lexi turned to Galen and Elizabeth. "We've been thinking a lot about PHASE. Abigail is an economics major, and she thinks that what you're doing makes a lot of sense, because it restores free market principles to the health care economy." She turned back to Abigail, who was looking at her in surprise. "See, I pay attention."

Abigail turned to her parents. "Mr. Douglas and Mrs. Rose have started a business to help people cover costs if they get ill. It doesn't rely on taxes or industry regulations, so it could stimulate research, and it can work for people at any economic level. I think it will change the health care system."

"But what they need is an unbiased spokesperson," Lexi said to Eddy. Elizabeth and Galen moved to speak. She turned back to them. "You do. I mean, who's going to take the word of an ex-industry millionaire? And a mom who lived through what you did is powerful, but it doesn't exactly lend itself to open debate about the merits of this as a business venture."

Abigail said, "My dad knows how to campaign. He's persuasive and he has the ear of the politicians who might turn away from you two. His presence might make people feel okay about engaging in a debate, and once people have kicked the tires some, they'll see what a great business this could be."

Abigail said, "Government and industry have been like ten people running the most important races of their lives, straight at each other, toward different finish lines. When they all collide and fall back to the ground, there's no one in the middle to blame. That void is the health care system. It doesn't stand on its own." It was Eddy's turn to protest. Abigail cut him off. "Hear me out, Dad. Until now, you've all got up and started blaming each other for being the evil mastermind, but it hasn't made any of the races less important, and it didn't help any of you go faster. What we're proposing is to realign the start and finish so you're all running in the same direction. People know that you and Mr. Douglas haven't always seen eye-to-eye, so can you imagine what a powerful statement it would be if you worked together on this?"

Lexi said peacefully to her father. "You know I think some things are meant to be. So, what if everything that has happened in all of our lives, from what made you friends to what made you fight, all of your decisions and everything you've ever cared about, has put you in the unique position now to really make a difference—together?"

Eddy and Galen glanced at each other for a split second, then both looked away. No one spoke for several minutes, though Harvard Square continued its hubbub. Finally, Abigail stood. "We're sorry to ambush you. Especially you, Mrs. Rose, because I have heard so many great things about you. But we couldn't see any other way. We just wanted you to consider the opportunity." She held out her hand to Galen and Elizabeth, and Eddy and Joy stood to go. "I'll see you later," she told Lexi. Then the Parkers left.

Galen didn't know how to feel about what had occurred or how Elizabeth felt. Lexi said, "Abigail and I are going to be friends no matter what you decide, so please don't think we're trying to pressure you that way."

Elizabeth said, "Your intentions are good."

57

AS SOON AS Eddy and Joy reached their room at the Cambridge-place Marriott, Eddy changed into his running clothes. Joy could tell that the meeting shook him up, but she had learned that when it came to Galen, it wouldn't help to push. So she closed the door behind him and hoped he would make the right decision.

Galen didn't say anything to Elizabeth on the way back from the meeting, and she didn't pry. When they reached the Cambridge condo, he just grabbed his running shoes and left. Elizabeth appreciated the effortless bond of motherhood she had experienced with Joy Parker that afternoon; she hoped the bond of fatherhood worked the same way.

Galen ran the familiar trail around the Charles River then cut over to the Harvard campus toward the freshman dormitories. When he got there, he saw Eddy staring up at the third floor window of their old room. Galen spun around and bumped into a group of students walking directly behind him. He mumbled an embarrassed apology. They laughed loudly and carried on their way.

The noise caused Eddy to look in that direction, and as soon as he saw Galen, he tensed. Neither could escape.

Galen was caught between his memories and his confusion about what had gone wrong—all of the turmoil that he didn't, and had never, understood. In so many ways, he still felt like he was eighteen years old, seeing Eddy for the first time, wondering what their encounter would hold for them both.

Eddy straightened his shoulders and walked purposefully toward him. "Galen." They both nodded. "You were struck with some nostalgia, too, I guess."

"I guess."

Eddy looked as if he expected Galen to say something else, but Galen wasn't going to be the one to give in. He'd had too many olive branches snapped before. If this rift were going to end, Eddy would have to do the work.

The two stared up at the window, where a body appeared now and again, the last straggler packing for summer. Eddy said jauntily, "Looks like our girls turned out well in spite of us."

It was a benign thing to say to any man who had been through the struggles of fatherhood, but not to Galen. The men stared at each other, two wolves circling, waiting for the other to strike. Eddy broke away. "Look, buddy, I didn't mean that the way it sounded. I was just making noise. Not that Lexi didn't turn out great, because she did. She seems really intelligent, like her dad. That's all I meant."

Galen cringed at the familiar word, "buddy", that drew out the feelings of longing and loss that had haunted him for so many years. But he needed to put his own issues aside to ensure his daughter's friendship was secure. "Abigail, too. It's good they're friends. Despite our example." It was more than he wanted to say.

Eddy started to speak and stopped several times before he responded, "Abigail needed a friend."

"Lexi, too." Galen paused. "Sera's death has been hard for her."

And there it was, the festering resentment. He blamed Eddy. If it hadn't been for the delays . . . . Galen could forgive losing his business; he was glad to be free of it after everything that had happened. But that it kept him from saving Sera—did Eddy even know what he had done?

The men exchanged stares, each trying to read the other's thoughts. Finally, Eddy said, "You know, my daughter told me before we met today that the right way looks different depending on where you stand. I didn't know what she meant until now."

Galen considered Lexi's similar statement. Could he forgive Eddy if he believed each of their hearts was in its own right place? Was Eddy even to blame?

Sera's words, her last gift, worked within him, coating his resentment like a pearl. *The thing about heroes is they care enough to try.* "Do you think good people can make bad decisions?" Galen said. His eyes pierced Eddy's brain, trying to see the answer inside.

Eddy blinked to break the intense gaze. A year ago, he would have responded no with certainty. But Abigail had awakened him to the hidden possibilities and human strengths that he had ignored for such a long time. How could all of his decisions have been good when there was so much he hadn't seen? Looking at Galen, who still bore shadows of the pale kid who never really connected with people, Eddy understood that Joy had seen through Galen's insecurity to his promise. Their daughter was living a normal, healthy life thanks to this man. Eddy was over-whelmed with regret. "I think the answer has to be yes."

Galen was surprised to hear Eddy's voice waver. He responded tentatively, "So, you think our daughters are pretty smart? That everything we've done wrong can be turned into something good?"

"How could they not be smart? Look where their genes came from." Eddy's eyes twinkled with a long-forgotten camaraderie.

Galen felt youth stir within him, the way he had felt when he embarked on his business a lifetime ago. He resurrected an old rejected offer. "So are we going to do this thing? This big idea of theirs that's going to change the world?"

Eddy extended his hand. "Partners?"

ACKNOWLEDGMENTS

To erin Khuê Ninh, the first person outside my family to read *The Neurology of Angels*: Thank you for your honest criticism and intelligent insights and for giving the story permission to be what it wanted to be.

To everyone who responded to the invitation to critique a stranger's work: I appreciate the donation of your time and each comment, criticism, and long period of silence. You taught me to fight the urge to defend my baby and instead find value in every reaction. Special thanks to Jennifer D. Williams, MaryAnn M., John L., Tatiana, and Paul S.

To Mom, Dad, and Sean: Thank you for believing I could do this. Thank you for cultivating my independence, for debates around the dinner table, and for being ready with your two cents—when asked. Most of all, thank you for supporting my life decisions even when they didn't make sense at the time; every experience of the last ten years has led to this project, in ways I never could have planned. I am proud to have you for my family.

ABOUT THE AUTHOR

Krista Tibbs studied neuroscience at MIT, holds an MBA in health sector management from Duke University, and spent three years in Washington, DC, where she developed a swing dance habit. She now works in the biotechnology industry conducting clinical research for diseases with unmet medical needs. Krista grew up in northern Maine and currently lives in Massachusetts.

Printed in the United States
204074BV00002B/106-525/P

9 780981 880303